Paul Burston grew up in South Wales listening to David Bowie, Soft Cell, Bronski Beat and The Smiths before moving to London in 1984. A journalist and broadcaster, his work has appeared in *Time Out*, the *Sunday Times*, *The Times*, the *Guardian*, the *Independent* and the *Independent on Sunday* and on Channel Four. He is the author of several books including the novels *Shameless* and *Star People*. He appeared in *I ♥ The 80s*, *Embarrassing 80s Moments* and other programmes with '80s' in the title. Visit his website at www.paulburston.com.

Also by Paul Burston

Star People
Shameless
What Are You Looking At?
Gutterheart
Queen's Country

as co-editor
A Queer Romance

Lovers and Losers

PAUL BURSTON

sphere

SPHERE

First published in Great Britain in 2007 by Sphere

A CIP catalogue record for this book
is available from the British Library.

ISBN 978-0-7515-3864-9

Papers used by Sphere are natural, recyclable products made
from wood grown in sustainable forests and certified in accordance
with the rules of the Forest Stewardship Council.

Typeset in Berkeley by M Rules
Printed and bound in Great Britain by
Clays Ltd, St Ives plc
Paper supplied by Hellefoss AS, Norway

Sphere
An imprint of
Little, Brown Book Group
Brettenham House
Lancaster Place
London WC2E 7EN

A Member of the Hachette Livre Group of Companies

www.littlebrown.co.uk

For my mother, and all the Katrinas

ACKNOWLEDGEMENTS

First and foremost, a huge thank you to those who took the time and shared their electric dreams with me, in particular Marc Almond, Princess Julia and Caroline McCartan. 'Love on ya,' as Mr Bowie used to say.

For brightening up the early 80s, thanks also to Boy George (who I once interviewed in a room full of Boy George dolls and other Culture Club memorabilia); Steve Strange (who insisted we sit outside even though it was freezing – he's from Wales, you know) and Pete Burns (who invited me into his lovely home and fed me chocolate cake followed by sushi).

Thanks also to Cary Archard, Gerard Boynton, Nichola Coulthard, Aruan Duval, Alma Evans, Darren Fawthrop, Suzi Feay, Simon Gage, David Hoyle, Gordon John, Andrew Loxton, Jamie McLeod, Jacqui Niven, Steve Pitron, Rupert Smith, Carl Stanley, Frances Williams, the late Vaughan Williams (for the houseplant song), Mark Wood and all the Myspacers.

And to Paulo Kadow, whose love and support keeps me going.

Last but not least, a big thank you to my agent Sophie Hicks, my editor Antonia Hodgson and everyone at Sphere, especially Jenny Fry, Caroline Hogg and Sarah Rustin.

CHAPTER ONE

As the taxi crawled its way along Warwick Road and past the Exhibition Centre where hordes of eighties pop fans used to call his name, Tony noticed the driver eyeing him up in the rear-view mirror. The cabbie was a shabby type with nicotine-stained hair and a photo of his kids taped to the dashboard, so there was nothing in that look to suggest anything untoward. It was simply the look of someone whose curiosity was about to get the better of him. Another minute or two and he would finally pluck up the courage, open his mouth and ask *that* question, the one people had been asking for years.

Tony was surprised it had taken him this long. Surprised, and if he was honest, a little disappointed. He'd been sitting in the back of this taxi for almost fifteen minutes and until now there hadn't been so much as a glimmer of recognition. He knew he'd put on a bit of weight lately, and his hair was going thin. But he hadn't aged that much, had he? Not so much that he was no longer recognisable? He sighed quietly to himself and stared out of the window.

Finally the driver spoke. 'You're him, aren't you?'

Tony smiled and confirmed that yes, he was indeed him, or at least he was the last time he looked.

'Oh, you know what I mean,' the driver went on. 'You're the one from that pop group. What were you called again?'

'Tony,' Tony replied. 'I was called Tony. Still am, in fact. But if you're referring to the group, we were called A Boy and His Diva.'

'That's right,' the driver said dreamily. 'A Boy and His Diva. God, that brings back some memories. The wife and I . . . Well, it's a bit embarrassing really, but we danced to one of your songs at our wedding.' He paused for effect. 'Give you two guesses which one.'

Tony felt his eyes glaze over. How many times had he heard this story? A hundred? A thousand? Always the same story, always the same song, always the same silly notion that it was written especially for them. He forced a smile. 'It wasn't "Lovers and Losers" by any chance, was it?'

The driver grinned. 'Got it in one! That was a great song. A few more like that and you'd probably still be around today. Not that I blame you for turning your back on it all. I'd hate to be famous, especially with all the paparazzi and the stalkers they get nowadays. It would do my head in. If you ask me, you were wise to get out when you did.'

Tony grimaced. 'You're probably right.'

'So what've you been doing with yourself all these years? Keeping busy?'

'Pretty busy.'

'And what about the girl? Katrina, wasn't it?'

'That's right, Katrina.'

'God, she had a voice on her. Not like these kids today. Whatever happened to her?'

Katrina. Sooner or later it always came back to Katrina. 'How's Katrina?' 'What's Katrina up to these days?' 'Whatever happened to Katrina?' The simple answer was,

Tony didn't know. But of course it was a lot more complicated than that. Katrina's whereabouts had been on his mind a great deal lately. Only now it wasn't just his troubled conscience or idle curiosity. Now there was an urgency to the question that hadn't existed a month ago. It was then that he got the call from his manager, the call that put an end to years of quiet desperation and offered the tantalising prospect of a second stab at the fame game. Finally he had an opportunity to be back in the public eye and instantly recognised by everyone, taxi drivers included.

Yes, Tony had been living a quiet life of late. In the words of the Japan song, boy the times were changing and the going had got rough. But the truth was, he hadn't turned his back on fame. If it were up to him, he'd be as famous now as he was twenty years ago. He'd be on the cover of Q magazine and between the pages of *Heat*. He'd be cuddling up to Phillip and Fern on *This Morning*, spilling his guts to Richard and Judy at teatime and hanging out with the 3 a.m. Girls every night of the week. He'd be a model celebrity, always willing to pose for photographers, always ready with a quick quote, always available. There'd be none of that Robbie Williams nonsense, none of that 'woe is me' crap. It made Tony sick to his stomach, the way today's stars complained about the pressures of fame, the constant scrutiny, the paparazzi. What he wouldn't give to have journalists rifling through his bins and photographers camped outside his door!

He dived into the shopping bags at his feet, rummaged around for a bit, and pulled out a CD. He turned it over in his hand, admiring the unfamiliar artwork and enjoying the sense of expectation as he slowly peeled off the cellophane wrap. Then he opened the plastic casing and removed the sleeve notes. He'd found the CD at Virgin, filed between Bowie and Boy George, which seemed appropriate in more ways than one. It was a rare Japanese import, so it was no wonder the artwork seemed strange and the sleeve notes were unintelligible. But where on earth did they find those photos? He barely recognised some of them. Had he really worn that mint-green jacket with the sleeves rolled up? And what did Katrina have on her head in that picture beside the Pyramids? Was it her hair, or some strange ceremonial head-dress stolen from the tomb below?

Tony smiled to himself. Those were the days, he thought. He was somebody then. Five consecutive Top Ten hits, a hairstyle that was imitated by thousands of teenagers across the country and a coke habit that was little short of legendary. Of course this was back in the eighties, when pop stars still had hairstyles and cocaine was a drug with class, enjoyed by rock royalty and city bankers with 'loadsa-money'. Back then, Tony couldn't pop out for a pint of milk without his picture appearing in the papers. That was one reason he never left the house without a full face of makeup. Press attention was a fact of life, and he loved every minute of it.

The press weren't always kind, of course. When their first single, 'Love Is A Pain (In The Heart)', was released in April 1983, the NME famously dismissed A Boy and His Diva as 'a couple of Talent Nite rejects from a suburban gay bar, an over-made-up tart and his equally ridiculous female side-kick, the kind of fag/hag combo that puts both parties to shame'. Sniggering over the song's title and its supposedly coded reference to the discomfort of anal intercourse, the reviewer went on to describe the band's style as 'a little bit Eurythmics, a little bit Yazoo, totally lacking in originality and utterly devoid of soul. This is the sound of someone flogging the space where a dead horse should be.'

But who needed the *NME* when there was *Smash Hits*? Interviewed shortly afterwards by Britain's best-selling pop magazine, Tony side-stepped the whole 'gay issue' by insisting that the band's name was meant to be taken ironically, 'with a large pinch of sodium chloride'. What he didn't say was that he actually found the name a bit embarrassing. It wasn't his idea. His manager had come up with it, insisting that it neatly summarised the band's character and ambitions. 'A Boy' because sexually ambiguous pop stars whose names contained the word 'boy' were proving extremely popular in the early eighties, as Boy George could happily testify. And 'Diva' because Katrina had always been a bit of a diva, even when she was plain old Katy Williams from Swansea.

Tony turned the CD over and read the track listing on the back. As with many imported greatest-hits packages, the term 'hit' had been applied rather loosely. There were twelve tracks on the CD, and even he was forced to admit that fewer than half of them could really be described as hits. The rest were either remixes, album tracks, or singles that had hovered around the lower reaches of the chart, worming their way into the affections of a few diehard fans before sinking without trace. A Boy and His Diva were not a band known for their longevity. They didn't constantly reinvent themselves and stage comeback after comeback, the way some of their contemporaries did. They didn't discover rock and prolong their careers by making it big in America. They didn't feed the world and become latter-day saints. Their time was up very quickly.

But what an amazing time it had been! Much to the surprise of the chairman of the record company, who'd signed the group on a whim and was already regretting his decision, 'Love Is A Pain (In The Heart)' entered the charts at Number 32. Usually a single had to be Top 30 before the artist responsible would be invited to perform on *Top of the Pops*, but as luck would have it, Shakin' Stevens broke his leg that week and Tony and Katrina were squeezed into his slot. Tony still remembered the thrill he felt at being driven to the *Top of the Pops* studio, and how it turned to something approaching disappointment the moment he was inside. He remembered how small the studio was, and how tacky it looked – not at all the way he'd imagined it from the comfort of his sofa. He remembered the producers shunting the studio audience around like sheep, and the cameramen shouting at the kids to get out of the way. He remembered watching Spandau Ballet miming to 'True' on the stage opposite and then finally the wait was over, the cameras moved into position and Jimmy Savile announced, 'For the first time ever on *Top of the Pops*, it's A Boy and His Diva!'

Then the crowd roared and the backing tape started and suddenly it didn't matter how small the studio was or how tacky it looked. This was it. His moment had arrived. After this, nothing would ever be the same again. That was how important *Top of the Pops* was back then. It didn't matter that the set had seen better days, or that the crowd were cheering for a band they'd probably never even heard of. This was the show Tony had grown up on, the one where he'd first seen Marc Bolan sing 'Get It On' with glitter on his cheeks, and

Bowie perform 'Starman' with his arm draped around Mick Ronson. As if that weren't daunting enough, by the early eighties *Top of the Pops* was regularly pulling in fifteen million viewers – enough to make or break a record overnight. So really it was no wonder that Katrina fluffed the intro to the song and that Tony forgot to look directly into the camera. They both knew how much was riding on this, their first ever appearance on the nation's favourite music show. Watching the clip again recently on *TOTP2*, Tony was struck by how nervous they looked. How nervous, and how painfully young.

Things went a little crazy after that. Boosted by their *Top of the Pops* appearance, the single climbed all the way to Number 2, held off the top spot by Spandau Ballet and 'True'. The whole Duran Duran/Spandau Ballet rivalry was at an all-time high then, so to come a close second to Spandau was hailed as a minor miracle. Celebrations were held at the Kensington Roof Gardens. Oysters were served and the champagne flowed. Industry bigwigs sucked on cigars and publicists buzzed around like flies. The guest list read like a *Who's Who* of eighties pop royalty. Photos from the night made their way into the tabloids. One had even made it into the CD he now held in his hand. It showed Tony rubbing shoulder pads with Martin Kemp while Katrina managed to force a smile out of Alannah Currie of the Thompson Twins (possibly with the name of a good milliner).

You wouldn't know it from the grinning photo of him and Katrina riding around on elephants, but the mood changed slightly when the second single, 'Touch', stalled at Number 12, despite the record company taking a leaf out of Duran Duran's book and packing Tony and Katrina off to Sri Lanka to work on their tans and film a multi-thousand-pound video.

But it was the third single that would guarantee them their place in pop history. No wonder it appeared twice on the CD – once at the beginning in its original version, and once at the end in what used to be called 'the twelve-inch'. Produced by Trevor Horn, and originally released in a daring gatefold picture sleeve that showed Tony and Katrina both naked with their heads imposed on each other's bodies and their genitals obscured by the little black stars usually found in porn magazines, 'Lovers and Losers' was a perfect slice of eighties synth pop – big, bombastic, overproduced and utterly irresistible. Crashing synths gave way to a chorus where Katrina urged listeners to 'love before you lose', while Tony's mournful tones warned of 'love's bitter tears, bigger than the sea'.

The lyrics were a bit pretentious, but then this was a time when bands were happy to call themselves Spandau Ballet and David Sylvian was busy quoting Sartre. Backed with a video shot by Godley and Creme and set in that early eighties emblem of decadence, a porn cinema, 'Lovers and Losers' went straight to the top of the charts and stayed there for five weeks. To this day, it was one of the songs most likely to be included on compilation CDs with titles like *Our Friends Electric* and *Eighties Synth Classics*. Not bad for a couple of Talent Nite rejects from a suburban gay bar.

All in all, 1983 was a big year for A Boy and His Diva. Their Christmas single, 'Angels At My Table', also went to Number 1. *Smash Hits* readers voted them Best Newcomers, Best Single for 'Lover and Losers' and Best Hairstyle for Tony's elaborate cut-and-dye job – black at the back, blond

8

on top, and held together with half a can of hairspray. In a few years' time, hairstyles like these would be identified as one of the main contributors to the hole in the ozone layer. But for now, nobody was interested in pointing fingers. They were are all far too busy cashing in on Tony and Katrina's success. As 1984 dawned, it looked as if nothing could possibly go wrong. But then nobody really knew then what horrors lay ahead. If they had, they might have acted a little differently. Whatever else Tony blamed himself for, he couldn't be held accountable for that.

Suddenly the cab lurched to a halt, jolting him back to reality.

'There you go,' the driver said. 'That's seventeen fifty, please.'

Tony took a twenty out of his wallet and handed it over. 'Keep the change.'

'Very kind of you, sir,' the driver said. 'If you don't mind me saying, you never answered my question – about what happened to Katrina.'

Tony managed a smile. 'Your guess is as good as mine.'

The day Mark died, his mother sat in a room full of strangers, inwardly grieving for a man she barely knew. A small woman with pale blue eyes and hair that was once mousy but had now faded to grey, Rose looked out of her depth and slightly befuddled, as if the full weight of her son's death hadn't quite sunk in yet.

For the past few days she felt as if she'd been on autopilot, doing whatever mothers were supposed to do in these situations and constantly questioning the sincerity of her own performance. Yesterday she'd tried to spoon-feed him some yoghurt, only his body was so weak he could barely swallow. She was afraid to hold him at first. Not for herself, but for fear that his bones might break, he was that thin. But the doctors assured her that it was okay, so for two hours this morning she lay next to him on the bed, conscious of how little space he took up, almost as if he were a child again, cuddled up with her after waking from a nightmare. Only this time the nightmare was real and he didn't wake up. He just lay there until finally the breathing stopped and the morphine spirited him away. And then he was gone, this son she hadn't seen in over ten years, this boy who'd grown into a man she couldn't bear to look at, lying dead in her arms. It was ironic really. She'd spent the past ten years pretending that he didn't exist, and at the moment he ceased to exist it was her arms that held him.

It was easy for others to judge. She'd seen the way they looked at her, these friends of his with their sad eyes and their false smiles, oozing resentment at the way she'd walked in and upstaged them all. They tried to hide it, tried to show some respect, tried to act as if she had every right to be here. But she wasn't fooled for a moment. There were a couple sitting across the room from her now, two men in checked shirts, huddled together over cups of coffee from the vending machine out in the corridor, secretly watching her, wondering what kind of monster would turn her back on her own son. But what did they know? They were only his friends. They didn't know what it felt like to be the mother of a gay child. They hadn't carried him inside them for nine months. They hadn't nurtured him. They hadn't watched him grow up and grow apart. They hadn't seen the son they loved become a stranger. They hadn't grieved for the grand-children they would never have. They hadn't felt that sense of loss. She hated this disease and everything it said about him. But at the very least it had done her one big favour. It had brought him back to her.

She'd always suspected that Mark was different. The signs were there from an early age. The gentle disposition, the fear of sports, the overabundance of female friendships, none of which developed into anything more than friends. But suspecting it was one thing. Having it rubbed in your face was a different thing entirely. By the time he was a teenager, the signs weren't just there. They were flashing like warning signs on the motorway. At fourteen he had his ear pierced. At fifteen he dyed his hair. At sixteen he started wearing eye-liner. She tried telling herself that it was just a phase, that this was what young people were into these days. She'd seen them on the telly – Boy George and Marc Almond and all those pretty boys in lip gloss. 'New Romantics' they called themselves, as if there was anything new or romantic about men acting like a bunch of poofs.

'I suppose he's gay as well, is he?' she said when she came home from work one day to find Mark watching some Soft Cell video with his friend Zoe.

'No, he's bisexual,' Mark replied, as if that somehow made it all right.

Then the posters of Jimmy Somerville went up on the wall and soon there was no use denying it. Her son was 'one of them'. That was what people said – 'one of them'. As if he was no longer a part of her but belonged to a different world entirely, a world apart where women were surplus to requirements and she wasn't welcome.

At eighteen he left home. The first chance he got, he was off to London. She tried to maintain contact at first, but then when AIDS started making headlines and he started mentioning boyfriends, she found it easier to simply push it all to the back of her mind. She didn't want to know about these men he was meeting or what they did together. The phone calls became shorter and less frequent, the visits home fewer and farther between. The last time she saw him was at his grandfather's funeral. He'd always been close to her father, possibly because he'd never really had a father of his own. Her husband wasn't really cut out for parenthood, and as soon as Mark was born he ran off with the woman who ran the local bridal shop (which showed a certain amount of commitment, she had to admit). At the funeral, mother and son sat together and cried, all differences set aside for the duration of the service. Then, as soon as it was over, he made his excuses and left. If she'd known then what fate had in store for him, she'd have forced him to stay.

The door opened and a woman came in. She looked up and smiled, grateful for a bit of female company. She'd met the woman earlier. She'd been kind enough to offer her a tissue. A small gesture, perhaps. But in the cold, clinical atmosphere of the hospital, small gestures could make a big difference.

'Can I get you anything, Mrs Taylor?' the woman asked. She was big, blonde, expensively dressed, with a kind face and smudges of mascara around her eyes.

'No thank you, dear,' Rose replied. 'I suppose I should really be thinking about getting home.'

The woman looked surprised. 'But you can't possibly go all that way tonight. Not on your own. Not in this weather.

Don't you have somewhere you could stay? They'll need you here anyway. You're his next of kin. There'll be papers to sign, arrangements to be made.'

Rose frowned. 'I hadn't thought of that. They never really explain these things properly, do they? I don't suppose you could recommend a cheap hotel?'

'I've got a better idea,' the woman said. 'Why don't you stay with me instead? It's not very far from here. There's plenty of room, and to be honest I could do with the company.'

'I couldn't possibly . . .' Rose began.

'Of course you could,' the woman replied. 'What kind of person would I be if I left you stranded in some hotel, tonight of all nights?'

Rose noticed the small gold crucifix nestled at the woman's throat. She thought for a moment. 'Did you know him well? My son?'

'We were pretty close, yes. We even shared a flat for a while.'

Rose caught her eye and the woman blushed. 'As friends, I mean,' she went on hurriedly. 'I could show you some photos if you like. Or we could just have a nice cup of tea and put our feet up. It's been a long day. You must be exhausted. I know I am.'

The older woman hesitated before answering. 'Thank you, a cup of tea would be nice. And please, call me Rose.'

The younger woman smiled. 'Nice to meet you, Rose. I'm Katrina.'

CHAPTER TWO

The Pontin's holiday camp in Prestatyn Sands, north Wales, wasn't known as a breeding ground for future pop icons. There were no tales of a young David Bowie ever having visited, for instance. Nor were there any reported sightings of Marc Bolan, Bryan Ferry or any of the glam rock gods who sent multicoloured shockwaves through the grim, grey Britain of the seventies. Yet it was here, one fateful day in the long, hot summer of 1976, that two of the brightest stars of the eighties first laid eyes on one another and a little piece of pop history was made.

Anthony Griffiths, aged sixteen of Bridgend, south Wales, had left his parents squabbling in their Swiss cabin-style chalet and was making his way towards the Dragon Bar in time for the under-eighteens' disco. Somewhere in the distance, 'Save Your Kisses For Me' by Brotherhood of Man was playing on a tinny transistor radio. Needless to say, it was not a good omen. Still he soldiered on. Dressed in a blue mohair sweater with black pegged trousers and a pair of see-through plastic sandals as worn by Bowie in *The Man Who Fell to Earth*, he cut quite a figure as he slouched past the groups of holidaymakers engrossed in games of crazy golf or developing skin cancer by the pool. His hair was dyed bright orange, heavy on top and falling over one eye, but chopped short at the neck. Again this was a look inspired by Bowie. Anthony prided himself on the fact that he was always the first person in Bridgend to imitate Bowie's latest style. By the time everyone else caught on, he'd already moved on to the next look. He and David were alike in so many ways.

Krazy Colour wasn't readily available in south Wales, so Anthony had been forced to improvise with Recital Super Blonde and a packet of red henna in order to achieve the desired shade of orange. Now, as the last rays of sunshine glinted off his freshly dyed hair, he became increasingly conscious of the looks he was generating. Grown men stopped and stared. Women whispered and children laughed. Of course this was nothing new. Anthony had been generating looks since the tender age of twelve, which was the age he was the first time he saw Bowie on *Top of the Pops*. Prior to this life-changing moment, he was just your average oversensitive adolescent with low self-esteem and a burgeoning acne problem. Then suddenly this strange, exotic creature was beamed into his living room, singing about little green men and flaunting his effeminacy like it was something to be proud of. His hair was orange and his face was white with makeup. And when he draped his arm around his guitarist's shoulder, revealing a limp wrist and white polished fingernails, Anthony blushed red and prayed for the ground to swallow him up. In short, he was smitten.

His parents insisted that he was too young to see Ziggy Stardust live in concert, but he made up for it by plastering his walls with posters of his idol and shaving off his eyebrows. When Bowie killed Ziggy off a year later, Anthony grieved for weeks. Without Bowie's light to guide him, his life seemed empty and meaningless. Nineteen seventy-four was a particularly bad year for British Bowie fans. With no live concerts to look forward to, and only a well-worn copy of *Diamond Dogs* for company, Anthony spent much of the year cocooned in his bedroom, reading George Orwell and experimenting with semi-permanent hair colours. And then when *David Live* came out, with its cover shot of an emaciated Bowie looking more like a corpse than a living legend, Anthony began to wonder if killing off Ziggy wasn't some kind of prophecy, a warning that his creator wasn't long for this world. It was only when his hero reappeared with *Young Americans*, dressed in a bum-freezer jacket and singing songs like 'Fame', that Anthony was finally able to relax. Bowie hadn't died after all. He'd simply gone disco.

Anthony had been going through some 'ch-ch-changes' of his own these past few years. Puberty had brought up a whole load of stuff, truths about himself that he was only just beginning to face. Not just the fact that he fancied boys, although obviously this would prove pretty momentous in a town where rugby-playing meatheads were the only available male role models. But even bigger than this was the realisation that he wanted to be famous. Even as Bowie sang about the perils of rock stardom, warning his fans that 'fame puts you there where things are hollow', Anthony was dreaming of a life less ordinary than his suburban existence allowed, a life of bright lights and adoring audiences, of luxury and limos.

It was these dreams that consoled him now, here in this stupid holiday camp with its stupid holidaymakers whose idea of a good time was another round of crazy golf. Their jeers were music to his ears, proof that however modest his present circumstances, he had never been and would never be one of them. It was easy to be ordinary. The world was full of ordinary people thinking ordinary thoughts and doing ordinary things. Few people had the imagination to think beyond their own experience. Fewer still had the ability to picture themselves as other people, or the courage to act out their fantasies and make them real. 'Don't dream it, be it', like the song from *Rocky Horror* said. Bowie had done it with Ziggy, and again with Aladdin Sane and the Thin White Duke. And Anthony would do it too. He already had the hairstyle. All he needed now was the talent or, failing that, the determination to succeed.

He approached the entrance to the Dragon Bar and there she was, with one hand clutching her skirt and the other waving a cigarette – the girl who would turn his world around.

Katy Williams was fifteen years old but looked two years older. Had she not been at Pontin's that day, it was unlikely that she and Anthony would ever have crossed paths. Katy's parents lived in Swansea, but she spent most of her time in Porthcawl, where she boarded at the local Catholic girls' school. Porthcawl was only seven miles away from Anthony's home town of Bridgend, but it may as well have been the other side of the world. St Agatha's had much to recommend it, but it was hardly the sort of place where Katy was likely to meet someone fitting Anthony's description.

It was often said of Katy that she would try the patience of a saint, and although there were no latter-day saints at St Agatha's, there were plenty of nuns who would testify to having their patience tried on a regular basis. Barely a week went by when she wasn't hauled before the Mother Superior over some misdeed or other, and her stubborn refusal to repent only made matters worse. It was during a reprimand over the correct wearing of school uniform that one of the nuns finally lost her temper and told her that the reason her parents had sent her to boarding school was because they obviously didn't love her. Deep down, Katy knew this wasn't true. But there were times when she felt the need to test the depths of their affection just the same.

Katy almost didn't make it to Pontin's at all. Two weeks ago she'd been caught out in a scam to skip the last week of school term, lying to the school authorities and informing them that her mother had been rushed into hospital and that her father was coming to pick her up a week early. Like many children indoctrinated in the ways of the Catholic Church, Katy could fake belief in almost anything. It was this ability that made her such an accomplished liar. Her tears were so convincing that the Mother Superior had no choice but to let her go. She then spent a week in Porthcawl, hanging around the sea front and sleeping on a friend's floor, until finally her father called the school to arrange to collect her and was informed that she'd already left.

Katy's father was not a man renowned for his sense of humour. A respected member of the British Cacti and Succulent Society, he had a hothouse full of exotic specimen plants and radiated little in the way of personal warmth. 'Prickly' was a word often applied to him, and not always in the context of his horticultural leanings. His parenting skills had been learnt mainly from his mother, who had produced seven children of her own and wasn't particularly fond of any of them. Like her, he was very big on discipline, and a little backward when it came to displays of affection or attempts at understanding. So when it was revealed to him that his precious daughter had lied to the school authorities and gone AWOL, his first instinct was to cancel the family holiday as punishment. It was only when his wife meekly pointed out that the deposit was non-refundable that he agreed to proceed with the holiday plans and decide on some other punishment at a later date.

Personally, Katy wouldn't have minded staying at home. Two weeks at Pontin's was punishment enough for anyone. It didn't matter how chirpy the yellowcoats were or how many activities they organised. The place was like a bloody concentration camp. (And yes, she did know what a concentration camp was. They'd taught her about the Second World War at St Agatha's, although obviously they left out the bit about the Pope being a Nazi sympathiser.)

It was only day four, and already she was bored out of her skull. Too self-conscious about her weight to strip down to her swimming costume, she'd avoided the pool and exhausted every other opportunity for mindless entertainment. She'd been go-karting and almost broken a nail. She'd ridden the rollercoaster and spotted the tattooed hunk on the dodgems. She'd even been reduced to joining the girl from the next chalet in a game of crazy golf. But today she decided she'd had enough of the holiday camp spirit and its forced sense of fun. It was time to break the monotony with a spot of shoplifting. Just after lunch she cried off a trip to the beach with her parents, complaining of a headache. As soon as they were gone, she ran down to the local town. Then she wandered into a chemist's shop, waited until the assistant was busy advising someone on the best way to treat sunstroke, and walked out with a packet of Clairol natural black hair dye.

Katy had often toyed with the idea of dyeing her hair. She dreamed of having it jet black and wild, like Patti Smith on the cover of *Horses*. What she'd give to be that thin! But failing that, the hairstyle would do nicely. She'd bought the album last year and had played it so often she knew all the lyrics off by heart. The opening words, 'Jesus died for somebody's sins but not mine' struck a particular chord. Unfortunately, the nuns at St Agatha's took as dim a view of girls colouring their hair as they did of blasphemy, and rebellious as Katy was, she wasn't willing to risk being expelled. But she wasn't at school any more. She was at Pontin's. And even if her hair went horribly wrong, she still had the whole of the summer holidays to grow it out.

Her hair hadn't gone horribly wrong – not exactly. Some bits were blacker than others, but then it was hard to apply hair dye evenly on your own, and even the purple bits behind her ears were a shade better than the mousy blonde she was this morning. As soon as it was done she realised that she'd have to go back to the chemist's and help herself to some darker makeup to complement her new hair colour. But now that she'd applied the purple eyeshadow and plum lipstick, it wasn't looking so bad. Her parents, of course, were bound to see things rather differently. In fact, they'd probably freak. She wasn't ready to face them just yet, so she decided to while away a few hours at the under-eighteens' disco and wait until the light faded before unveiling her new look.

She was standing outside the Dragon Bar, checking her skirt for dye stains and smoking a Sobranie, when she spotted a boy with bright orange hair walking towards her. As he approached she took a long drag on her cigarette and fixed him with a cocky grin. 'I like your hair,' she said. 'Who do you think you are? David Bowie?'

Some friendships take years to develop. Others are forged overnight. That night at the under-eighteens' disco, Anthony and Katy discovered what a perfect match they were. Not that their bond was based on anything so vulgar as sexual attraction. Anthony had already decided that his interests lay elsewhere, and Katy wasn't so naive as to assume that a boy with dyed orange hair would be interested in her in that way. In fact, she rather welcomed the fact that he wasn't. One of the disadvantages of going to an all-girls' school was that she didn't meet many boys, and when she did, the encounters were always fraught with the possibility of sex. To finally meet a boy she might actually consider a friend was a refreshing change.

The DJ claimed never to have heard of Patti Smith and refused to play anything by 'that bloody poofter' David Bowie. Instead, he served up a string of painfully familiar hits by inoffensive acts like the Brotherhood of Man, Dr Hook and the Bay City Rollers. But Anthony and Katy didn't really mind. They danced together for a bit, Anthony trying to impress with his mime artist moves, Katy trying not to laugh as he struggled to find an opening in an imaginary sheet of glass. When 'Devil Woman' came on, she played him at his own game, prowling around the dance floor like a Hammer horror vamp (which, with her black hair and purple lips, she resembled more closely than she realised).

Then, when the opening strains of 'Disco Duck' pushed the joke that little bit too far, they retired to a corner and talked.

'So do you go out dancing a lot?' Katy asked.

Anthony shrugged. 'There's not a lot of places to go in Bridgend. I go to the rugby club disco sometimes.'

Katy widened her eyes. 'Not with your hair like that! Don't you get picked on?'

'I used to,' Anthony said. 'Before the sixth form. Then most of the rugby boys left and the few that stayed on suddenly became strangely protective of me. They still see me as a freak, but I'm *their* freak and nobody else is allowed to have a go at me.'

Huddled together on plastic chairs under the disco lights, drinking Vimto and struggling to make themselves heard, they looked just like a typical couple of teenagers on a first date. They swapped life stories. They shared their tastes in music. Anthony told her about travelling down to Wembley the previous month to catch Bowie on the Station to Station tour.

'It was amazing,' he gushed. 'There was all this bright white light and him in his white shirt and black waistcoat. It was like something from a German expressionist film, not like a rock concert at all.'

'How many German expressionist films have you seen?' Katy asked, clearly impressed.

'None,' said Anthony.

'And how many rock concerts?'

'Just that one. But everyone said it was like no rock concert they'd ever been to.'

Having got Bowie out of the way, the conversation turned to subjects closer to home. They discussed religion and

Katy's parents' decision to send her to a Catholic girls' school despite the fact that they were hardly what she would call practising Catholics.

'I wouldn't be an only child if they were,' she said, and although it took Anthony a moment or two to work out what she meant, he nodded sagely as if religious observance and family planning were subjects he'd already given a lot of thought to.

Gradually they worked through their differences and found some common ground. And like countless teenagers before them, they discovered that what they really shared was a heightened sense of drama and a certain pride in their own outsiderdom. They boasted about being unpopular. They bitched about how boring school was, and how nobody understood them, and how they wished they could just run away to London and rent a flat somewhere and live on Pot Noodles. And by the time the evening finally drew to a close with couples smooching together to 'Silly Love Songs', they'd made a solemn vow to be friends for ever.

CHAPTER THREE

Tony arrived home to find a pizza menu poking through the letterbox and the house every bit as empty as when he'd left it. Home was a white stucco-fronted three-storey town house off the Fulham Road, purchased with the proceeds from A Boy and His Diva's first single, 'Love Is A Pain (In The Heart)', way back in 1983. There wasn't much love in the place, although the costs of converting a perfectly decent house into a palace fit for pop royalty had certainly pained his wallet. It was lucky for Tony that he'd written most of the hits himself and was therefore entitled to the lion's share of the royalties. The lifestyle of the rich and famous didn't come cheap, and even if he was no longer as rich or as famous as he'd have liked, he was still intent on keeping up appearances.

He closed the door behind him, placed his shopping bags on the table in the hall and, remembering that the fridge was practically empty and that it would soon be time for dinner, glanced at the pizza menu. This being fashionable Fulham, the pizzas were freshly baked in a wood-burning oven and came with a variety of gourmet toppings including goat's cheese and truffle oil. And to think there was a time when frozen pizza was considered the height of sophistication! He toyed with the idea of Canadian bacon, bell pepper and

Monterey Jack cheese, before catching a glimpse of his waistline in the hallway mirror and remembering that he was supposed to be on a diet.

The entrance hall led directly into the main reception room, which was dominated by a huge marble fireplace spotted during a shopping trip to Milan and shipped over at considerable expense. In front of the fireplace lay a sheep-skin rug. Above it hung a portrait of Tony by Pierre et Gilles, commissioned from the masters of pop iconography in 1990 and depicting him as an eternally youthful thirty-year-old with a bleeding heart and a flawless complexion. Bleached wooden floors, cream and gold walls, a glass coffee table and two large cream leather sofas completed the look.

The high-definition plasma screen TV had been left on all day (an easy habit to fall into when you lived alone), and as Tony entered the room his attention was immediately drawn to the latest music/exercise video from Madonna. He grabbed the remote and switched channels. Madonna's triumphant posturing was the last thing he needed today. How she'd managed to survive all these years he had no idea, but one thing he knew for certain. Talent had very little to do with it. (Tony and Madonna's paths had crossed briefly in 1984. She was on the way up and he, despite his best efforts, was very clearly on the way down. Needless to say, she didn't waste too much time getting to know him.)

He walked through to the kitchen, the sound of *The Simpsons* burbling away in the background. He loved *The Simpsons*. Sometimes he would spend an entire afternoon watching several episodes back to back, marvelling at how subversive the show was and congratulating himself on picking up the wealth of pop cultural references and sly in-jokes.

He could probably write a book on the subject, and probably would if he weren't so busy pursuing other projects.

He opened the Smeg fridge and was surprised to find half a lettuce and some leftover roast chicken together with the usual bottles of champagne he kept in case there were any visitors he wanted to impress. The lettuce was a bit limp, but add some mayonnaise and you'd never know the difference. And the chicken couldn't have been there for more than a couple of days. So that was dinner taken care of.

The vibration in his trouser pocket told him his mobile was ringing. It was his manager. 'Hi, Dan, what's up?'

'Good news. I've just heard back from Channel Seven. They've agreed your fee and the contract is being biked over to you as we speak. Just sign it while the courier waits and I'll go over it later. Sorry it's been such a drag but finally it looks as if we're all set to rock and roll. The show starts on Monday.'

'Monday? But I thought you said it didn't start for another two weeks.'

'The producers were worried about press leaks, so they brought it forward.'

Tony felt a sudden panic attack coming on. 'But Monday's too soon. It doesn't give me enough time.'

'What do you need time for? Like I said, we're all set.'

'You mean you've found her?'

'Katrina? No, not yet. But I do have some very good leads. But let's not dwell on that now. That's for me to sort out. You just concentrate on getting yourself into shape. We want you looking your best for the TV cameras. This show is going to be huge, I can just feel it.'

'Let's hope so. Do we know who the other celebrities are yet?'

'I did ask, but they're not giving away too many details at this stage. Like I said, they're worried about people leaking stuff to the press. It's all a bit hush-hush.'

'Well, so long as we're talking proper celebrities. I don't want to arrive and find that I'm stuck for three weeks with some bimbo whose only claim to fame is that she once slept with a fading Hollywood actor or a member of the England football team.'

'It may not be three whole weeks. Remember, you might get voted out before that.'

'Thanks for the vote of confidence! The point is, I'm only doing this to help pave the way for a new record deal. And for that to work, I need to be seen with the right sort of people. I'm not sharing my spotlight with some Z-list glamour model.'

'There's no worries on that score. I spoke to the producer this morning and he assures me that all the celebrities are household names. There won't be a face there the viewers won't recognise.'

Tony sighed. 'Well, that's a relief.'

'There's just one thing. It's a bit awkward really, but about the recognition factor . . . The producer wanted to know if you could do your hair the way it used to be, y'know, back when you were famous.'

'Well, thanks for that, Dan. Thanks a lot. And I suppose you told him it wouldn't be a problem?'

'Kind of. But it won't be, will it?'

Tony wandered into the hallway and gazed at his reflection in the mirror. He ran a hand over his head and tugged at his thinning locks. 'No,' he said, confidently. 'It won't be a problem.'

Katrina's flat was only a short drive away. The area was called Bloomsbury, and the place they'd driven from was called Goodge Street. The AIDS ward at the Middlesex Hospital wasn't actually in Middlesex, but in the middle of London. Even the name of the street sounded a bit queer.

'Here's your tea, Rose.'

Rose looked up from the sofa to see Katrina hovering with two steaming mugs of tea. Not cups as promised, but mugs. And the tea had been made from tea bags, no doubt. She hadn't been in the kitchen long enough to have gone through the ritual of using a teapot. She seemed nice enough, but judging from the way the flat was decorated, she wasn't very big on tradition. Rose's eyes were drawn to a large ceramic leopard standing guard next to the fireplace, the mantel of which was home to a menagerie of smaller animal figurines including a coiled cobra, a winged lion and what appeared to be some sort of dragon. Katrina was either a disgruntled teenager trapped in a forty-year-old woman's body, or some kind of witch. So much for the crucifix round her neck.

'Sorry about the mug,' Katrina said as she lowered herself into the armchair opposite and placed her tea on the glass coffee table between them. 'I've never been one for cups and saucers. A bull in a china shop, that's me. They wouldn't last long around here.'

'A mug is fine,' Rose replied, though she couldn't help recalling that Katrina's invitation had specified 'a nice cup of tea', and to her mind a proper cup of tea meant exactly that – a cup.

They sat in silence for a while, quietly sipping their tea. Rose's eyes wandered around the room, taking in the textured

28

walls, the red velvet curtains at the window and the thick white carpet underfoot. It was a big room – the carpet seemed to go on for miles – and at the opposite end to where they were sitting was a large dining table with six chairs in black ash. It was like being in an episode of *Through the Keyhole* and trying to guess the identity of the famous home-owner, most of whom she'd never heard of anyway. Who'd live in a house like this? Frankly, she didn't have a clue.

Finally Katrina spoke. 'I'm glad you could stay,' she said. 'It'll give us time to get to know each other.'

Rose smiled stiffly. She went to take a sip of tea, then stopped. 'Why did he die?' she said suddenly.

Katrina looked shocked, then puzzled. She obviously hadn't been expecting this. But what had she been expecting exactly? How was a person supposed to behave in these circumstances? Was it the done thing for a mother who'd rejected her only son to speak so bluntly of his death? What was the right thing to say?

'But I thought you knew,' Katrina said cautiously. 'He had—'

Rose cut her off. 'I know what he had. But I thought they could cure it nowadays, with these new drugs.'

'I'm afraid not,' Katrina said. 'It's a bit more complicated than that. The drugs have made a big difference, of course. They work for a lot of people. But not for everyone. Not always.'

Rose nodded and took a sip of tea. There was a long silence as she tried to process the information she'd been given, not really understanding it. Through the window she could hear the steady rumble of traffic, people heading to unknown destinations, life carrying on as normal.

'It must have been hard for you,' Katrina said finally. 'Seeing Mark again after all these years. But I'm glad you came. It meant a lot to him, I'm sure.'

Rose felt her hackles rise. 'He was my son,' she said sharply. 'What else was I supposed to do?'

'Of course,' Katrina said quickly. 'I didn't mean to suggest . . . It's just that, well, I know you and Mark didn't always see eye to eye on a few things. But I also know how much he loved you, and I know it would have been a great comfort to him, having you at the hospital like that.'

Rose studied her for a moment. 'You seem to know an awful lot,' she said. 'Do you have any children of your own?'

Katrina faltered. 'No. No, I don't.'

'Then forgive me for saying so, but I don't think you know half as much as you think you do.'

'You're probably right and I probably don't. But I did know Mark. And I know that this is what he'd have wanted. You back in his life.'

Rose's voice softened. 'I think it's a bit late for that, dear.'

Katrina leaned forward in her armchair. 'But it needn't be,' she said. 'Don't you see? It's not too late for you to get to know your son again. It's not too late for you to show him how much you care. There's still the funeral arrangements to take care of. And there's his flat. Someone needs to sort through his stuff and decide what to keep and what to give to charity. You could be a part of all that. You could stay here for a few days and we could make the arrangements together.'

Rose eyed her warily. 'You seem to have given this a lot of thought. I'm not one of those people who likes to outstay my welcome. And what about my clothes? I only have a few things with me.'

'Then we'll wash them, or you can borrow some of mine. And you wouldn't be outstaying your welcome. You'd be helping me. I can't go through this alone. And neither should you. It'll be easier for both of us if we do it together.'

Rose shifted uncomfortably in her seat. She looked away for a few moments, and when she turned back her eyes were wet. 'Why are you doing this?' she asked.

'Doing what?'

'Why are you being so nice to me? The other people at the hospital, his other friends ... Well, they weren't rude exactly, but I could tell they didn't approve of me. But you, you're different. First you invite me into your home, and now this. Why aren't you more like the others?'

Katrina smiled. 'Well, for one thing, I'm not a gay man. Don't get me wrong. Some of my best friends are gay men. And this lot are okay when you get to know them. It's just that they can be a bit defensive sometimes. Life's one long battle for a lot of them, and sometimes they forget that people like you aren't always the enemy. It's different for me. I'm a woman. We tend to see the wider picture. And as a woman I think it's probably a little easier for me to imagine what you're going through.'

Rose blushed. 'I'm sorry for what I said before, about you not having children of your own. I didn't mean anything by it.'

Katrina stood up. 'I know you didn't. Now, are you ready for more tea, or can I get you something stronger? A night-cap perhaps?'

'A brandy would be nice, though I don't think I'll sleep much tonight. Maybe you could show me some of those photos you mentioned.'

'Are you sure you're up to seeing them now?'

Rose nodded. 'I'm sure.'

So Katrina brought the brandy and dug out her photo album and for the next half-hour they sat together on the sofa, two women from very different worlds who barely knew one another but who both, in their own ways, had loved the same man.

'This one was taken in Rome,' Katrina said, pointing to a photo of herself and Mark posed beside the Trevi Fountain.

'He looks very handsome,' Rose said softly.

'He was,' Katrina replied, tracing the edge of the photograph with her finger. 'Very handsome. Especially then.'

'And where was this one taken?' Rose asked, pointing to another photo. This time Mark was standing alone, dressed completely in white with a silver cowboy hat on his head.

'That one was taken in Miami,' Katrina answered. 'New Year's Eve, 1999. I wasn't there that night. That was more of a boys' holiday.'

Rose grunted and placed her brandy on the coffee table. 'I'm sorry,' she said. 'Do you think I could use the bathroom?'

'Of course,' Katrina replied, her face still buried in the photograph album. 'It's just along the hallway, second door on the right.'

Rose found the bathroom easily enough, though she was a little taken aback at how long the hallway was. It was like the inside of a hotel. Were all the flats in Bloomsbury this big? she wondered. And what did a woman like Katrina need with all these rooms? You could fit a large family in this flat, yet here she was living all alone.

The bathroom was all mosaic tiles and Italian marble,

with a large sunken bath and a separate shower, big enough for two. The wash basin had a glass surround and those wall-mounted taps she could never work out how to use. Even the toilet paper felt strange to the touch, impossibly soft, as if it had been dipped in fabric conditioner. She tore off a few sheets and quickly dabbed her eyes and gave her nose a good blow. The paper smelt of lavender. She gazed at her reflection in the mirror and saw the gold record hanging above the toilet. She turned to inspect it.

The record was framed, with a red velvet background and an inscription that read: 'Presented to A Boy and His Diva to recognise sales in the United Kingdom of more than 750,000 copies of the single "Lovers and Losers", 1983'. Rose stared at it for a moment, recognising neither the name of the pop group nor the title of the song. But evidently this meant that Katrina had some connection to the music business, which would explain her strange taste in home furnishings.

She dabbed her eyes again and checked her reflection once more before making her way along the hallway and back to the living room. As she approached the room she heard the unmistakable sound of a woman weeping. She coughed gently and Katrina immediately slammed shut the photo album in her lap and pushed it aside.

'Sorry about this,' she said, wiping her eyes with the back of her hand. 'Sometimes it feels like I'm always crying over gay men.'

Rose looked at her blankly. 'I'm not sure I understand, dear.'

Katrina smiled up at her. 'No,' she said. 'I don't suppose you do.'

CHAPTER FOUR

For seventeen-year-old soul boy Anthony Griffiths, 1977 didn't get off to an auspicious start. With Johnny Mathis at the top of the charts, closely followed by David Soul and then Leo Sayer, it didn't look as if this would be a particularly good year for pop music. Even Bowie's eagerly awaited *Low* album proved a major disappointment, comprising as it did only half a dozen proper songs and a load of instrumentals, suggesting that, for the first time in his career, the normally erudite Bowie was literally lost for words. The vocal style was numb, almost lobotomised, lacking the theatrics of Ziggy or the tortured soul inflections of *Station to Station*. Even the record sleeve seemed uninspired. The Thin White Duke was sporting the exact same look he'd worn on his last album, which left his many imitators frantically searching for a new act to follow. As a disillusioned Anthony told Katy after throwing his copy of *Low* across the room in what he hoped was a grand gesture, 'If that's the best he can come up with, it's no wonder he's keeping such a low profile.'

But all this was forgotten (if not entirely forgiven) with the arrival of the Sex Pistols. The band had already dented the charts the previous November with 'Anarchy in the UK'. Their much-publicised foul-mouthed appearance on the *Today* programme with Bill Grundy had been the talk of the sixth-form common room, and had given Anthony's parents plenty to say about the youth of today and how you never heard the Beatles swear, or even Elvis for that matter. But this was nothing compared to the chorus of disapproval that greeted their next move. As the nation prepared to hang out the bunting for the Queen's Silver Jubilee celebrations, it was the release of 'God Save the Queen' that finally persuaded Anthony to ditch his soul-boy wedge and invest in a pair of bondage trousers.

The haircut was easy. Taking punk's DIY aesthetic to heart, he simply borrowed the scissors from his mother's sewing kit and chopped it off in front of the mirror. Unfortunately, the trousers posed more of a problem. Bondage trousers weren't readily available on the mean streets of Bridgend, where the local brand jeans, known as Gentle Folk, were still very much in vogue. High-waisted and bell-bottomed, with patch pockets large enough to fit an A4 folder, the jeans came in various shades of blue and were worn with pride by the sort of people who thought platform shoes were still the height of fashion. And much as it amused Anthony to think that the favourite jeans in Wales were Gentle Folk, even if some of the people weren't, that didn't help him in his efforts to transform himself from last year's soul boy into this year's punk. Even Cardiff was stuck in the dark ages so far as punk fashions were concerned. If he wanted the look he'd have to travel further afield. He'd have to go to London. Luckily, he had a bit of extra money at his disposal, having taken a Saturday job selling open-necked shirts and white polyester trousers to would-be John Travoltas while he studied for his A levels. It wasn't the most rewarding job in the world, but at least it meant he could afford to splash out on some new clothes for himself every once in a while.

'So when are we going?' Katy asked when Anthony made the announcement one Wednesday night over pints of snakebite at the Royal Oak on Park Street. The Oak was their favourite haunt – a grotty old pub where most of the punters were aged fifty or over, and were either too long in the tooth or too short-sighted to care what the youngsters were wearing or whether they were really old enough to be served alcohol. It may have lacked the energy of younger, more happening establishments like the Three Horseshoes, and getting there may have entailed a dash of death across the dual carriageway, but at least they weren't at the mercy of marauding gangs of rugby boys.

'Who said anything about you coming?' Anthony replied. 'Some things a boy has to do by himself. This is a rite of passage, a bit like a girl's first period or the first time you catch your parents having sex. I think it's something I should do alone.'

'Aw, Anthony!' Katy wailed. 'That's not fair. My parents have gone away for two weeks, and they left me money to buy food. If I lived on baked beans, I could easily afford the train fare. I was planning on having a party, but a trip to London sounds so much better.'

Anthony grinned. 'Only joking,' he said. 'Of course you can come. But mind you don't go too mad with the baked beans. I don't want you farting all the way to London.'

So the following Saturday Anthony phoned in sick to work, and shortly after nine a.m. they boarded the train to

Paddington. Katy didn't fart once – at least not so as Anthony noticed – and by eleven thirty they were off the train and worming their way through the crowds of Saturday shoppers and on to the Underground. As the westbound Circle Line train pulled out of Paddington and headed in the direction of Sloane Square, the semi-focused dream of London slowly became a reality.

If the truth be told, Katy had been to London once before. But she was only seven at the time and all she could really remember was the reptile house at London Zoo. It was there that her fascination with snakes began. Her fascination with London came much later, fuelled by the escapism of pop music and endless conversations with Anthony about what life would be like when they lived in the big city.

As for Anthony, he'd travelled down to Wembley the previous year. But that wasn't about seeing London. That was about seeing Bowie. And although, for him, the two were somehow related, he hadn't taken time to venture far from the concert hall, fearing that he might miss the start of the show.

This was different. The two of them together, riding on the Underground, heading for the world famous King's Road and the shop where the Sex Pistols were first formed! And it wasn't even lunchtime! They had the whole day ahead of them. Maybe if they were lucky they'd see Johnny Rotten. Or if not him, then maybe one of the lesser-known punk icons. Sue Catwoman perhaps, or one of the Bromley Contingent. Barely able to contain his excitement, Anthony smiled at Katy across the crowded Tube carriage and she grinned back at him, knowing exactly what he was thinking without him having to say a word.

The King's Road was like nothing they'd ever seen. People dressed for a day out in the country crossed paths with teddy boys and punks in black leather jackets and mohawks a foot high. And it was long. The road seemed to go on for ever. On and on they walked, past boutiques selling designer dresses and antique markets selling second-hand dinner suits. Outside a pub, a gang of punks were posing for photographers, beer bottles in hand, faces contorted into looks of disdain even as they accepted payment for their efforts. Then there were rows of houses, a few trees, and a cinema showing *Star Wars*. And still no end in sight.

'It's no wonder they call it World's End,' Katy huffed. 'You have to walk halfway across the world to get there.'

The shop they were looking for used to be called SEX, but was now called Seditionaries and sold 'Clothes for Heroes'. The brainchild of punk svengali Malcolm McLaren and fashion designer Vivienne Westwood, it was famous for two things – the clothes for sale inside, and the teenagers who would hang around for hours outside, daring one another to go in. Perversely, the clock hanging in the shopfront showed thirteen hours in a day and went backwards, so nobody was ever entirely sure how long they'd been standing there.

'Have you seen that clock?' Katy said, nudging Anthony's arm. 'That's mad, that is.'

'Time waits for no man,' Anthony replied airily and swept inside, dragging Katy behind him.

He spotted the trousers immediately. Red tartan, with matching bum-flaps, zips up the legs and straps at the knees.

'Sixty pounds!' Katy almost choked.

'Shut up, Katy,' Anthony hissed. 'God, you sound just like my mum! It's my money. I'll spend it how I like.'

'Yeah, but sixty pounds!' Katy repeated. 'You could buy three pairs of trousers with that. I thought punk was supposed to be about anarchy. Daylight robbery more like.'

She soon changed her mind when she saw Anthony step out of the changing room with the trousers on. 'They look really lush,' she said. 'I want a pair.'

'You can't have a pair. They look much better on boys. Why don't you buy a nice PVC miniskirt instead?'

'With my thighs? You must be joking!'

'It doesn't matter what size your thighs are. That's the great thing about punk. You can wear whatever you want, even if you look hideous in it. Look at Jordan in those fishnet stockings. There must have been a bloody big catch that day.'

Jordan, the shop's amply proportioned, blonde beehived sales assistant, turned and fixed them with a look that could turn milk sour.

Katy smiled at her. 'Sorry,' she said. 'We're from Wales.'

They arrived back in Bridgend just before seven thirty. They had planned to take a later train, but after wandering the King's Road for a few hours, Anthony decided he was bored and couldn't wait to get home and put his new look together. In fact, the train had barely left Paddington when he disappeared into the toilet with his carrier bag and came back with his bondage trousers on. It was a shame he couldn't afford a ripped T-shirt from Seditionaries. He particularly liked the one with the two cowboys, naked from the waist down with their cocks practically touching. But at £30, that would have been stretching his budget a bit. Still, all was not lost. He had a plain white T-shirt at home his mother had bought for him a week earlier. With a little help from Katy, whose creative skills had already earned her an O level in art, he was confident that he could turn a humble T-shirt into something fit for a teenage white punk.

Anthony's house was one of a long row of Victorian terraces that ran all the way from the bus station, past the old hospital where he had had his tonsils taken out, and under the railway bridge to the council estate where, once, he fell off his Chopper bike and chipped a tooth. It was a fairly ordinary house, no mansion, but big enough for himself, his parents and the second child they'd always planned but hadn't got around to producing. Whether this was the cause of his parents' many arguments, Anthony didn't dare say. But whenever they did argue, the third bedroom came in very handy.

The moment he turned his key in the front door he could hear his mother in the back kitchen, swapping gossip with Auntie Alma in tones of barely disguised glee. 'She never!' 'She did!' 'Well, of all the . . .' 'Well this is it, see, Myra. It's the quiet ones you have to look out for.' It struck him that nobody would ever accuse his mother or Alma of being especially quiet, which presumably meant that they were above suspicion.

Alma wasn't really Anthony's auntie, just a long-standing friend of his mother's. How long-standing was a matter of some dispute, mainly between his mum and her somewhat hazy powers of recollection. 'I've been friends with Alma for twenty-seven years,' she announced one Christmas after a few too many Cinzanos. 'No, thirty-three years! No, nineteen years!'

Anthony gently closed the door and gestured for Katy to follow him up the stairs.

'Is that you, Anthony?' His mother's voice rang out down the hall.

'Yeah, I'm just going up to my room.'

'Well come and say hello to Auntie Alma first. She hasn't seen you in weeks. And is that Katy with you? Bring her in too.'

It was true that Auntie Alma hadn't seen Anthony for some time, and was therefore unfamiliar with the latest developments. The orange hair dye she'd seen before, but not the new punk hairstyle. Combined with the bondage trousers, it was a look that was bound to provoke a reaction, particularly from a woman in her forties who had her hair set in the same beige bouffant every week.

Sure enough, Alma's eyes practically popped out of her head. 'How will you get a proper job looking like that?' she asked.

'Oh, he doesn't want a proper job, Alma,' his mother chipped in. She was in full throttle now and relishing every moment. Bosom heaving, she pulled back her chin and pursed her lips until she was confident she had everyone's full attention.

'He wants to go to college in London,' she announced finally, allowing a slight pause for the full impact of this revelation to sink in. 'He wants to do drama.' She pronounced 'London' and 'drama' as if they were the most exotic concepts in the world, as foreign to her as Demis Roussos or chilli con carne.

'Drama?' Alma chortled. 'Well you don't need to run off to

London for that, love. There's plenty of drama round here. You should come round my house. It's one drama after another.' She turned her attention to Katy. 'And what have you been buying, love?'

Katy clutched her carrier bag and shifted uncomfortably in her Doctor Marten boots. 'It's just a skirt,' she said quietly.

'Well give us a look then,' Alma said, pointing at the bag and gesticulating wildly.

Reluctantly, Katy opened the bag and took out a black PVC skirt with buckles on one side and silver chains hanging down the front. Anthony smirked. His mother and Alma exchanged glances. Nobody spoke for a moment.

'Ooh, it's a bit risky, isn't it?' Alma said with a roll of her eyes.

'I think you mean risqué,' Anthony sniggered. 'It's called bondage gear. It's supposed to look like the clothes worn by prostitutes.'

Alma gave a little shudder. 'I could never be a prostitute,' she said, as if this was a viable career option for a woman at her time of life, and one she'd given a considerable amount of thought to. What her husband would have made of this, Anthony didn't dare speculate.

'I wouldn't mind the clothes so much,' Alma went on. 'But I couldn't stand the thought of having to go with a dwarf or something, and them climbing all over you with their little hands. It would turn my stomach, it would.'

Anthony stared at her, began to say something, then thought better of it. Some things were better left unsaid. He turned to his mum. 'Is it okay if Katy stays over tonight?' he asked. 'Her parents are away, and we thought we might go into town later.'

'Of course it is, love,' his mother replied. 'There's always a bed here for Katy. She knows that.'

'Thank you, Mrs Griffiths.' Katy smiled.

His mother smiled back, then turned to Anthony and sighed. 'Though why she'd want to be seen with you looking like that, I haven't a clue.'

They left the house an hour later, Katy in her PVC skirt, Anthony in his tartan bondage trousers and white T-shirt with the sleeves torn off and the word 'Anarchy' scrawled across the front in black marker pen. The following week a photograph of Anthony in his new punk ensemble appeared in the pages of the *Glamorgan Gazette*. It was the beginning of a great love affair.

CHAPTER FIVE

Rose woke to the rumble of delivery vans thundering down the streets below. At home it would have been the gentle hum of the milk float – the only sound to break the early morning silence in her quiet cul-de-sac. But she wasn't at home. She was in London, where rich people lived alone in flats big enough for entire families and traffic roared through the night without a thought for grieving women or people trying to sleep.

She hadn't slept much. It wasn't the fault of the bed, which was more comfortable than any she'd ever slept in, if a little larger than necessary. The mattress seemed to mould itself to the shape of her body, making her strangely weightless. Nor, if she was honest, was it the fault of the traffic. She'd slept through far worse than that, particularly in the early days of her marriage. Her husband's sexual demands had never been that great, but his snoring was a different story.

No, what had kept her awake half the night were the thoughts running through her head. Thoughts of Mark and what a bad mother she'd been. Thoughts of Katrina and the love in her eyes when she looked at those photos. From what she'd said, it sounded as though Katrina had been a better mother to him than she'd been herself. She couldn't have been much older than Mark, but she certainly appeared to have loved him the way a mother should – unconditionally. Which was more than could be said for the woman who gave birth to him.

She remembered it as if it were yesterday. Lying in that hospital bed, cradling her baby boy in her arms, feeling worn out and weepy but oh so happy. Where had it all gone wrong? How had she gone from that happy hospital bed to the one she'd sat beside yesterday, watching helplessly as the son she barely knew took his final breath? Terrible memories came flooding back to her. Things she'd said, like the time she told him she wished he'd never been born. Things she'd done, like the time she emptied the contents of his wardrobe into bin bags and threw them on the bonfire. Things she could only hope he'd forgiven her for now that it was too late to put them right.

Suddenly she felt her eyes burn and her chest tighten. She sank back under the covers and buried her face in the duvet. For a few minutes she lay there, quietly choking on her own tears. Was this what real grief felt like? She thought she'd grieved when her father died, but it was nothing compared to this. The convulsions were so strong, it felt as if her stomach was being ripped out. She remembered reading somewhere that there was no word for a parent who loses a child, because the mere thought of such a thing was too awful to even contemplate. You weren't supposed to outlive your children. That wasn't the way it was supposed to be. It wasn't part of God's plan.

None of this was God's work, she was certain of that. No matter what the Old Testament said, she couldn't believe that her God would take away a life like this. She'd heard them on the radio, those Tory lords and Anglican bishops, pontificating about the sin of homosexuality. There was a time when she might have listened to what they had to say, might even have found herself nodding in agreement with some of it. After her husband left, there was a period when the Church was everything to her and she swallowed everything its leaders said, no matter how harsh it sounded.

But not any more. She'd let Mark down enough when he was alive. She wouldn't deny him now he was dead. The funeral would be her chance to make amends. It would be everything a proper funeral should be. A church filled with mourners, the best floral arrangements money could buy, a few well-chosen hymns, and then afterwards he'd be buried in the family plot, next to his beloved grandfather, home at last.

There was a gentle knock on the door and Katrina popped her head in. She had no makeup on and looked puffy around the eyes. Her blonde hair was pulled back off her face, and her roots were beginning to show.

'Did you sleep okay?' she asked.

'Not really, dear.'

'No, me neither. I've made some tea and there's a choice of cereal or bacon and eggs if you're really hungry.'

'Maybe just a slice of toast.'

Ten minutes later they were facing each other across the breakfast table, Katrina in her fluffy white bathrobe with a half-eaten bowl of muesli, Rose in her sensible skirt and blouse with a slice of toast going cold on her plate.

'I suppose we should start making plans for the funeral,' Katrina said, more briskly than she'd intended. It was awful, the way things came out at times like this. Of course it didn't help that her house guest was a total stranger to her, as unfathomable in her way as death itself. How were you supposed to discuss funeral arrangements with a grieving mother who'd rejected her only son for being gay and was only reunited with him as he lay on his deathbed? What was the correct tone to take?

'I was thinking the very same thing,' Rose said, and for an awful moment Katrina thought she'd read her mind. 'There's a church in Swindon where Mark was christened,' the older woman continued. 'I've not been in a while, but I'm sure the vicar would allow us to hold it there. The cemetery where his grandfather is buried is nearby. I know it's a bit far for all of his friends to come, but since he's going to be buried there anyway . . .'

Katrina looked at her blankly. 'But I thought you knew,' she said.

'Knew what?'

'Mark left very specific instructions in his will. He didn't want to be buried in Swindon. In fact, he didn't want to be buried at all. He wanted to be cremated here in London. And he didn't want a traditional service. He wanted people to remember him the way he was. He didn't want some vicar he didn't know rewriting history or telling people how they should feel.'

Rose looked ashen. 'But that can't be,' she said. 'Yesterday, when you asked me to stay, you said we could arrange things together. You made it sound as though I actually had a choice about the way my son's funeral was conducted. Now you're telling me that my feelings don't matter. I don't understand.'

'I'm not saying that,' Katrina said firmly. 'I'm not saying

that at all. All I'm saying is that Mark had certain ideas about what should happen after he was gone, and a traditional burial wasn't one of them.'

Rose sniffed and dabbed her eyes. 'Well, it's not right. It's not the way these things are supposed to be done.'

'Right or not, it's what he wanted.' Katrina paused and smiled. 'Mark had plenty of time to plan his own funeral,' she said. 'That was the one advantage he had, knowing he was going to die. I think we should honour his wishes, don't you?'

Tony wasn't having a very good morning. First he woke with a thumping headache, brought on no doubt by the detox diet he'd sworn to follow before stepping in front of the television cameras. Then his dreams of relaunching his career took a turn for the worse when he popped out for a pint of semi-skimmed milk and spotted the headline in the *Daily Mirror*. In fact, he didn't so much spot it as have his attention drawn to it by Mr Jivani, his friendly local Asian shopkeeper.

'I see you are in the newspapers again, Mr Tony,' he said, smiling, which raised Tony's hopes for a moment before fate stepped in and delivered a crushing blow to his ego. He was hoping to make headlines, but this wasn't quite what he had in mind. 'Eighties has-been to join nation's favourite weather girl in new reality show' was the headline. He could barely bring himself to read the rest of the story, but of course his curiosity got the better of him and he returned home with the paper folded under his arm.

'Tony Griffiths, of eighties pop duo A Boy and His Diva, is

set to take part in a new reality show for Channel Seven,' the story went. 'Griffiths, once famous for his gravity-defying black and blond hairdo, hasn't had a hit since 1984. He last made headlines in 2005, when he was charged with possession of a controlled substance. No doubt he'll be hoping that previous convictions don't come back to haunt him when he swaps his designer clothes for a prison uniform and takes his place inside *The Clink*. The show, which starts on Monday, features ten celebrities who will be locked in a maximum-security prison and asked to perform a number of back-breaking tasks as decided by you, the viewing public. Punishments for failing to complete the tasks will include solitary confinement and loss of meal privileges. Griffiths, whose hits included "Lovers and Losers", is said to be planning a comeback. He'll be joined in *The Clink* by weather girl Tamsin Applegate and by Ritchie Taylor, lead singer with the Brit award-winning group Fag Endz. Let's hope one of them can lend poor Tony a hairdryer. The last time he was seen out in public, his hair looked like something previously worn by Elton John.'

Tony phoned his manager straight away.

'You've seen it, then,' Dan said. He sounded annoyingly blasé about the whole thing, almost as if it was something he'd been anticipating for weeks.

'Yes, I've seen it,' Tony snapped. 'What the hell is going on, Dan? How could you let this happen?'

'It's not so bad,' Dan assured him. 'There are far worse things in life than being called a has-been. They could have called you a never-was.'

'Well excuse me while I count my blessings,' Tony hissed. 'As a matter of fact, I'm fully aware that there are worse things in life than being called a has-been. One thing worse than being called a has-been is discovering that I'm about to be locked in a prison cell.'

'Oh, that,' Dan said cautiously.

'Yes, that,' Tony replied. '*I'm a Celebrity* meets *Celebrity Big Brother*, that's how you described the show to me. Nobody said anything about a prison.'

'Didn't they?' Dan sounded distracted, as if he'd suddenly remembered something far more important he ought to be doing, preferably on the other side of the world. 'Well, you know what these producers are like. They have to keep upping the ante. Celebrities alone are no guarantee of good ratings any more. They have to find new ways to keep the viewing figures up. First they put them in the jungle. Then it was a tropical island. Then it was a farm. Now it's prison.'

'Well I'd rather be stuck in the jungle than behind bars,' Tony said. 'And a few weeks on a tropical island sounds like my idea of heaven. Even the farm sounds like a holiday camp compared to this.'

'It won't be that bad,' Dan said soothingly. 'Besides, there's not a lot either of us can do about it now. It's too late to back out. I biked your contract over to them first thing this morning. It's all signed, sealed and delivered. Pull out now and they'll sue you for breach of contract. And don't forget, you really need the exposure. I hate to remind you of this, but without this show I can't offer any guarantees that I'll be able to find you a new record deal.'

At the mention of a new record deal, Tony instantly perked up. 'So have there been any developments? How are things shaping up?'

'They're ticking along. I've made some calls, sounded a

few people out. I think I've managed to generate some inter-est. But to be honest, it really all depends on how well you come across on this show. You know how it is these days, Tony. It's one big bloody popularity contest. If the public likes you, the record companies will like you too.'

'And Katrina?'

'I'm still working on it. Nobody has heard from her in years. Wherever she's hiding, she obviously doesn't want to be found. But if she's still around, I'll find her. And as I'm sure I don't have to tell you, I can be very persuasive. Whatever her reservations, it won't take me long to talk her round. It'll be fine. Trust me.'

'And in the mean time I have to share a prison cell with Ritchie fucking Taylor.'

'Is that so bad? I've never understood why you hate that kid so much. What's he ever done to you?'

A good question. And the simple answer was, absolutely nothing. But animosity didn't always need a reason, partic-ularly when it was fostered by one slightly over-the-hill gay singer-songwriter and directed towards another, far younger, far prettier model with a bigger audience and a better hairline. And besides, there were more than enough reasons to take an instant dislike to someone like Ritchie Taylor. Fag Endz were one of those annoying pseudo-rock groups who borrowed their look and sound wholesale from the sort of New Wave bands they were far too young to remember, and who wore their politics on the sleeves of their skinny-fit jackets. Lyrically, they shared Morrissey's fondness for bits of rough, one of their earliest hits being the defiantly upbeat 'Buggered In Borstal'. Ritchie himself was openly gay, staunchly vegetarian, and to top it all he came from Cardiff and chose to sing in an overly exaggerated Welsh accent.

'I just don't like him, that's all,' Tony grumbled.

'Well maybe when you've got to know him a bit better you'll change your mind,' Dan said. 'I'd have thought that you two had a lot in common. You're both gay. You're both musical. And judging by his accent, I'd hazard a guess and say that you're both Welsh.'

'Oh for fuck's sake, Dan,' Tony practically screamed. 'Have you listened to the ridiculous way he sings? Nobody is that Welsh!'

CHAPTER SIX

A scream rang out from behind a closed door marked 'Katy's Room' and echoed down the stairs of the well-kept semi-detached property Mr Richard Williams and his lovely wife Linda were proud to call home. Behind the door, their teenage daughter lay sprawled across her bed, surrounded by posters of Siouxsie and the Banshees and listening to their debut album *The Scream* at full volume. After another heated argument with her father, her hair had been dyed with a semi-permanent hair colour that started off black but had already faded to a purplish brown. As if to compensate for this, her clothes were the blackest items she could find in her wardrobe. A black suede skirt was teamed with a black T-shirt and a black woolly cardigan. The eyeliner pencil she had used to draw panda circles around her eyes was also black. And her mood? Black.

It was the middle of November, and John Travolta and Olivia Newton-John were enjoying their seventh week at the top of the charts with 'Summer Nights'. *Grease* was the word, and people were queuing round the block to watch a film in which thirty-year-old actors played at being teenagers and broke into song at the drop of a cliché. Even Olivia's transformation from shy cheerleader to cat-suited temptress failed to persuade Katy that this was something worth getting excited about. Punk was supposed to have revolutionised the music industry, and the best 1978 could offer was a fifties revival with dancing cheerleaders and hunks in letter sweaters. How much worse could it get?

A bit worse, perhaps. She could be at St Agatha's. Half-term had ended days ago, but thanks to a particularly virulent throat infection she was still at home with her parents in Swansea, listening to the Banshees, sucking honey and lemon Strepsils and wondering what to do with the rest of her life. Ahead of her, another year of school loomed like a prison sentence. She was seventeen and she felt as if the world was passing her by. Girls younger than her had money in their pockets and jobs in local pubs and restaurants. Yet here she was, supposedly studying for her A levels, when really all she wanted to do was follow in Siouxsie's footsteps. What use were A levels when you dreamed of becoming a punk icon? It all seemed so pointless. She'd have considered suicide, but if she killed herself today she'd never know if the Boomtown Rats made it to Number 1. 'It's a rat trap and you've been caught.' She knew the feeling well.

To top it all, her best friend in the world had swanned off to London, leaving her to face the horrors of Swansea all alone. Starting a new life in London was something she and Anthony had dreamed about since the day they met, and for the past year it had been their main topic of conversation as he crammed for his exams and applied to various colleges. He'd had several interviews, mainly for courses he wasn't remotely interested in but which were offered by colleges within travelling distance of London. Then he found a course he really liked the sound of – a BA combined honours in drama and English, at St Mary's College in Twickenham.

'It's not really London,' he told her. 'More like Middlesex. But it's only forty minutes to Waterloo, and with a full grant and a student railcard I can easily afford the train fare.'

So he went for an interview and, following an audition in which he gave a moving performance as a man trapped inside a glass box, they offered him a place. He only needed two A-level passes, so when he failed his history exam it didn't really matter. He still had a B in English and a C in religious studies. One phone call and it was all confirmed. He was in. And then he was gone. Just like that.

He'd written to her, of course. Every week she waited for his letters, and every week they arrived in black envelopes with silver handwriting, addressed to 'The Diva Katy Williams' and filled with tantalising accounts of nights at the theatre and days spent languishing in bed writing poetry. She wrote back, wondering if he ever went to lectures and asking if there was a place on his course for her. She was only joking, of course, but behind the humour lay the quiet desperation of someone who'd been left behind.

Her mother's voice echoed up the stairs, barely audible over the sonic assault of 'Hong Kong Garden'. 'Katy! Your tea's ready!'

She turned the music down and opened the bedroom door an inch. 'I'm not hungry,' she shouted back, but she knew there was no point in arguing.

Sure enough, her father wasted little time in asserting his authority. 'Come down and eat your tea right now, young lady,' he bellowed. 'You've been up in that room all day. It's not good for you.' This from the man who spent most of his spare time in an overheated greenhouse, tending his precious plants. The way he went on, you'd swear he was Mr Sociable himself.

She trudged down the stairs and took her place at the table, careful to avoid her father's eyes. Her mother buzzed back and forth from the kitchen, all hot plates and nervous smiles. Finally she sat down and the nightly ritual began. 'Get it down you, love, before it goes cold.'

Katy stared at her plate. Lamb chops. She hated lamb chops. There was a song on the Banshees album called 'Carcass', which just about summed up her feelings towards the food on her plate. Maybe now was the time to consider becoming a vegetarian. 'I don't think I can eat this, Mum.'

'What's the matter? Aren't they done? I grilled them for fifteen minutes.'

'It's not that. I just don't like the thought of eating lamb. It doesn't seem right somehow.'

'Oh, well . . . Is there something else I can get you? I think there's some cold ham in the fridge.'

Her father slammed his fist on the table. 'She'll eat what she's given,' he said, which was her mother's cue to stop being so ridiculous and caving in to her daughter's every whim.

'Right,' her mum said and pursed her lips. She looked as if she might be about to cry.

'But Dad . . .' Katy began.

Her father lowered his knife and fork and glowered at her across the table. 'You'll eat what's on your plate, young lady,' he said. 'And then as soon as you've washed the dishes you can go upstairs and get your stuff packed for the morning. I'm taking you back to school.'

Anthony was putting the final touches to a poem he'd been working on. He'd been feeling pretty inspired in the poetry department lately. Yesterday he'd composed a tongue-in-cheek number entitled 'Never Trust A Dwarf (With Sex On His Mind)', written in memory of his Auntie Alma's comments about the demands placed on prostitutes and the peculiar horrors of men with little hands. Maybe it was a sign that he was more homesick than he cared to admit, but today's poem was an altogether more sombre affair. Entitled 'The Shadow Explodes', it was full of pent-up aggression and extended metaphors involving shattered mirrors and moving shadows. It also hinted at something vaguely sexual, once shrouded in secrecy but now emerging into the light. The last line was: 'Youth and I stand together, joined in the flesh.' Anthony was especially pleased with that line. It sounded sexy but vaguely apocalyptic, like something Bowie might have written around the time of *Diamond Dogs*. Some people might have interpreted 'The Shadow Explodes' as a coming-out poem, but Anthony wouldn't hear of such a thing. He simply liked the sound of the words.

In the absence of a suitable garret, he'd composed his poem in Room 107, Old House Hall of Residence, St Mary's College, Waldegrave Road, Twickenham, Middlesex TW1 4SX. He knew the address off by heart, as well he might. This was his room, the first address he could truly call his own, and it gave him a great sense of pride just to be able to recite it at will. The room wasn't very big, or very much to look at. A single bed took up most of the floor space. Next to the window was a small sink where he brushed his teeth and sometimes urinated when he was caught short during the night. The curtains were a revolting shade of green, and the radiator was a large grey monstrosity that went from freezing cold to scalding hot and back again in accordance with the whim of the college authorities and regardless of the weather.

But it was home, and in the short time he'd been here he'd made it his own. The walls were plastered with posters, mostly old favourites from his bedroom in Wales, but with a few recent additions. Over the door, Kate Bush gazed down with crimped hair and a somewhat sorrowful expression. Maybe someone had informed her that *Lionheart* wasn't a patch on *The Kick Inside* (although Anthony did love 'Wow', arguably the greatest song about stage fright ever written by a schoolgirl poetess turned freaky pop star. And the reference to a failed 'movie queen' busy 'hitting the Vaseline' hadn't gone completely over his head either). Next to the bed, a poster for Derek Jarman's *Jubilee* signalled a growing awareness of experimental film, some of which Anthony had actually seen. Above his desk, a poster for Lindsay Kemp's *Flowers* reminded him of a night at Sadler's Wells, watching the man who mentored both Bowie and Bush and who was still a force to be reckoned with, regardless of what the critics said. The wardrobe doors were covered in postcards and cuttings from magazines. Pictures of male dancers in tights and punk boys in eyeliner featured heavily.

Anthony himself was no longer sporting the punk look he'd worn for his interview, and which had prompted one of his lecturers to remark that he looked like Johnny Rotten. His hair had returned to its natural brown and was in an overgrown bob, no longer short and spiky but not quite long. His bondage trousers had been cast aside in favour of skinny black jeans, worn with a leather bomber jacket and a plunging V-neck T-shirt which gave him a slightly androgynous look. It was the look worn by Bowie in the 'Heroes' video, the album of which sat on the shelf next to the stereo, together with albums by Kate Bush, Kraftwerk, Iggy Pop and a group of men in makeup who looked like the New York Dolls but who came from south London and went by the unlikely name of Japan.

Anthony had bought a lot of records recently. A lot of records, and an awful lot of clothes. The day his grant cheque came through, he went out and spent close to £400 on items he deemed necessary to get him through his first term of college. The fact that this left him with very little to actually live on didn't bother him in the slightest. He could always do as others did and live off an overdraft. Besides, man could not live by bread alone, even if it was Mother's Pride and would keep for six days if wrapped in a carrier bag and hung outside the window. Anthony's culinary skills barely stretched to beans on toast, and what he saved on food bills he had no guilt spending on the finer things in life. Obviously he needed his leather bomber jacket to keep him warm during these cold winter nights. And clearly he couldn't be seen dead in last year's bondage trousers, not with papers like the *Daily Mirror* showing people how to achieve the punk look by ripping up their clothes and pretending they'd had their nose pierced. Black jeans didn't show the dirt, which saved money on the launderette, and everyone needed at least one Vivienne Westwood T-shirt in their wardrobe. Anthony had two, including the naked cowboy T-shirt he'd first admired a year ago but hadn't found the courage to wear just yet.

The reason for this was simple. Much to his dismay, college

life wasn't quite as liberating as he'd imagined. In fact, there were just as many rugby boys roaming the campus at St Mary's as there were roaming the streets back home. The irony of the situation wasn't lost on him. Having fled from a place where rugby was practically a religion, it was pretty galling to discover that he'd be sharing a campus with a load of rugby boys for another three years. The two biggest departments were the drama department and what was laughingly referred to as 'sports science'. So far as Anthony could tell, this involved drinking copious amounts of beer and playing rugby several days a week before qualifying for a job as a games teacher and terrorising future generations of awkward teenagers with hair issues and no interest in sport.

The rugby boys liked to get their practice in at night, when they would return from the student union bar tanked up on cheap beer and run amok with the fire hose, smashing through the glass panels above fellow residents' doors and soaking everything inside. That was when they weren't turning on one of their own, dragging him into the showers and rubbing toothpaste into his testicles or shaving off his pubic hair. It was for this reason that Anthony always avoided taking a shower after eleven p.m., although there was a certain amount of titillation in watching fit young lads horsing around with a fire hose or whipping one another with wet towels. One night they were even rumoured to have tied someone naked to a chair and taken turns simulating a scene from *Deliverance*. And they had the nerve to call him queer!

There was another student who received just as many soakings as Anthony, and who was also labelled queer. His name was James and he lived just down the hall in Room 113. He was also studying drama, and he and Anthony had exchanged the occasional nod and the odd word during lectures or in the drama studio. James had a head of blond curls and a lip that would curl into a camp approximation of a snarl at the slightest provocation. He came from High Wycombe and had trained for a couple of years as a dancer before deciding that a degree in drama offered a wider range of career options. His passion for dance had never left him, and he was often to be seen pirouetting around the playing fields or pointing his toes at the Porter's Lodge. Anthony kept James at a safe distance. He might smile at him across the courtyard, but he would never consider sitting down and eating with him in the canteen. Even for an exhibitionist like Anthony, James drew far too much attention to himself, and since Anthony had absolutely no desire to have sex with him, there was no reason on earth why they should be friends.

So he wasn't entirely pleased when he heard a knock on his door and opened it to find James standing there with one hand on his hip and the other held mid-air with the knuckles still clenched. Anthony checked the hall for rugby boys and was relieved to find that there was no one else around.

'There's a call for you,' James said. 'On the pay phone. Some girl. It sounds pretty urgent.'

'Right,' Anthony replied. 'Er, thanks.' He looked around for his keys, but couldn't see them. 'Would you mind keeping an eye on my room? I won't be long.'

'Take as long as you like,' James smiled, stepping into the room and unfurling himself on the bed. 'I'm not going anywhere.'

Anthony ran down the hall, already doubting the wisdom

of his decision. But any thoughts of James getting too comfortable on his bed were soon forgotten when he picked up the phone.

'Anthony! Thank God you're there.'

'Katy. What's wrong? Is everything okay?'

'Nothing's wrong. Well, that's not quite true, but I'm okay. The thing is, I've made a decision. I'm coming to London.'

'To visit? Great! When?'

'Not to visit. To live. And I'm coming tonight. My train leaves in five minutes.'

Ultimately, it didn't matter that Katy had made her decision to run away from home long before picking up the phone. It didn't matter that Anthony tried to talk her out of it, and only agreed to put her up in his room for a few nights on condition she phoned her parents as soon as she arrived. From this day forth, Katy's father would refer to Anthony Griffiths as the boy who led his little girl astray.

CHAPTER SEVEN

After breakfast, Katrina suggested they drive over to Mark's flat and make a start sorting through his things.

'Tell me if you're not feeling up to it,' she said. 'I can always go alone. But I think it might help.'

Still smarting from the news about the funeral arrangements, Rose nodded meekly.

The journey didn't take long, but the view of London couldn't have been more different. Mark's flat was south of the river, on the ninth floor of a tower block overlooking an old pub and a car park littered with broken glass. Katrina parked the car and led Rose into the lift. It smelled of stale urine and cigarettes.

'He lived here?' Rose asked, dismayed.

'For the past couple of years, yes,' Katrina replied. 'It's not so bad once you're inside.'

That's easy for you to say, Rose thought. You with your four bedrooms and your posh flat in Bloomsbury. But she said nothing. This promised to be difficult enough, without any added tension.

Katrina was right, in any case. The place didn't look so bad from the inside. It was cheery at least. A terracotta hallway led to a bright yellow living room with a large sofa, a small dining table and chairs and a piano. What the piano was doing there, Rose had no idea. Mark had been for one piano lesson when he was seven years old, but other than that he'd never shown the slightest aptitude for music.

'I didn't know Mark played the piano,' she said.

'Oh, yes,' Katrina replied. 'He wasn't bad actually, considering how late he started. His teacher said he could have been a concert pianist if he'd had the right training. Hidden talents, eh?'

They walked on into the kitchen, which was bright and airy and filled with house plants. Orchids lined the windowsill. A large ornamental fig stood next to the fridge. Ferns grew from glazed pots and spider plants trailed from hanging baskets.

'I pop in and water them every few days,' Katrina explained. 'He really loved his plants. I promised him faithfully that I wouldn't let them die.' She bit her lip. 'Why don't you go and make yourself comfortable and I'll put the kettle on.'

Sensing that Katrina needed a moment alone, Rose retreated into the hallway and hovered there for a moment, not sure which way to turn. On her left was a door which opened into the bathroom. Switching on the light, she was confronted with a large framed photograph of a bare-chested man rising up out of the ocean and staring straight back at her. She switched off the light and pulled the door closed. Directly ahead of her was another door, which she assumed must lead to the bedroom. She didn't dare look inside. She was frightened of what she might find in there. She turned right into the living room and lowered herself on to the sofa.

It felt strange being here, here in this flat where her son had lived and she had never visited. Every unfamiliar sight felt like an accusation. There was the table she'd never eaten off. There was the television she'd never watched. There was the stereo she'd never listened to. There was the piano she'd never heard him play. And there on top of it were the framed photographs she'd never seen, the memories she'd never been part of.

She stood and walked over to the piano. The first photo that caught her eye was of Mark and a blond man she recognised from the hospital. They were lying on a beach somewhere, squinting up at the camera with their hands shielding their eyes, both smiling happily. She wondered who the blond man was. A friend perhaps? Or someone more important? She couldn't put her next thought into words. Was 'boyfriend' the correct term? It sounded silly, the sort of thing a teenager might say. Was 'partner' more appropriate? 'Lover' sounded too melodramatic, and made her think of things she'd rather not dwell on.

She turned her attention to the next photo, which offered the far less challenging sight of Mark dressed in a dinner suit, looking terribly handsome and slightly embarrassed. The photo appeared to have been taken in this very room, and fairly recently judging from the weight loss in his face. Rose picked it up and held it to her chest, as if somehow this might bring him closer. As she stood there, quietly fighting back the tears, her eyes slowly focused on a much smaller photo, tucked away behind the others. It was in a silver frame and showed a younger-looking Mark with a girl of about five perched on his shoulders. The image was too small to make out the features clearly, but Rose could see that the girl was a pretty little thing with mousy hair and a gap in her teeth.

The door opened and Katrina appeared with a tray laden with china teacups, saucers, a bowl of sugar, a tiny milk jug and a large teapot. Rose was pleased to see that her son had standards, even if some of his friends didn't.

'Who's the blond man in this photograph?' she asked.

Katrina came and stood beside her. 'Oh, that's Peter,' she said, smiling. 'I think you met him briefly at the hospital.'

'And were he and Mark . . . What was the nature of their relationship?'

'They were together, for a while. But that was a long time ago. They were friends mainly. Good friends. Peter's a very special person. You'd like him.'

Rose forced a smile. 'I'm sure. And who's the little girl?'

Katrina looked distracted. 'What little girl?'

'This little girl. Here in this photograph.'

Katrina leaned forward and stared at the photo. 'Do you know, I really have no idea,' she said, shaking her head. 'Maybe it's one of the neighbours' kids. Mark really had a way with children. And you know what some of these estates are like. Kids running around everywhere. You don't know who they belong to half the time. Now, shall we have some tea?'

Katrina turned and walked briskly over to the table, and as she did so Rose thought she detected a slight stiffening of the back and a flushing of the cheeks. Maybe it was just the emotional demands of the day, but suddenly Katrina looked like a woman who was hiding something.

If some journalist were to turn up on his doorstep and ask him to name the one major difference between the pop stars of the eighties and the pop stars of today, Tony would have answered without hesitation. 'We had faces then,' he'd have said. 'We didn't need a team of stylists to create a look for us. We did it ourselves. We were creative. We had imagination. To some casual observers it may have looked like a mere headscarf, or a load of bangles, or a white stripe painted across someone's face. But to us it was a personal style statement. It said that here was someone who saw the world in a different way, someone who thought for themselves. Most pop stars today couldn't think their way out of a plastic bag. In my day they'd have taken that plastic bag and turned it into an outfit.'

It was a slightly ridiculous thing to say, of course. He knew that. Being slightly ridiculous was part and parcel of being a pop star, and never more so than in the eighties. But it also happened to be true. Tony had never relied on anyone to teach him how to dress. He may have taken inspiration from certain people. He may have borrowed the odd fashion tip here and there. But by the time he became a fully fledged pop icon, Tony was his own special creation. The black leather jodhpurs, the fox-fur coats, the French berets, the crimson-striped Cossack trousers and silk capes – each item was hand picked by him personally, each outfit assembled without a thought spared for what others were wearing or what the rules were. No stylists suffered to create the looks that wowed *Smash Hits* readers and dazzled audiences on *Top of the Pops*. He didn't need them then and he didn't need them now. All he'd ever needed was his own unique sense of style. That, and a damn good hairdresser.

Luckily he had just the man for the job. Keith at Cutz had been doing Tony's hair for years. Cutz was one of those reassuringly overpriced salons from back in the days when 'unisex' still sounded daring, and Keith was the salon's chief stylist, as famous in his way as some of the people whose follicles he regularly fingered. It was Keith who'd helped create the hairstyle for which Tony was best remembered. Inspired by the boldness of punk and the super-strong-hold gels of the early eighties, they'd experimented with a variety of styles before hitting on the dramatic blond and black creation that became Tony's crowning glory.

Since then they'd been through so much together – the late eighties mullet, the early nineties moptop, the mohawk, the faux-hawk, the Hoxton fin, the first worrying signs of male pattern baldness. Through all the pressures of being a pop star, through all the disappointments of the past twenty years, Keith had never let Tony down. Even when the fans deserted him and the record company informed him that nobody wanted to buy his records any more, Keith was there to soothe away his troubles, liven up his tresses and send him back on his way, looking and feeling every inch the star again. The man was nothing short of a miracle worker. So of course it was no surprise that it was Keith he turned to now, on the day when his name was back in the papers and a miracle was needed more than ever.

Getting an appointment hadn't been easy. Keith was always in great demand, and Tony wasn't the only famous person to benefit from his magic touch. But it was a measure of their friendship, not to mention the vast sums of money Tony had spent over the years, that on the morning in question a few last-minute phone calls were made and a vacant slot was found in Keith's busy diary.

'Good to see you again, Tony,' Keith said as he escorted

him to his chair. 'How's it going, mate?' Like many gay men in the business of styling other people's hair, Keith tended to overcompensate for the perceived queenliness of his profession by affecting a Cockney accent. In actual fact he came from Woking.

'Not bad,' Tony replied. 'Not bad at all. I suppose you've heard about this TV show I'm doing?'

'Heard about it? Tanya hasn't stopped talking about it since the moment she walked through the door.'

Tanya, the salon's chief colourist, looked up and smiled. 'Good for you, Tony. It's about time we had some proper stars on the telly.'

'I'm a bit worried about it, to be honest,' Tony said. 'I've seen the way they edit some of these shows. What if I come across as a total wanker?'

'Course you won't, mate,' Keith assured him. 'You'll steal the show. Trust me. I watch a lot of reality TV. I know about these things.'

Tony smiled. 'Thanks for the vote of confidence.'

'No problem, mate. So, what can we do for you today?'

'Well, it's a bit of a tall order, really,' Tony said. 'But I need my hair the way it used to be, back in the day. This isn't my idea, I hasten to add. It's for the programme.'

'No problem,' Keith said, though he didn't look entirely convinced. He ran his fingers through Tony's hair and stood back for a moment, arms folded, with one hand under his chin. 'I think it can be done,' he said finally, as if he were a structural engineer asked to assess the possibility of erecting a suspension bridge over the Grand Canyon. 'It's going to take a bit of time and a lot of product, but I think we can manage it.'

'Take all the time you need,' Tony said. 'I'm not in any great hurry.'

'Perfect,' Keith said, and sent him off to be shampooed.

Twenty minutes later he was back in the chair, with Keith buzzing around with hair grips and two colourists standing by. And so began the process of turning back the years with nothing more than a pair of scissors, some highly skilled hands and enough peroxide to tame a thousand female moustaches or one slightly thinning head of middle-aged male hair.

'I see that Ritchie Taylor is going to be locked up with you,' Keith said. 'Lucky you.'

'Do you know him?' Tony asked.

'Know him? I've been doing his hair for years! Remember that black spiky do he was sporting at the Brits? That was one of my creations.'

'Right,' Tony said. 'It looked great. I remember thinking that at the time. "God, that guy's hair looks great." So what's he like?'

'Ritchie? Oh, he's a total sweetie. Trust me. You'll love him. Cute too. And not short in the trouser department, if you catch my drift.'

Tony did catch his drift, and rather wished he hadn't. Ritchie Taylor already had youth, beauty and great swathes of the CD-buying public on his side. Was it really necessary for him to be hung like a donkey as well?

'What about the weather girl?' Tony asked. 'Tamsin something-or-other.'

'Applegate,' Keith said. 'Well, let's just say the outlook isn't quite as sunny as her image suggests. There are a few storm clouds on Miss Applegate's horizon, not to mention a number of damp patches she'd rather not talk about.'

The conversation went on like this for the next twenty minutes. Then the colourists applied various shades of black and blond to Tony's hair before whisking him off to the back of the salon and popping him under a dryer. It took another forty minutes for the colour to develop, and a further fifteen to establish if these were indeed the correct shades as specified by Keith, or merely an approximation. Tanya was brought over to inspect the results and confirmed that, yes, the entire operation had been a complete success. Then it was time for a deep-conditioning treatment and a chance for Tony to flip through this week's *Heat*. With any luck it would be his face on the cover in a few weeks, and not some gurning nonentity from *Big Brother*. Finally, Keith returned to apply the finishing touches and the whole look was revealed.

Tony stared at the mirror, barely able to believe the picture staring back at him. His hair had been completely transformed. The back and sides were an almost blue-black, but somehow multi-toned and more natural-looking than he'd expected. Tiny wisps of black framed his face, emphasising his cheekbones and improving the contours of his face considerably. But it was the top that really took his breath away. What was once thin and lifeless was now thick and golden and bursting with vitality, like a field of ripened corn. It was like looking at a photograph of himself from twenty years ago.

'Yes,' he said happily, blown away by his own blondness. 'Yes, that's perfect.'

CHAPTER EIGHT

'Sorry, you're not blond enough,' said the man dressed as the Milky Bar Kid. 'You can't come in looking like that. Only blonds.'

The object of his derision was a fat girl with hair that was once brown and was on its way to being blond, but appeared to have got stuck halfway and was now a curious shade of orange. Anywhere else, this might have evoked pity. Here, it was more likely to provoke scorn and outrage at such a flagrant disregard for the all-important door policy.

It was Tuesday night, and Anthony and Katy were queuing outside Billy's. A tiny basement club on Dean Street, Billy's had been the talk of the town for months. In a former life it had been known as the Gargoyle Club, and catered to the likes of Noël Coward and Tallulah Bankhead. But the years had taken their toll and until fairly recently the club had been reduced to providing a safe haven for Soho sex workers. Then a group of disillusioned punks decided to open a club there, and suddenly the world and its wife were beating a path to its door.

Tuesday night was Bowie night, and attracted a mixture of former punks, closet Bowie fans, cross-dressers and people whose idea of a good time was to go out wearing the first ridiculous thing that came into their head. The man dressed as the Milky Bar Kid was known as Steve Strange, and seemed to take a certain delight in turning people away from his club, not because they looked as if they might cause trouble, but because they simply weren't fashionable enough.

'And to think he comes from Newbridge!' Katy exclaimed. 'I'd like to see him try that nonsense there. They'd skin him alive.'

'Let's just go,' Anthony said. 'I can't be bothered waiting, just to be told we can't come in.'

'We're not going anywhere,' Katy frowned. 'It's taken us an hour just to get here. We're getting into that club even if we have to bleach our hair right here in the street. Wait a minute, I've just had an idea.'

And with that she left Anthony holding their place in the queue and disappeared into the dark. It was a cold January night, and as he stood there waiting for her to reappear, Anthony seriously considered sloping off to Waterloo and catching the first train back to Twickenham. He'd gone to a lot of effort getting ready for tonight. He'd spent over an hour on his hair alone. The white dinner jacket he'd found at the local Oxfam shop went well with his black jeans, but it had been a bugger to clean. The heavy black eyeliner looked suitably dramatic, but it had nearly got him beaten up by a gang of football supporters on the way through Leicester Square. And now to be unceremoniously turned away by some pillock in a cowboy hat was more than he could stomach.

Besides, he had lectures in the morning. The second term at college was proving a lot tougher than the first. He couldn't rely on his wits to get him through the next three months the way they'd got him through the last. Essays were required, not to mention an 'observation file' filled with personal and provocative thoughts about life, art and the various productions he'd seen so far. And at some point he'd have to decide which areas of study he wanted to concentrate on next term, and it was hard to do that when he'd missed most of his lectures through oversleeping or lack of interest. It was all right for Katy. Her job as a barmaid didn't demand much in the way of concentration. She should try staying awake through a lecture on the Living Theatre after a few hours' sleep. It was more like the Theatre of the Dead.

Suddenly Katy was back, brandishing a can of Ultra Hair Glo spray-in hair colour she'd purchased from the late-night chemist, and some last-minute accessories she'd lifted from a skip on the corner of Old Compton Street. 'Tilt your head down while I spray your hair,' she said. 'And tie this around your neck.'

'What is it?'

'What does it look like? It's a piece of bubble wrap. I know it looks crap now, but once I've sprayed it it'll look fabulous.'

Minutes later they were standing under the watchful eye of Steve Strange, Anthony with his makeshift collar, Katy in her matching bubble-wrap skirt, both with their hair (and a large part of their faces) sprayed blond. There was a moment's hesitation, then much to Anthony's surprise they were waved in.

As they descended the stairs, Katy turned to him and smiled triumphantly. 'See,' she said. 'I told you we'd get in. Stick with me, kid. I'll show you the world.'

The world of Billy's was a little different to the world outside. As they entered the crowded basement, Bowie's 'Joe the Lion' was playing and the air was heavy with sweat and thick with hairspray. As Bowie sang, 'You will be like your dreams tonight', it struck Anthony that people here had obviously taken him at his word, and that some people's dreams were a little more ambitious than others. There were men dressed as Arabian knights, women dressed as Little Bo Peep, and someone of indeterminate gender dressed as Marilyn Monroe. There were pillbox hats, lace veils, kilts, kimonos and jackboots. Women preened, men queued for the ladies' loos and people of both sexes sucked in their cheeks to make themselves look even more emaciated than they looked already. It was like a scene from 1930s Berlin, but without the imminent threat of a Nazi dictatorship or a song-and-dance number from Liza Minnelli.

Huddled at the bar, determined to make their first can of lager last an hour at least, Anthony and Katy soaked it all up. There couldn't have been more than two hundred and fifty people squeezed into this room, but to them it felt like the centre of the universe. A rumour was circulating that Mick Jagger had been turned away, which made everyone feel even more important. So what if Jagger had sold millions of records? He was yesterday's news, once cool but no longer hip enough to make it past the door.

The dance floor was no bigger than a postage stamp, and of course there were no records by the Rolling Stones play-ing. The music was a mixture of Bowie, Human League, Japan, Kraftwerk, Roxy Music, Siouxsie and a sprinkling of torch songs from Marlene Dietrich. Not that the crowd seemed to notice what song was playing, or when the music changed. They simply continued with their strange robotic dancing – lips out, cheeks in, eyes staring straight ahead.

Katy spotted a woman with her breasts exposed and nudged Anthony. He followed her gaze and that was when he saw him – a small, skinny queen with a curly blond hairdo, his body shrink-wrapped in black rubber and PVC, tottering around on Cuban heels.

'Shit, it's James,' Anthony hissed. 'What's he doing here?'

'The same as us, I imagine,' Katy replied. 'Why are you always so mean to him? He seems nice enough.'

'You be nice to him if you want to,' Anthony sniffed. 'Just leave me out of it.'

James waved and made his way over to the bar. 'Fancy seeing you here,' he said.

'Yes, fancy,' Anthony replied. 'I didn't know you were into all this.'

'I'm not,' James said. 'I only come here to catch the straight guys with their guard down. I love a straight guy in makeup. So much sexier than the queens at the Sombrero, don't you think?'

'I wouldn't know. We're here for the music, and to make a style statement, of course.'

'So I see,' James said, casting an appraising eye over Anthony's sprayed blond hair and bubble-wrap collar. 'So is bubble wrap the new PVC, or are you wearing that for a bet?'

'Stop it, you two,' Katy chipped in. 'Honestly, you're worse than a couple of girls.'

'Talking of which, have you seen the guy dressed as Marilyn?' James said. 'I overheard someone chatting him up earlier. They asked him what his name was, and he said

"Marilyn". Then they said, "No, your real name", and he said, "Norma Jean". How weird is that?'

'About as weird as you lusting after straight men,' Anthony said. 'What makes you think any straight guy is going to fancy you?'

'It's all the same when the light's off,' James replied coolly. 'And I haven't met a straight guy yet who'd turn down the offer of a quick blow-job in the loos.'

'You're disgusting,' Anthony said.

'And you're too uptight,' James laughed. 'Let your hair down, or are you worried your makeup might run? Talking of which, is your hair supposed to be like that?'

'Like what?'

'Like . . . dripping.'

Anthony touched his hair and looked down at his white dinner jacket. His hair was indeed dripping. Tiny drops of liquid were falling from his head and landing on his jacket, where they blossomed into yellow blotches like piss stains in the snow.

'Shit! This fucking hair colour is running,' Anthony said, and looked accusingly at Katy.

'Don't blame me,' she said. 'At least it got us inside. And mine seems okay.'

'Oh well, that's all right then,' Anthony snapped.

'Don't worry,' James laughed. 'Most of it is catching in your collar. See, fashionable and practical. Who'd have thought that bubble wrap could be so versatile?'

It took Anthony the best part of an hour to recover from the trauma of seeing his hair turn his jacket yellow, and even now he wasn't in the best of moods. He'd washed the remaining colour from his hair, and removed what stains he could from the sleeves of his jacket. His hair was slicked back and his jaw set in a grimace.

'Nobody even noticed,' Katy assured him. 'They're all far too self-obsessed to pay attention to anyone else.'

'That's where you're wrong,' Anthony replied. 'In case you hadn't noticed, this room is full of people desperately trying to outdo one another. And the first rule of any contest is that you always keep a close eye on the competition.'

'Maybe nobody sees you as competition,' James said sweetly. 'I mean that in the nicest possible way, of course.'

'Of course.' Anthony smiled bitterly.

'Anyway, it's all over now,' Katy said. 'Let's just try and forget about it and have a dance.'

'Being Boiled' by the Human League was playing, prompting Anthony to pull a face. 'I can't dance to this,' he said sulkily. 'Maybe if they play something a bit livelier. Joy Division, for instance.'

'Joy Division?' James repeated. 'Lively? Are you mad?'

'I was being ironic,' Anthony said flatly.

'Well stay here and be ironic on your own,' Katy said. 'I'm going for a dance. Coming, James?'

'Yes, James,' Anthony said mockingly. 'Time to show Katy some of your dance moves. Run along.'

And with that they were off, disappearing into a sea of white frills. Anthony watched as James lifted his arms high above his head and twirled around on the dance floor, dislodging several hats and elaborate head-dresses as he did so. A hint of a smile played on Anthony's lips, until he remembered that he was supposed to be in a bad mood. He moved to the far end of the bar and stood there, scowling at anyone who dared to catch his eye.

Unfortunately, he was in a club where scowls were worn for a variety of reasons, and could therefore be interpreted in any number of ways. There was the scowl that said, 'I'm too cool for this world'; the scowl that said, 'I am incapable of a spontaneous gesture'; the scowl that said, 'If I smile my makeup might crack'; and the scowl that said, 'I've got mascara in my eye.' There was also the scowl that said, 'I'm trying desperately hard to be cool but deep down I really want someone to come over and talk to me', and sadly for Anthony, this was precisely how his scowl was interpreted by the man currently staring at him from across the room.

'Hello, my name's Les,' he said, sidling over. He was dressed in a shiny silver suit and wore his hair in a rockabilly quiff. Even worse, he looked about thirty, which made him practically ancient in Anthony's eyes.

'Do you mind if I stand here?' Les went on.

'Do what you like,' Anthony replied. 'It's a free country.'

'Ah, but is it?' Les said. 'Is it really? The politicians tell us we're free, but everywhere I look today I see people in chains. Why is that?'

Anthony stared at him. 'Maybe you go to the wrong kind of clubs.'

Les smiled. 'Good answer. Maybe you're right . . . er, sorry, I didn't quite catch your name.'

'Anthony.'

'Anthony,' Les repeated, rolling the word around his mouth like a fine wine. 'What a wonderful name. Strong and masculine, yet ripe with literary allusion. And where, might I ask, is your Cleopatra?'

'If you mean my friend, she's dancing,' Anthony said. 'And I don't mean to be rude, but if you're trying to chat me up, you're wasting your time.'

'Really?' Les replied. 'Why is that?'

Anthony frowned. 'Because I don't fancy you.'

Les smiled knowingly. 'If only life were that simple. You have so much to learn.'

'Well I think I've learned quite enough about you, thanks,' Anthony said, moving away. 'If you don't mind, I think I'll take a walk.'

Les grabbed his arm and held it tight. 'No need to be hasty,' he said, softening his grip slightly. 'Surely it wouldn't hurt to allow me to buy you a drink?'

Anthony's first instinct was to run, but then he remembered how little money he had in his pocket. 'Sure,' he said. 'I'll have a vodka and Coke.'

'Let's make that a large one, shall we?' Les said, all smiles again.

'Why not?' Anthony replied, displaying far more confidence than he was actually feeling. 'So, what do you do, Les?'

Les reached into his jacket pocket and took out a cigarette case. He removed a long, thin purple cigarette and lit it, very artfully. 'Sobranie?'

Anthony shook his head.

'I'm in the music business,' Les said, producing a business card from his trouser pocket and pressing it into Anthony's hand. 'I help to make people's dreams come true. Now tell me, Anthony, do you have any dreams you'd like to share with me?'

CHAPTER NINE

Katrina and Rose were busy dividing up Mark's possessions, putting some things into bin bags and others into boxes. They started in the kitchen, where the house plants were the first things to be assigned a new home.

'I'll take them back to mine,' Katrina volunteered, putting the first of many leafy green refugees into a shallow box on the kitchen table. 'Unless you want any of them, of course.'

Rose shook her head. 'I can't be doing with house plants. I can never keep them alive for long.'

'They can be a bit temperamental sometimes, can't they?' Katrina said, holding a spider plant in her hand and combing the leaves with her fingers. 'My father's a firm believer in the idea that plants need their own space, preferably in a greenhouse at the bottom of the garden. But there's something special about having them living close to you. They complement us perfectly, you know. We breathe in oxygen and breathe out carbon dioxide, and they do the exact opposite. It's a totally symbiotic relationship.'

Rose looked at her blankly. 'The garden's the place for plants. You can't go far wrong with a few busy lizzies.'

'Mark was very good with house plants,' Katrina went on. 'It's all in the watering, apparently. Too much and they drown, too little and the roots dry out. Little and often, that's the key with most of them. And misting. They like misting. I remember Mark had one of those little aerosol bottles of water you use to cool yourself in the sun. He used to spray them with that. We used to joke about it, but he really loved his plants. He even wrote a song about them.'

Rose frowned. 'A song?'

'Yes,' Katrina said, smiling to herself. 'He used to play it sometimes on the piano. "Buy yourself a tiny house plant, someone to tell your troubles to, no matter what you tell it, it will never tell on you."'

Rose was unimpressed. 'It doesn't sound like much of a song.'

'Not when I sing it like that, no,' Katrina replied. 'There were a couple more verses, but I can't remember them now.'

'Did he write a lot of them?' Rose asked. 'Songs, I mean.'

'Not a lot, no. It was just a bit of fun, really. Something to entertain his friends with.'

'You were in a pop group once, weren't you?' Rose said. 'And quite a popular one, judging by that gold disc I saw in your bathroom.'

Katrina put the spider plant in the box and smiled. 'That was a very long time ago. Now, shall we make a start on the living room?'

Ten minutes later they were sitting at opposite ends of the sofa, packing CDs into boxes. The boxes would be taken back to Katrina's and, according to instructions set out in Mark's will, their contents distributed between close friends and deserving charities. Peter and another unnamed friend were coming to remove the sofa and other larger items of furniture tomorrow.

'What about the flat?' Rose asked.

'The rent is paid up until the end of the month,' Katrina said.

'Council?'

'Ex-council. The woman who used to live here bought it for a fraction of what it's worth, for the sole purpose of renting it out. She charges three times what it used to cost her and lives hundreds of miles away. Quite comfortably, I should imagine.'

Rose frowned. 'I'm not sure I approve of that sort of thing.'

Katrina laughed. 'I'm not sure I approve of a lot of things that happened under Mrs Thatcher.'

Rose tightened her lips. 'I make it a rule never to discuss politics,' she said, busying herself with the lid from one of the boxes. 'It only leads to arguments.'

Katrina stopped what she was doing and set a handful of CDs down on the sofa. Jimmy Somerville's face stared up at her, reminding her of what Mark had gone through, daring her not to let the matter drop. 'What are you so afraid of, Rose?'

'Me? I'm not afraid of anything. I just think some things are best left unsaid, that's all.'

'Like the way you left things with Mark all those years?'

Rose patted her hair. 'I don't know what you mean.'

'I think you do,' Katrina said firmly. 'Why didn't you talk to him? When he told you he was gay, why didn't you discuss it with him? Were you ashamed? Embarrassed? Or maybe you were worried that it was your fault?'

Rose turned, her eyes flashing. 'Oh, that's right!' she said. 'Now I see what this is all about. Now I know why you wanted me here. It's so you could punish me, isn't it? Go on then. Tell me what a bad mother I was!'

'I don't think you were a bad mother,' Katrina said patiently. 'I'm just trying to understand, that's all.'

But Rose wasn't listening. She stood up from the sofa and walked over to the window. Her right hand gripped the window frame as she spoke. 'I never drove my son away,' she said. 'My door was always open. He knew where I was. He was the one who stopped calling.' She didn't sound entirely convinced by this, which might have explained why she was clinging to the window frame for support.

'But you left him no choice, did you?' Katrina said. 'What sort of relationship could he hope to have with you when you refused to discuss the fact that he was gay? It was a major part of his life, and you wouldn't even talk about it. That was hard on him, Rose. Don't get me wrong. I'm glad you came to the hospital, and I'm glad that you were able to spend some time with him before he died. I just wish you'd shared your feelings a lot sooner, that's all.'

Rose turned to face her again, her cheeks flushed. 'I see,' she said coldly. 'Well, I'm sorry I was such a disappointment to you both. I'm sorry I find it difficult to talk about these things. I'm sorry there's a huge chunk of my son's life that I wasn't part of. I'm sorry he's dead, and I'm sorry if you think I could have done more for him when he was alive. But it wasn't easy for me either. None of this has been easy for me. Just being here now, here in this flat, it breaks my heart to look around at all his things and not recognise any of them.'

Her eyes filled with tears, and suddenly Katrina was reminded that this was an old woman she was dealing with. A difficult old woman perhaps, and one who hadn't always behaved in the best way possible. But an old woman nevertheless, and one who'd just witnessed her only son die a terrible death.

'No, I'm the one who's sorry,' Katrina said. 'I shouldn't have said some of those things. It's a difficult time for all of us. Maybe you need a few moments to yourself. Why don't I leave you to finish packing these CDs and I'll go and make a start in the bedroom.'

'If you like,' Rose replied and turned back to the window. She took a moment to compose herself, gazing out at the harsh urban landscape below. Her dreams of London were never like this. Imagine waking up each morning and seeing that spread before you, a sprawling mass of concrete and cars and walls covered with graffiti. Imagine stepping into a urine-soaked lift every day, or braving the gangs of teenage hoodies huddled outside. This was no place for the vulnerable, least of all someone contemplating his own death. The mere thought of it made her sick with grief.

She turned away from the window, walked over to the sofa and picked up the CDs Katrina had left lying there. She recognised Jimmy Somerville's face immediately. 'Mr Potato Head', that was what they used to call him. And then there was Boy George and some other man with long hair and makeup. Finally she came to a CD with a picture of a boy and a girl on the cover. That was a step in the right direction at least. Although on second thoughts, the boy looked a bit suspect. Bleached hair and a smile you couldn't trust. The girl looked nice enough, even if the hair was a bit tarty. Black and spiky, it looked as if it could benefit from a good conditioning treatment. The face was sweet, though, what she could see of it under all that makeup. Sweet, and strangely familiar.

Rose looked at the name printed across the top of the CD. 'A Boy and His Diva'. The same name she'd seen on that gold disc back at the flat. So it was her. It was Katrina. Rose wondered what it must have been like to be in a pop group and have your face on the cover of a CD. She wondered if that was why Katrina didn't have any children of her own. She'd been so busy selling records, she'd left it too late to start a family. That would explain her reaction to that girl in the photo. The woman was obviously regretting some of the decisions she'd made. A lot of these career women did, apparently, which was why so many of them were crying out for IVF at forty. This was a subject on which Rose was rather well informed. She'd watched a programme about it just the other week on the telly.

She put the CDs down and made her way to the bedroom. The door was wide open and Katrina was sitting on the bed, clutching a man's woolly jumper to her chest and sobbing gently. Rose coughed to alert her to her presence. This was getting to be quite a habit, she thought.

But this time Katrina didn't wipe her eyes or try to laugh the situation off. She simply sat there, the tears rolling down her cheeks.

'What's the matter, dear?' Rose asked.

Katrina looked up, her face a mess of mascara. 'I don't know what to do with this jumper.'

'Well, it looks too old and worn to be much use to anyone,' Rose said. 'Maybe we should just throw it away.'

'I can't,' Katrina wailed.

'Why ever not?'

'Because it was a part of him,' Katrina replied, and fell to pieces, crying uncontrollably.

With that, Rose instantly forgot that they'd just been arguing. She forgot that she'd only met this woman for the first time yesterday. She forgot everything that usually prevented her from reaching out and touching another human being and she sat down on the bed and held Katrina to her.

'I feel so empty,' Katrina wailed, her whole body shaking.

'I know,' Rose said.

Katrina looked up at her. 'No you don't,' she sobbed. 'You don't know at all.'

Tony left Cutz with a spring in his step and his sights on the future. What was it they used to say, back in the seventies? 'The future belongs to those who can smell it coming.' Well, Tony could smell it all right. Even with the stench of exhaust fumes and the lingering whiff of peroxide, his senses had never felt keener. He was ready to sniff out and seize whatever opportunities came his way. He was master of his own fate, king of the world. And all because he had a new hairdo.

Of course it wasn't really a new hairdo, more a reworking of an old classic. But what a reworking! Keith had really excelled himself this time. Pausing to study his reflection in a shop window, Tony took a moment to inspect Keith's handiwork. It was a first-class job, no doubt about it. Even in the full glare of the sun, his hair looked fuller and more healthy than it had looked in years. This called for a celebration. A little early afternoon shopping on Bond Street perhaps? Or maybe a trip to Harvey Nicks? He mulled it over for a moment. Then his mind began to wander until, finally, his thoughts focused on a small bag of white powder.

It was a while since Tony had indulged in anything stronger than a double espresso. His drugs counsellor had warned him that he would have moments like this, and that for someone with his history of addiction, even the occasional lapse was playing with fire. 'One line is too much, and a thousand is never enough' – that was the advice they'd given him. But what was he supposed to do with a piece of double-speak like that? Write a song around it? God knows he'd tried, but somehow songs written about drugs were a bit like conversations he'd had while under the influence. They seemed great at the time, but when he sat down and thought about them afterwards they didn't seem nearly as profound. The only person who'd really pinned down the experience of cocaine on record was Bowie, and he only did it by simultaneously acknowledging his drug use and denying its impact on his behaviour. 'It's not the side effects of the cocaine,' he sang on *Station to Station*. 'I'm thinking that it must be love.' What better way to sum up the endless cycle of addiction and denial?

Maybe it was the effect of all the chemicals he'd inhaled at the hairdresser's, but inside Tony's head a little voice was telling him to ignore the warnings of his drugs counsellor, ignore the fact that he was a recovering drug addict, ignore all the evidence suggesting that cocaine was highly addictive, and make that call. Why shouldn't he indulge himself every now and then? It wasn't as if he couldn't afford it. The producers of *The Clink* were paying him handsomely, and once the show was over, who knew what new doors would open? A second chance at pop stardom wasn't beyond the realms of possibility. He already had the hairstyle. If a gram of coke was what he wanted, then a gram of coke was what he should have. He still had his dealer's number stored in his phone, just in case of emergencies. He made the call and ten minutes later he was in the back of a taxi, speeding across Soho.

Tony's dealer was called Alex and he lived in a rooftop apartment in Covent Garden, purchased with the proceeds from various celebrities' secret addictions. He'd already talked Tony into buying two grams – 'To make it worth my while' – and by the time he reached Alex's building Tony had decided to increase his order to four. It was easier that way, and by buying in bulk he would probably qualify for a discount. He paid the cab driver and was disappointed when there wasn't so much as a flicker of recognition. Still, all that was about to change. He pressed the buzzer and took the lift up to the fifth floor.

Alex answered the door in a pair of track pants, the shape of his cock clearly visible through the folds of the fabric. Not only was he not wearing any underwear, he was also shirtless, and his impressive chest brushed against Tony's arm as he ushered him inside and steered him towards the large zebra-print sofa.

'Like the look of my new sofa, Tony? I got it from Heal's. Cost me an arm and a leg, but I figured it was worth it.'

'It looks great,' Tony said, though the truth was he liked the look of Alex a lot more, especially today when there was so much of him on display. Alex's muscular good looks were the stuff of phone sex ad fantasies. Had he not discovered his true calling as a drug dealer, he could just as easily have found gainful employment as a male escort. A few years short of forty, and not quite classically handsome, he had the broken nose of a boy who'd played a lot of rugby and the finely sculpted body of a man who spent more hours at the gym than was strictly heterosexual. That said, his sexuality was a matter of some dispute. Rather like the male escorts with whom he shared a fair number of his clients, Alex preferred to be all things to all people and was therefore committed to retaining an air of mystery whenever possible. Still Tony couldn't help noting that he'd chosen to answer the door half dressed, and that he clearly loved the attention. And was it just his imagination, or was the bulge in Alex's track pants bigger now than it had been a moment ago?

'So how are things, Tony?' Alex said, sitting next to him on the sofa and stretching provocatively. 'I haven't heard from you in a while. How's tricks?'

'Oh, you know,' Tony mumbled. 'Can't complain.'

Alex stretched again and the top of his pubes peeped out over his track pants. Tony couldn't help noticing that they were neatly trimmed, adding further fuel to his already feverish imagination.

'I was starting to think you'd found yourself a new supplier,' Alex said, idly picking a bit of fluff from his belly button. 'I thought you'd turned your back on me, so to speak.'

Tony blushed. 'I've been a bit busy,' he said, averting his eyes.

'So I hear,' Alex said. 'Saw your name in the paper today. *The Clink*, eh? Sounds pretty horny.'

'Horny?' Tony repeated, his mouth suddenly dry.

'Locked up like that. I'm assuming you won't be sharing a cell with any of the women. Just a bunch of lads locked up together. Should be right up your street. So, are you ready to sample the merchandise?'

Tony gulped. 'Sorry?'

'The old Peruvian marching powder. Fancy a line?'

'Sure,' Tony said. 'I mean, it's what I'm here for, right?'

Alex gave a lopsided grin and leapt up from the sofa. He disappeared into the kitchen, returning a few minutes later with half a dozen lines neatly arranged on a plate and an erection straining against the elasticated waistband of his track pants.

'After you,' he said, handing Tony a rolled-up note and holding the plate a few inches from his nose.

'Thanks,' Tony said, and snorted a fat line.

'Good stuff, eh?' Alex said, taking back the note and helping himself.

'Great,' Tony replied as he felt his teeth go numb and his libido rising.

'I like your hair, by the way,' Alex said, placing the plate on the sofa and standing with his crotch level with Tony's head. 'Very nice.'

'Thanks,' Tony said. 'Good of you to notice.' He tried not to stare at the swelling in Alex's groin, but it was a losing battle and he knew it.

Alex clearly knew it too. 'What are friends for?' he said, grinning.

There was a moment's silence.

'And since we're friends, I was hoping you could help me with this,' Alex said, finally springing his erection free from his track pants and waving it in Tony's face. Then, just to ensure that he had Tony's undivided attention, he took a bag of cocaine from his pocket and sprinkled a small amount of powder along the length of his shaft, until his penis resembled something you might find in a patisserie window.

'There,' Alex said. 'Now you can snort and blow at the same time.'

As he took Alex's cock in his mouth, it suddenly dawned on Tony that this was no ordinary drug deal.

CHAPTER TEN

Two major events took place as the seventies drew to a close and a new decade dawned. Katy and Anthony were party to both of them.

The first was the opening of a new gay club, far bigger than any that had gone before.

'What are you doing tonight?' James asked Anthony one day as they were leaving a lecture on the alienation effect in Brechtian theatre, both feeling suitably alienated.

'Nothing much,' Anthony replied. 'I'll probably just meet Katy for a drink.'

'Great,' said James. 'Call her and tell her to meet us at the station at nine. I'm taking you to Heaven.'

'What's that?' Anthony asked.

'What's that?' James laughed. 'Only the biggest gay club London has ever seen. It's the opening night tonight. What's the matter with you? Don't you read *Gay News*?'

'Why would I?' Anthony replied sweetly. 'When I have you to do it for me?'

'So,' said James. 'Do you want to come or not?'

Once it was established that yes, Anthony did want to come, there was only the small matter of what to wear. Anthony was keen to dress as outlandishly as possible, but James warned him against it.

'Save it for the Blitz,' he said, the Blitz being the latest Steve Strange club, where, every Tuesday, James, Anthony and Katy would compete to see who could generate the most attention. The three of them were spending a lot of time together lately, not because Anthony's opinion of James had changed or because Katy's opinion of James carried more weight, but simply because James was now the proud owner of a sewing machine. Anthony could tease James all he liked, but in a world where people were judged on the novelty value of their clothes, a friend with a sewing machine was a serious asset. With some second-hand shirts, a few offcuts and some sequins and lace liberated from the college wardrobe department, James could run up a new outfit for a fraction of what it cost in the shops.

Still, he refused to have anything to do with his sewing machine today. 'We can't turn up looking like freaks,' he said. 'This is a gay club. People will laugh at us.'

'I thought gay clubs were all about expressing yourself,' Anthony pouted.

'Not this one,' James said. 'This one's about checked shirts and handlebar moustaches, and men dressed like members of the Village People.'

He was right, too. Queuing outside the club later that night, Anthony was glad he'd left his glad rags at home. The crowd were every bit as conservative as James had predicted. Unless you counted leather chaps and cowboy hats as the height of fashion, which Anthony certainly didn't.

Heaven was located under the arches at Charing Cross, in what was once a club called Global Village. As they descended the stairs, Dan Hartman's 'Relight My Fire' was playing, prompting a disapproving look from Anthony. Still, even he was forced to admit that the venue itself was pretty impressive. A lot of money had been spent converting an old roller disco into the largest gay club in the known universe, and it showed. The main dance floor went on for miles, and there were lots of other rooms to explore upstairs. The lights were fantastic too. It was just the music and the people he couldn't stand.

'It's not so bad,' Katy insisted. Personally, she was in her element. She'd never seen so much male flesh on display. And as much as she liked the Blitz, the men here were far more to her taste. The moustaches reminded her of home and the men she used to see working the fairground in Porthcawl. If she turned a blind eye to the leather shorts and colour-coded handkerchiefs, she could almost picture some of these men as straight.

But Anthony wasn't having any of it. 'I can't stay here,' he announced, all of twenty minutes after they'd arrived. 'You stay if you want to. I'm going to the Sombrero. If this is the future of gay clubbing, I'd rather live in the past.'

James had already disappeared, lured away by a man dressed as a motorcycle cop and a full bottle of poppers, so Katy didn't feel she was left with much of a choice.

'I wouldn't mind,' Anthony said afterwards, 'but cowboys and motorcycle cops are such American stereotypes. That whole look has nothing to do with London. How can anyone take it seriously?'

Katy's thoughts immediately turned to Anthony in his Cossack outfit, but she kept well buttoned.

Thankfully, there were fewer disappointments at the other big occasion that month, namely watching Bowie on the

New Year's Eve special edition of *The Kenny Everett Video Show*. Having discovered that James was also a Bowie fan (though mainly of the Ziggy Stardust period), Anthony had graciously agreed to allow him to spend the evening with him and Katy, glued to the TV set in the otherwise barely furnished living room they now shared with three other housemates a short walk from the college campus. Luckily for James, two of the three other housemates had gone home for Christmas, which meant that he had a bed for the night and wouldn't have to fork out for a taxi back to his digs in New Malden. The third housemate, a Glaswegian girl named Jenny, had been invited to a Hogmanay party in Putney and wouldn't be back until sometime the following day.

'We've got the whole house to ourselves,' Katy announced when Anthony and James returned from the off-licence, weighed down with cans of lager.

'Fantastic!' James cried, and immediately rushed upstairs to test the springs in Jenny's bed. Five minutes later he was back, declaring the bed a far better option than the two others he'd tried and not seeming to care that, while the owners of those beds had given him express permission to use them, Jenny hadn't even been asked.

'Jenny won't mind,' Anthony said casually, although of course he knew perfectly well that she would. Jenny minded if he accidentally used the last drop of milk in the morning, so it was safe to assume that she wouldn't take too kindly to a man she barely knew sleeping in her bed. But Anthony didn't let a little thing like personal space bother him, unless it was his own of course. Besides, Jenny wasn't someone he'd have chosen to share a house with. Her friends were boring, and she had an irritating habit of sitting up late at night, playing the guitar and singing 'The Streets of London' to anyone too polite or too pissed to leave the room. In short, Jenny was the housemate from hell, and it wouldn't have bothered Anthony in the slightest if she came home, found James in her bed and announced that she was moving out.

It was left to Katy to defend Jenny's space and suggest that, comfortable though Jenny's bed might be, it probably wasn't a good idea to invade her room without first obtaining her permission. 'You can sleep in my bed,' she told James. 'And I'll sleep in one of the spare rooms. That way, there'll be no strange men in anyone's bed.'

'And let's face it, James,' Anthony chipped in, 'you are a very strange man.'

Once the sleeping arrangements were agreed, it was soon time to settle down on the sofa, crack open a few cans and await the start of the show. There had been rumours that Gary Numan was also due to appear tonight, but thankfully such fears proved unfounded. (Anthony was pleased to note that, while James wasn't a total Bowie fan, he was sufficiently well informed to recognise Numan's whole act as a cheap rip-off, from the *Low*-era deadpan vocals right down to the icy stare. Anthony had now revised his opinion of *Low*, rating it the most innovative album of Bowie's career. To see another act shamelessly recycling those themes and ideas made his blood boil. The world didn't need a Bowie impersonator, for the simple reason that the original was as productive now as he'd ever been, releasing three albums in the past three years, or four if you counted the live double album, *Stage*.)

Even without Numan's presence, it was generally agreed that the show didn't get off to a promising start. There was a moment's doubt when Bowie first appeared, playing the straight man to Everett's funny guy.

'I'm not sure about this,' James said. 'It's not as bad as that Christmas show he did with Bing Crosby, but I'm not convinced he's really cut out for this Mr Light Entertainment thing. Give me the bisexual alien from Mars any day.'

But any reservations were cast aside the moment Bowie reappeared to perform. First there was the strangeness of the set, which bore a striking resemblance to a padded cell. Then there was the choice of song. For his final performance of the seventies, the most forward-thinking rock icon of the decade chose not to showcase his latest single, or even a track from his recent *Lodger* album, but to go right back to where it all began, with a rerecorded, acoustic version of 'Space Oddity'. Cool and measured, with a spare, elegant arrangement, the song felt eerily restrained, and was infinitely more chilling than anything Numan could have come up with.

The moment it was over, Anthony turned to Katy and grinned.

'Welcome to the eighties,' he said, raising his can of lager. 'Here's to the future of futurism!'

For Katy, both of these events would soon be overshadowed by a third. On 2 January, her parents announced that they were filing for divorce.

'I just woke up and realised that I didn't love him any more,' her mother said when she phoned with the news.

'Are you sure this isn't just a bad hangover?' Katy asked. 'Lots of people wake up with someone on New Year's Day and wonder why they're there.'

'It isn't New Year's Day,' her mum replied. 'And this isn't a hangover. My head feels clearer now than it's felt in years.'

'Well that's just great, Mum,' Katy wailed. 'Perfect timing as always. I thought you and dad were supposed to be Conservatives. Isn't that why you voted for that awful Thatcher woman? Whatever happened to family values and sticking with tradition?'

'I don't know why you're having a go at me. You couldn't even be bothered to come home for Christmas. And you know as well as I do that your father can be extremely diffi-cult at Christmas time. Well, he pushed me too far this year. And it's me who has to put up with him, day in, day out. It's not even as if you live here any more.'

'Well that's just great,' Katy said. 'Blame me for your mar-riage ending.'

'But I *don't* blame you,' her mother replied.

And the truth was, she didn't. But deep down, Katy did. Ever since she'd left home, she'd felt a burden of responsi-bility for the way tensions had grown between her parents. It was a known fact that some couples only stayed together for the sake of the children, so by flying the nest she felt that she'd precipitated the break-up of her parents' marriage.

She spent the next few weeks holed up in her room, refus-ing Anthony's offers of nights out to help take her mind off things, and only emerging to use the bathroom, go to work, or pick at tins of tuna and sweetcorn she mixed together with a large dollop of mayonnaise and pushed aside after a few mouthfuls. Apart from that, she didn't really eat, and her weight began to drop dramatically. But even that wasn't enough to give her the lift she needed. She still had plenty of reasons to feel sorry for herself. She hated her job. She hated her parents. And to top it all, Pink Floyd's 'Another Brick in the Wall' was playing constantly on the radio. A new decade had begun and Pink bloody Floyd were at Number 1. So much for Johnny Rotten and his 'I Hate Pink Floyd' T-shirt. So now it was official. The punk revolution *had* failed.

By the end of January, Anthony's patience had run out.

'Right,' he said one Saturday morning, bursting into Katy's room and throwing open the curtains. 'This has gone on long enough. Get dressed. That's assuming you can find something that still fits. You look like you've dropped about four dress sizes. Find something to cover your nakedness and meet me downstairs. We're going shopping.'

'I can't afford to go shopping,' Katy grumbled. 'In case you haven't noticed, I work in a bar, not an investment bank.'

'I don't care,' Anthony said. 'The sales are on. You're going shopping and I'm coming with you. My grant cheque comes through in a couple of days, and I'm still not up to the limit on my overdraft. You can pay me back later.'

'That's really kind of you, Anthony, but I couldn't . . .'

'Just call me your flexible friend. Now, no more arguments. Get yourself dressed. I'll see you downstairs in ten minutes.'

'Ten minutes? I need at least half an hour.'

Anthony looked at her. 'What you need is a complete makeover. But failing that, we'll settle for a new outfit. Fifteen minutes, then I'm off.'

Twenty minutes later, Katy bounced down the stairs in a baggy pullover and black jeans, her hair tied back and just a touch of makeup on her face.

Anthony grinned. 'Mother Courage, I presume?'

'Shut your mouth, gay boy,' Katy snapped, then smiled to

let him know she wasn't serious. 'Any more quips like that and I'm going straight back to bed.'

'Well you're certainly going straight,' Anthony said. 'Where did you find that pullover? Dorothy Perkins?'

'I can't help it if my clothes all hang on me,' Katy said, though it was clear from the look on her face that she wasn't really complaining.

Anthony studied her for a moment. 'You do look a lot thinner,' he said thoughtfully. 'In fact, I think you may even squeeze into something from PX.'

PX was a clothes shop in Covent Garden. It was where Steve Strange sometimes worked when he wasn't hosting the Blitz, and was largely to blame for the hordes of punters currently turning up at the club in German military gear. Lately the shop had been experimenting with frilly velvet suits with stark white puritan collars, and it was this look Anthony had in mind for Katy.

Katy wasn't convinced. 'I'll look a right prat in one of those.'

But Anthony was very persuasive, and by the time he'd escorted her to Covent Garden and led her past the painfully trendy shopfront, Katy was forced to concede that he might have a point. Surrounded by the very latest in industrial chic fittings, gazing at her reflection in the dressing room mirror, there was no denying the fact that, in her current shape, this was a look that suited her very well. The trousers really flattered her thighs, while the frilly detail on the jacket was feminine enough to prevent her from being mistaken for a bull dyke.

'But I really can't afford this,' she said, turning to admire herself from a different angle.

'Nonsense,' Anthony replied. 'When something looks that good on you, you can't afford not to buy it. Besides, you're not buying it. I am.'

'I'll pay you back,' she said. 'Every penny. As soon as I can.'

'No rush,' he said and pulled out his chequebook. Minutes later, Katy emerged from PX the proud owner of a purple velvet suit, her punk days well and truly behind her.

'All you need now is a haircut,' Anthony said as they walked up Endell Street. 'Then you'll be a whole new person.'

'No I won't,' she laughed. 'It's just a new outfit.'

'It feels good, though, doesn't it?'

Katy grinned. 'Yeah. It feels really good.'

CHAPTER ELEVEN

Tony was having trouble sleeping. Maybe it was the shameful memory of what had happened with Alex. Maybe it was the worrying thought that, two days from now, he'd be locked in a prison cell and competing for the love of the public with the likes of Ritchie Taylor. Or maybe it was simply the fact that, despite telling himself he'd only dip into the four grams of coke he'd purchased from Alex, he'd managed to work his way through two grams by the end of the afternoon and a further gram this evening. This was in addition to the free samples he'd enjoyed at Alex's flat, often with his host's cock in his mouth at the same time. That was the trouble with coke. One line was too much, and a thousand was never enough. The more you had, the more you wanted. And the more you wanted, the less you cared about little things like money, dignity and lack of sleep.

It was no use, he decided. He couldn't sleep while there was still coke in the house. He'd just have to get up, go downstairs and finish off that fourth gram. It was the only sensible thing to do.

The coke was on the coffee table, next to the Japanese import CD he'd bought a few days ago. The CD had the inspired title of *A Boy and His Diva – Greatest Hits* and boasted a cover photo of Katrina with her head resting on

Tony's shoulder. Her eyes were closed while he stared directly into the camera, wide-eyed and wearing as much makeup as the human face could possibly accommodate. The inspiration for the photo had come from the cover of Bowie's *Pin Ups*, with Katrina playing Twiggy to his Ziggy. And no, she hadn't been too pleased about it either.

There were still some coke crumbs on the CD cover, and as he racked up a couple of lines it suddenly struck him that he was snorting coke off his own face. So this was the true meaning of the phrase 'off your face', he thought, and snorted the first line. He waited a moment before swapping nostrils and hoovering up the second.

He remembered the first time he ever snorted cocaine. It was 1983, 'Love Is A Pain (In The Heart)' was riding high in the charts, and he and Katrina were waking up to the realities of international promotion. For Tony, those first few months of pop stardom would always be summed up by the title of that Culture Club book, *When Cameras Go Crazy*. Only it wasn't just cameras that went crazy for him and Katrina. It was everything. His itinerary was completely mad. A typical day would find him leaving the house at six thirty to arrive in Paris for ten a.m., then leaving Paris at noon, arriving in Germany at two p.m., checking into a hotel for two hours of interviews, having something to eat and a shower, then jetting off somewhere else, maybe to do a couple of TV shows in Belgium, before catching a flight back to London.

Tony didn't mind the travelling at first. The only time he'd flown before was on a family holiday to Spain when he was ten, so there was a certain novelty involved in jetting off to different countries several times a week. And of course it was exciting to be picked up in a limo and to fly first class and stay in the finest hotels. But the novelty soon wore off. The excitement faded. There were too many limos, too many airports, too many countries and far too many interviews. And not just press interviews but TV and radio appearances too. Soon it got to the stage where he didn't know which interviewer he was talking to, or which question he'd just been asked. Once, during an interview with a journalist from a French fanzine, Tony responded to a question about the inspiration behind his lyrics with a passionate account of why he loved Brussels, and how no one did french fries like the Belgians.

But Germany was where he really came unstuck. Their version of *Top of the Pops* was a show called *Formula One*, and it was so tacky it made the British show seem the height of sophistication. The German fanzines were totally intrusive, and would happily ask him outright if he was gay or what sort of men he went for. And back then Germany was the biggest record market in Europe. It was the one that really mattered. So naturally it followed that he and Katrina were destined to spend a lot of time there, proving themselves worthy of the massive investment their record company had placed in them.

It was in Germany that Tony's drug problems began. As he was quick to discover, the demands on a pop star were far greater than he could ever have imagined. What he didn't know – at least not yet – was how he could possibly keep up with them. Then one night in Berlin he found the answer. He was at a party, swapping small talk with the likes of Nina Hagen, when his publicist noticed he was flagging and offered him a line of cocaine. He'd been offered coke before, of course, but had always turned it down, remembering how Bowie nearly lost his mind in the mid seventies and deciding that this was one form of experimentation he could happily do without. But exhaustion had got the better of him and before he knew it he was crouched in a toilet cubicle, snorting a fat line off the toilet seat.

Nothing would ever be as good as that first line. But that didn't stop Tony from trying to relive the experience. Soon he had a dealer in every port. He became far more animated in interviews, and would happily party the night away in whatever city he happened to find himself in. And because coke was seen as such a vital part of the music industry, as essential to its survival as synthesisers and drum machines, nobody ever stopped to ask if Tony's drug consumption was getting out of hand. As the schedules became more gruelling, his dependency grew. Soon he couldn't get out of bed without chopping a line. And by the time 'Lovers and Losers' was at Number 1 and A Boy and His Diva were at the height of their success, Tony was in the grip of an addiction so strong it nearly cost him his septum. Long before Danniella Westbrook made a name for herself as the soap star with half her nose missing, Tony was undergoing reconstructive surgery to prevent his nose from caving in.

He stopped for a while after that. But then after the hits dried up and he and Katrina went their separate ways, his cocaine use began to increase again. Some might say that he contributed to his own downfall, and many did. But then as Tony always said, at least he avoided the mid-eighties career move of becoming a heroin addict, thus proving that Boy George wasn't quite the trendsetter he once was. Steve Strange followed George down pretty much the same path, of course. But then poor Steve was never really anyone's idea of a talented musician, which made his subsequent disappearance all the more inevitable. At least Tony had his talent to fall back on.

And fall back on it he did. Stubbornly refusing to accept defeat, he released a couple of solo singles, none of which made much of an impact on the charts. Then in 1985 he travelled to Japan in search of inspiration, only to discover that David Sylvian was right and that 'life can be cruel, life in Tokyo'. He was staying at the Keio Plaza Hotel – a little expensive, but suitably star-studded for a man of his station. Wandering one day in Kamakura, stopping to admire a temple in the shape of a giant Buddha, he spotted a squirrel scurrying towards him with a cuteness that was pure Disney. However, the whole scene soon turned more manga than Disney when the squirrel scampered across his canvas slip-ons, sank its claws into his bare ankle and disappeared up the leg of his Yohji Yamamoto blue silk trousers, only stopping short of his genitals when he instinctively cupped them with both hands. Not that it made a great deal of difference. Within an hour his leg had swollen up to twice its normal size and was covered with weeping sores. If only he'd worn leg-warmers! At least then he might have spared himself the indignity of being rushed to hospital, where a doctor prescribed antibiotics and tetanus shots while displaying the apparent lack of emotion for which the Japanese were famous.

The British tabloids weren't quite as tactful. 'Squirrel-haired pop freak attacked by Tufty' was one of the headlines. 'Japanese squirrel nuts about Tony' was another. And they were some of the kinder mentions he received that year.

Soon the knives were out for Tony. And then when AIDS really hit home, it was open season on all sexually ambiguous pop stars, himself included. Homophobia was licensed. Thatcher called for a return to traditional moral values and declared war on local councils who 'promoted' homosexuality. As the first AIDS casualties were laid to rest, the tabloids spoke of homosexuals 'swirling in a cesspit of their own making'. The mood was one of guilt and fear and punishment for the excesses of the earlier part of the decade. Tony even wrote a song about it, 'Generations of Loss'. Sadly it wasn't a hit. Nor were the two singles that followed. In 1986 he made one last appearance on *Top of the Pops* before his record company finally decided to cut their losses and terminated his contract.

By the time the nineties arrived, Tony had all but given up hope of resurrecting his career. Hope died sometime in the late eighties, a tragedy brought on by Thatcherism, AIDS, and Stock, Aitken and Waterman. But still Tony refused to crawl away quietly. In some ways, he felt he had a moral duty to stand and fight. He was a survivor, one of the lucky ones. He owed it to the memory of his dead friends not to give up now. And what other choice did he have? What was a former pop singer supposed to do? It was a question he'd been asking himself ever since. And before the night was over, he would ask himself the same question again, many times over.

Several miles away in Bloomsbury, someone else was having a restless night. Rose had never seen a gram of cocaine, and probably wouldn't have known what to do with it if she did.

But she didn't need any stimulants coursing through her veins. She had more than enough reasons to lie awake, mulling over the day's events, wondering what she was doing here, trying to find some small comfort in the fact that she'd been to see her son's flat. She could have gone back to Swindon, slept in her own bed and waited for news of the funeral. But instead she'd stayed and been shown around the flat where he had lived. It had been difficult, of course. More difficult than she'd ever imagined, if she was honest. But it had been worth staying in London for, surely? Just to be in the same room, to share the same physical space. Somehow it had brought him closer.

But not nearly as close as she'd have liked. He was still a stranger to her, more so now than when he was alive. It was the same when her father died. Death brought its own little mysteries. Even when you thought you knew someone, their death could hit you in ways you never expected. For Rose, grief had always been a very private emotion. She didn't go in for all this public mourning over dead popes and people's princesses. She kept her feelings to herself, maybe allowing herself a few tears at the funeral, but nothing too excessive, nothing that would draw too much attention. Which was why, when Katrina had broken down this afternoon, she was surprised to find herself comforting her. Usually she recoiled in horror from such scenes.

Heaven knows what further scenes would unfold at the funeral. Weeping women she could just about cope with. Weeping men were a different kettle of fish. And from what she'd seen, Mark's friends weren't ones for dignified silence and stiff upper lips. Their type rarely were. She could just picture it now. A room full of wailing men, and she and

Katrina left to hold everything together, the way women were often required to do. Men were such weak creatures in many ways. Maybe that was why they prided themselves on acting tough. And why they often vanished at the first sign of trouble.

She'd been thinking about Mark's father a lot lately. Vernon. Her Vernon, with his Italian suits and his shiny black quiff. Vernon the charmer, the man all the women went weak at the knees over. He was a handsome devil in those days, there was no denying that. Whatever else he turned out to be, he was a fine figure of a man. He could charm the pants off any woman he fancied, and when it emerged that he fancied Rose, she couldn't believe her luck. Suddenly she was no longer Rose the invisible woman, Rose the lonely, Rose the wallflower. She was Rose the girlfriend of the most eligible bachelor in town, Rose the fiancée, Rose the wife.

Two years down the line she was Rose the abandoned woman, Rose the divorcée, Rose the single mother. People had said it wouldn't last, that Vernon was too good a catch to ever be truly satisfied with someone like her. Oh, she was pretty enough in those days. Bright blue eyes, mousy hair, a nice smile. But she was nothing special. She didn't generate admiring looks everywhere she went. She didn't have suitors lined up and waiting. Not like him.

She saw him once, after the divorce, in Bristol of all places. He was still with her, that woman from the bridal shop. Bride Ideas – what a stupid name for a shop that was. She hadn't changed much. Still blonde. Still quite pretty in a homely sort of way. But him! He'd aged so badly, she almost didn't recognise him at first. His hair was thinning, his skin was grey, and he looked far shorter than she remembered, as if he had the weight of the world on his shoulders, pressing him down. He wasn't such a great catch now. But she'd have taken him back in an instant, for Mark's sake as much as hers. A boy needs a father, that's what everyone said. But after Vernon, she never found a man she could trust, let alone consider marrying.

Still, there was no point dwelling on the past. There were more pressing matters to consider, the funeral for one. She still wasn't happy about the arrangements. If she had her way Mark would be buried in the local cemetery, where she could visit his grave as often as she liked. She had a lot of making up to do, and tending his grave would be one way of doing it. But it wasn't up to her. Katrina had made that much clear. She might have been a blubbering mess this afternoon, but she had a will of iron. Women like Katrina were probably used to having things their own way, Rose thought. She'd heard about these pop divas and their impossible demands. Not that she doubted Katrina's sincerity. From the way she'd behaved today, it was clear that she had loved Mark a great deal. But even without the issue of Mark's will, Rose had little doubt that she and Katrina would have been fighting over the funeral arrangements, and that in all probability Katrina would have had her way in the end.

As it was, she seemed keen to impress upon Rose that this funeral was for her as much as anyone else, and that she should play a part in making the arrangements. The body would be cremated, as specified in Mark's will. The ashes would be scattered at a later date.

'But beyond that, it's for us to decide what shape the funeral should take,' Katrina had said before going to bed.

'Have a think about it, Rose. We can discuss it further in the morning.'

Well, Rose had thought about it. She'd thought about little else for the past few hours. But after today's events she was beginning to doubt whether she was in any position to decide what should happen at her son's funeral. His friends obviously knew Mark a lot better than she did. It had taken a visit to his flat for her to learn that he liked house plants and that he played the piano. What other secrets were there, waiting to be discovered? What else didn't she know?

CHAPTER TWELVE

It took Katy four months to pay Anthony back for the suit she had bought at PX. It was a long four months in which very little happened. Anthony went to lectures and agonised over what to wear each week to the Blitz. She went to work and struggled to maintain her new weight with the aid of diet pills and the occasional dab of speed. Neither of them was particularly pleased when The Jam became the biggest band in Britain, and when May dawned there was nothing to suggest that this month would be any more exciting than the previous four. On 1 May, Blondie were enjoying their second Number 1 of the year with 'Call Me'. Two days later, they were knocked off the top spot by a bunch of singing dustmen called Dexy's Midnight Runners and a song called 'Geno'. So far, so depressing.

But then an extraordinary thing happened. It was like a visit from God. David Bowie came to the Blitz. And in a cruel twist of fate, it was the one night that Anthony wasn't there. An accident with Katy's crimping irons prevented him from leaving the house that night, and he was reduced to hearing the news second-hand from James the following morning.

'It was amazing,' James said, clearly relishing the fact that he was the bearer of such glad tidings. 'Everyone was throwing themselves at him. Except me, of course. I just stood at the bar, nonchalantly. I wanted to rush over and tell him how Ziggy saved me from my own rock-and-roll suicide, but I figured he must hear that sort of thing all the time. I wish I'd been a bit more pushy now. It turns out he was looking for extras for his new video.'

Anthony was sitting on the sofa, flicking through a new magazine called *The Face* and waiting for the hot oil treatment he'd applied ten minutes ago to repair the worst of the damage to his hair. 'It says here that RCA don't even have a release date for his next record,' he said. 'So how he can be casting for a new video, I've no idea.'

'Well that's what happened,' James said irritably. 'Steve Strange and a couple of girls were hand-picked and whisked off to some secret location first thing this morning. Imagine! David Bowie picking you to be in his new video. It doesn't get much more glamorous than that!'

'Lucky bitches,' Katy said. 'I expect we'll hear more about it next week.'

'If Steve Strange has anything to do with it, we won't hear anything else for months,' Anthony said and turned back to his magazine. Despite being hailed as 'the first new rock magazine of the 1980s' and 'licensed to thrill', he couldn't find anything in *The Face* that struck him as either particularly new or particularly thrilling. A feature on The Specials was followed by a feature on Ian Dury, a photospread on Madness and a lone shot of Paul Weller.

'God, this magazine is boring,' Anthony said finally. 'Just what the world needs. Another magazine devoted to a load of old mods. I thought this was supposed to be 1980, not 1966.'

'There's a picture of Debbie Harry in there somewhere,'

Katy offered. 'And there's a photo of some people at the Blitz at the back.'

'With James in it, no doubt,' Anthony said. 'Or were you too busy sucking up to David Bowie?'

'You're in a lovely mood today,' James replied. 'I was going to offer to sew some lace on that new shirt you bought last week, but if that's your attitude I won't bother. Love that towel on your head, by the way. You should wear it more often.'

'He scorched his fringe with my crimpers,' Katy said. 'Don't take any notice of him. He's just jealous because you were there and he wasn't.'

Anthony gave a hollow laugh. 'Me? Jealous? You must be joking.'

But he couldn't hide his true colours for long. He avoided the Blitz for weeks, but when he and Katy returned the following month, Bowie's visit was still the main topic of conversation. Anthony practically bit the head off one poor boy who'd been invited to sit at Bowie's table and hadn't stopped talking about it since. But the biggest giveaway was when the video for 'Ashes to Ashes' was shown on *Top of the Pops*. There was Bowie in his pierrot costume, sinking into a lake. And there was Steve Strange and three girls dressed in ecclesiastical robes, walking behind Bowie with a bulldozer following closely behind. By now, it was common knowledge among regulars at the Blitz that the video had been shot not in some glamorous foreign location, but on the beach at Southend. But even this was no comfort to Anthony. By the end of the video, he was apoplectic.

'That should have been us walking in front of that bulldozer,' he said, turning to Katy with a crazed look in his eyes. 'If it wasn't for those bloody crimpers, we'd be famous by now!'

Maybe it was because Bowie had given the club his official blessing, or maybe it was just a question of timing, but soon the media couldn't keep away from the Blitz, and faces familiar to Anthony, James and Katy began to appear in the papers on a fairly regular basis. The club's cloakroom attendant, a spiky queen named George O'Dowd, reinvented himself as Boy George and took to dressing up as Boudicca, all for the benefit of waiting photographers. As predicted, Steve Strange didn't stop talking about the day he spent shooting the video for 'Ashes to Ashes', although much to everyone's surprise he did risk alienating his newfound friend and was quoted in the papers as saying that Bowie had stolen the pierrot look from him.

Katy found it all highly amusing, and would often tease Anthony about his attempts to compete with the likes of Steve and George, turning up at the Blitz dressed in the most ridiculous outfits he could lay his hands on.

'It's just meant to be a bit of fun, remember?' she said one evening when he appeared in a pair of brown leather breeches, a billowing yellow blouse and a beekeeper's hat.

'For you, maybe,' Anthony replied grimly. 'I mean business.'

And he wasn't the only one. By now, Bowie had released his follow-up single to 'Ashes to Ashes'. A dance-floor filler of the first order, 'Fashion' poked fun at the style fascists and warned of the dangers of taking yourself too seriously. But the message was lost on most of the people who attended the Blitz, who danced along quite happily to the song while continuing to take themselves very seriously indeed. They were encouraged no end by the media, which decided that the so-called Cult With No Name really ought to have one and, unable to decide on one, promptly came up with two. Soon Steve Strange and friends were known as the Blitz Kids to some, the New Romantics to others. And now that a new trend had been formally identified, the record labels weren't far behind. Record companies who had missed the passing bandwagon with punk were determined not to miss out a second time around. Suddenly the club was awash with A&R men eager to sign up anyone with a half-decent wardrobe and even a passing interest in music.

The Blitz already had its own house band, a group of straight lads from Islington who dressed in yards of tartan and rejoiced in the name of Spandau Ballet. But much to everyone's surprise, it was Steve Strange who was the first to secure a record deal. His band, Visage, released their first single, 'Fade to Grey', in November. Backed by a video directed by Godley and Creme, the single went to Number 2 in the charts and within a matter of weeks Steve was a bona fide pop star, interviewed in *Smash Hits* and photographed swilling champagne with the likes of Britt Ekland.

By now, Anthony's jealousy knew no bounds.

'What's Steve Strange got that I haven't?' he asked Katy one night over a TV dinner of Welsh rarebit.

'A band?' Katy replied. 'Not to mention a record contract, a hit single and a shitload of money. I think that just about covers it.'

'Very funny,' Anthony snapped. 'What I mean is, Steve

isn't really a musician, is he? If he can become a pop star, anyone can.'

Katy chewed on a mouthful of cheese on toast. 'I suppose so,' she said thoughtfully. 'But that's nothing new, is it? Most of the punk bands couldn't play an instrument to save their lives.'

'Exactly,' Anthony said. 'So why don't we?'

'What? Start a band?'

'Yes.'

'Seriously?'

'Yes, seriously.'

Katy considered it for a moment. 'Well for one thing, neither of us can sing.'

'Do you call what Steve Strange does singing? And how do you know you can't sing? Have you tried?'

'Not since school, unless you count singing in the shower.'

'Well it's a start. I'm sure Steve never sang in the shower. He'd have shattered the glass.'

'But what about the music? Neither of us can play an instrument. I don't think the recorder counts.'

'But you just said yourself that most of the punk bands couldn't play. And besides, we don't need to play proper instruments. We can just buy a synthesiser instead.'

Katy frowned. 'I don't think it's quite as simple as that. Don't you need to know something about computers?'

'So we get someone to teach us. There's a guy at college who works with computers. I can ask him.'

Katy looked at him. 'You're really serious about this, aren't you?'

Anthony grinned. 'I've never been more serious in my life.'

A week later, Anthony came home from college with a spotty lad in glasses and a Wasp synthesiser. Katy was on her way out to work and met them at the door.

'Where did you get that?' she asked, staring at the keyboard with its tangle of coloured wires, sockets and knobs.

'This is Ian,' Anthony replied. 'Ian is one of the technicians at college. And Ian, this is Katy. She's usually quite polite but she appears to have forgotten her manners today.'

'Sorry,' Katy said quickly. 'I'm just surprised to see you with that synthesiser, that's all.'

Anthony shook his head. 'O ye of little faith,' he said solemnly. 'Now, if you'll just move out of the way, we'll get this baby upstairs.'

Katy went to work feeling slightly disgruntled. She'd known Anthony for four years, and had shared a house with him for the best part of eighteen months, but she'd never seen him like this. He was like a different person, more focused than before, but somehow less fun. Maybe it was simply part of growing up. He'd be twenty-one next birthday. She'd be twenty herself in a couple of months. Maybe it was time she focused on something more than pulling pints and dressing up for the Blitz. Still, she couldn't help feeling that this was all happening too quickly. The feeling stayed with her all evening. Then shortly before midnight she came home to the sound of breaking glass, crashing waves and the whirr of helicopter blades. No, it wasn't the world coming to an end. It was Anthony, playing with his new toy.

'Is that you, Katy?' he yelled down the stairs.

'No, it's Steve Strange,' she shouted back. 'He's come to check out the competition.'

119

'Well tell him to come up and listen to this. I think I've just written our first hit single.'

He hadn't, of course. All he'd really done was flesh out one of his old poems with some very basic sound effects. But it was a step in the right direction at least. He made a similar amount of progress the following day, and the day after that. Then the days turned into weeks, and the weeks turned into months. Lectures were missed, coursework was set aside. Even his personal appearance suffered. Sometimes he left his makeup on for days, only washing it off when his hair got so dirty he was forced to take a shower. But slowly he got to grips with his new piece of technology. Finally, he was sufficiently confident in his ability to invite Katy up to his room for what he described as 'a playback session'.

'Right,' he said, positioning her on the bed and taking his place behind the keyboard. 'Now, whatever you do, don't laugh. I know I'm not the best singer in the world. This is just to give you an idea of what I've been working on.'

'Okay,' she said, smiling. 'I promise I won't laugh. Now play that funky music, white boy.'

'It isn't funky,' he corrected her. 'It's futuristic. Right. Here goes.'

Katy couldn't believe her ears. It was true that Anthony wasn't the greatest singer in the world. But even his feeble vocals couldn't detract from the fact that what she was hearing was every bit as good as some of the stuff they played at the Blitz, better in some cases. Was it really possible that he'd acquired so much musical ability in such a short space of time?

'Fucking hell, Anthony!' she shouted as the music faded. 'Where did you learn to write stuff like this? It's really good.'

'Wait, I haven't finished yet,' he said quickly. 'Listen to this next song. This is the best one, I reckon.'

So Katy listened, and her admiration grew, and by the end of the next song she had stars in her eyes and a big stupid grin on her face.

'That was brilliant,' she gushed.

'Really?'

'Yes, really. What's it called?'

Anthony grinned. 'It's called "The Shadow Explodes". It's based on a poem I wrote when I was still at college. And it'll sound even better when you sing it. I wrote the lyrics out for you on this piece of paper. Shall we give it a go?'

Katy blushed and leapt up from the bed. 'I'm not sure. My throat feels a bit dry. Maybe another time.'

Anthony thrust the piece of paper at her. 'Not so fast, missy. I sang for you. Now it's your turn.'

'But I really don't feel comfortable with you looking at me.'

'Then I won't look at you. See, I'm facing the other way. Now, wait for my cue and we'll give it a go.'

It took a while to get the timing right and to overcome her fears, but by the fourth attempt Katy was finally relaxed enough to give it her best shot. She forgot that her throat was dry and that Anthony was in the room. She forgot that the last time she was required to sing for an audience she was still at school. She remembered the words written on the piece of paper she held in her hand, and when she opened her mouth, the sound came up from somewhere deep in her stomach.

And much to her amazement, she discovered that Anthony was right. His song sounded even better when she sang it.

CHAPTER THIRTEEN

Katrina made the announcement over breakfast. 'I've been thinking about the funeral,' she said, pushing her bowl of muesli aside and placing her hands on the table, all very businesslike.

Rose sipped her tea and smiled cautiously across the fruit bowl. 'Oh yes.'

'Yes, and I was thinking it would be nice if you said a few words.'

Rose looked horrified. 'Me?'

'Well, you are his mother.'

'I know, but I wouldn't know what to say. I'm no good at standing up and speaking in front of a room full of strangers.'

Katrina's eyes narrowed ever so slightly. 'But it won't be a room full of strangers, will it, Rose? I'll be there, and Peter you met at the hospital. And if you're worried about what to say, we can always sit down together and work on something if you want. I know people say you should just say what-ever's in your heart, but sometimes it helps to have something prepared.'

'But I . . .'

Katrina smiled. 'I think it's what Mark would have wanted, don't you?'

Rose blinked. So that was it, was it? End of discussion. 'It's what Mark would have wanted.' Which, roughly translated, meant 'It's the least you can do.' How could she argue with that? Never mind that she was terrified of public speaking, or that she didn't know how to put her feelings into words. She was the mother of the deceased, and as such her duties extended to standing before an audience packed with his friends, most of whom had already formed an unfavourable impression of her, and grieving for all to see. It was all right for Katrina. She was used to performing in public. She probably didn't know the meaning of stage fright.

Rose looked at her. 'And what about you? Will you be singing at the funeral?'

Now it was Katrina's turn to look horrified. 'Singing? No. I haven't sung in years.'

'Why ever not?'

'I just haven't, that's all. People change. Life moves on.'

'But surely you must miss it? I know I would. To be blessed with a gift like that. It's not something you just throw away, is it?'

Katrina smiled and mumbled something about gifts not always being the blessings they were cracked up to be.

Rose frowned. 'Well, I think that's terrible. I mean, if you're lucky enough have a talent like that, I think you have a duty to use it.'

'I did use it,' Katrina said flatly. 'I used it well. And then one day it started using me, and that's when I knew it was time to stop.'

Rose looked at her, not really understanding what she meant but sensing that this wasn't a subject Katrina was keen to discuss. Well maybe it was time she had a taste of her own medicine. Maybe then she'd think twice before pressuring other people to do things they didn't want to do.

'So how successful were you?' Rose asked. 'Were you very famous?'

Katrina nodded, her expression a mixture of embarrassment and stubborn pride. 'Pretty famous, yes. I mean, I wasn't as big as Madonna or anything like that. But I had my fifteen minutes.'

Rose didn't care much for Madonna. She considered her vulgar and foul-mouthed, more like a stripper than a singer. But that was what people seemed to like these days. Maybe if Katrina swore like a trooper and exposed her breasts she'd still be selling records too.

'And were you still famous when you met Mark?' Rose asked.

Katrina fiddled with her hair. 'Not really. To him, maybe. He used to joke that he was my number one fan. But deep down I think we both knew it was over by then.'

'But you were still singing?'

'I'd sing for Mark sometimes. He liked me to sing for him. He said it was like having his own personal diva. But I wasn't recording or performing much any more. That all came to an end pretty soon after the band split.'

Rose felt a sudden pang of pity. 'You seem to have done pretty well out of it, though. I mean, you have a lovely home. You can't be doing too badly.'

Katrina smiled and reeled off a list of things to do with accountants and investments and property.

Rose half listened, not really taking it in. 'And what about the boy you used to sing with?' she said when Katrina had finished. 'Him with the funny hair.'

Katrina laughed. 'Tony? He did a little better out of it than me.'

'Do you still see much of him?'

'No. We haven't spoken in a long time.'

'You had a falling-out?'

'Something like that. Right, I'll just clear these dishes away and then we can finish sorting through those boxes from yesterday.'

Katrina took the breakfast things and loaded them into the dishwasher. Rose watched her, wondering what could have driven a woman with such obvious strength of character to suddenly stop singing and turn her back on everything she'd ever worked for. It must have been something pretty traumatic, to have had such a profound and lasting impact. It made Rose wonder what it would take to restore someone's faith in their ability, once it had been shaken like that. And then she had an idea.

'I've just been thinking about the funeral,' she said.

'Great,' Katrina replied, turning to her and smiling brightly. 'Have you thought about what you'd like to say?'

'Not exactly,' Rose said. 'But I do have an idea I hope you'll consider. I suppose you'd call it a deal really. I'll promise to get up and say a few words if you promise to sing. You said yourself that Mark loved to hear you sing. I think it's what he would have wanted. Don't you?'

The press call for *The Clink* took place outside Wandsworth Prison at eleven a.m. Tony arrived to find the majority of his fellow celebs already assembled, wrapped in winter coats and tucking into Danish pastries and coffee. Wondering when he'd next have the opportunity to savour a Danish, Tony took two and gulped them down.

Someone patted him on the back and a piece of pastry shot out of his mouth and landed in the hairnet of one of the catering staff.

'Sorry,' Tony said, and turned to see his manager sidling up beside him with a broad smile on his face.

'Looking good, Tony. Love the hair.'

Tony wiped his mouth with a paper napkin and looked his manager up and down. 'You're not looking so bad yourself, Dan. Been away?'

Dan fancied himself as a bit of a Jude Law lookalike. In truth, he wasn't nearly as good-looking or half as popular with the ladies, although today his somewhat misshapen features were enjoying the benefits of a golden tan.

'The old Costa del Solarium, Tony. I know people say they cause skin cancer, but you've got to take a few chances in life or you might as well be dead.'

Tony gave him a look. 'Any news on Katrina?'

Dan smiled. 'Yes, actually, I do have something for you. Don't get too excited. It's only an email address, I'm afraid. But at least it's a start.'

'So who've we got here?' Tony asked. He looked around for Ritchie Taylor and, unable to find him, began to entertain the fantasy that he might have pulled out.

'Well I've just been informed that Ritchie is running late,' Dan said. 'That pretty little peach over there is Tamsin Applegate.'

Tony looked and saw one of those interchangeable blondes who seemed to have spread through the television schedules like a virus, replicating themselves everywhere from *GMTV* to *Hollyoaks* to *The Bill*. 'Sorry,' he said. 'I'm none the wiser.'

'She's the weather girl I told you about,' Dan said, and immediately began to undress her with his eyes. Since Tamsin was the only person brave enough to have ventured out without a coat and didn't appear to be wearing much in the way of a skirt, this didn't take very long. 'Mmm,' Dan said with a lascivious grin. 'She can feel my warm front any day.'

Tony rolled his eyes. Then a frown formed on his face as he focused on a large woman with cropped hair, a yellowing complexion, grey sunken eyes and a lip ring. 'Who's the troglodyke?' he said, horrified at the thought of being stuck with such a creature for even a few hours, never mind days or possibly even weeks.

'You mean the rug-muncher with the nose ring?' Dan said, tearing his eyes away from Tamsin Applegate for a moment. 'That's Kim Radclyffe. She hosts a phone-in show on Radio Five. Rumour has it she's on male hormones, which would help explain the facial hair.'

Tony laughed. 'She's certainly got a good face for radio.'

Dan grunted and went back to leering at the nation's favourite weather girl. Moments later he was distracted by the appearance of a publicity girl from Channel Seven, who welcomed everyone to the launch before introducing the presenter of the show, Kelly Gibbon. A busty blonde with a private school education and barely enough intelligence to read an autocue, Kelly was familiar to late-night television viewers from her groundbreaking show on celebrity plastic surgery, *Stars and Scars*. Physically speaking, she had no scars of her own, or at least none that she was willing to admit to. Emotionally speaking, it was rather a different story. Beneath the fake tan and blonde hair extensions beat the damaged heart of a girl whose daddy left home when she was eight, and whose stepfather lavished on her all manner of material possessions and loved her a little too often and in ways her mother wouldn't have been too thrilled to find out about. Dan knew none of this, nor would it have bothered him to learn that Kelly regularly cried herself to sleep and had twice overdosed on sleeping pills. Her screen image was all he was interested in. That, and her occasional spread in *Loaded*.

There was muted applause as Kelly took the stand and proceeded to recite from some hand-held notes, complete with a rundown of those celebrities brave enough to enter *The Clink*. This was extremely useful, as few of the journalists present could name more than four of the people they were expected to write about. Apart from those already identified by Dan, Tony learned that the remaining celebrities were a former soap star, the daughter of a famous politician, a disgraced game show host, a south London rapper, a member of a girl band he'd never heard of and a Brazilian porn star who rejoiced in the name of Hercules Brasil.

'I'm going to take a wild guess and assume that's not his real name,' Tony said in a whisper.

'Actually, I'm told that's the name on his birth certificate,' Dan whispered back. 'It makes you wonder what his parents were thinking. Who knows? Maybe they wanted a porn star for a son.'

'Straight porn or gay?'

Dan smirked. 'What do you think? He says he's straight, but gay porn pays better.'

'And the men have bigger breasts,' Tony added, and they both laughed.

On the platform, Kelly was struggling to fill time until the final celebrity arrived.

'Tamsin rates herself seven out of ten in the looks department,' she said, nervously. 'Though I'm sure some of the gentlemen here will beg to differ on that one. She likes gardening and meditation, and her favourite colour is pink.'

There was a pause while Kelly consulted her notes, and then she was off again. 'Kim's proudest moment was when Sandi Toksvig phoned in to her radio show, and her favourite colour is yellow . . . Hercules doesn't have a favourite colour, but he does like swimming, going to the gym and, er, sleeping . . . Finella became famous when her father, Clive Banks, was MP for Wandsworth and was found to be suffering from Alzheimer's. She is now a spokesperson for Alzheimer's Awareness and hopes to raise funds for the charity with the release of her version of the Take That classic "Never Forget" later this year.'

'I have to say, some of these people aren't exactly my idea of household names,' Tony said.

'Mine neither,' Dan replied. 'But that's good news for you, isn't it? Less competition.'

As if on cue, a cheer went up as a limousine rolled into view and every photographer present turned to capture the arrival of Ritchie Taylor. He might have been a bit of a poof, but Ritchie had done Britain proud these past couple of years, even beating Robbie in the all-important bid to conquer America. The same photographers who hounded George Michael on Hampstead Heath and drove Michael Barrymore to New Zealand were different men when Ritchie was around. Heterosexual to a man, they had even been known to acknowledge just how attractive they found him. And as luck would have it, today was one of those times. As Ritchie stepped out of his limo, looking particularly fetching in a shiny black suit and blue-black hair, the photographer standing nearest to Tony turned to him with a look of barely disguised love in his eyes, the kind usually reserved for football matches.

'Proper pretty, though, ain't he?' he said breathlessly.

And the worst part of it was that Tony was forced to agree. As he stood and smiled for the photographers, there was no denying the fact that Ritchie Taylor was indeed pretty. Proper pretty, in fact.

CHAPTER FOURTEEN

'Oh my God!' Katy screamed. 'Anthony! Quick! You have to see this! Adam Ant's on *Top of the Pops*, dressed like a highwayman. It's the campest thing you've ever seen!'

Anthony came running into the living room, his hair canary yellow and dripping wet from the shower. 'Somehow I doubt that very much,' he said, settling himself on the sofa. 'But I'm willing to be proved wrong.'

Anthony was still undecided on the whole Adam Ant question. Of course he could see the appeal. When Adam first appeared on *Top of the Pops*, stripped to the waist for 'Dog Eat Dog' or singing about 'a new royal family, a wild nobility', there was a raw sexiness about his performance that made a refreshing change from the likes of nerdy Elvis Costello, cheesy David Essex and boring Barry Manilow. And although he was never tempted to paint a white stripe across his nose or tie bits of ribbon in his hair, Anthony was quite taken with the Ant image and its blend of teenage tribalism and swashbuckling heroics. But something had changed in the year since *Kings of the Wild Frontier*. Twelve months of overexposure had robbed the former punk icon of the very thing that made him special. Adam wasn't so noble any more, or so wild. And the only frontier he was crossing now was the one from irrepressibly cool to irredeemably naff. Seeing the dandy highwayman leap from trees or swing from chandeliers, it was hard to believe that this was the man who had once walked down the King's Road with the words 'Fuck me' carved into his back.

'This isn't camp,' Anthony said. 'It's crap. It's pantomime. If you ask me, he's blown it. His career is as good as over.'

Katy didn't take her eyes off the television. 'He's still pretty though, isn't he?' she said.

Anthony shrugged. 'I suppose so. If you like that sort of thing.'

Katy laughed. 'Oh, c'mon, Anthony. Don't tell me you wouldn't shag him if you had the chance.'

'That's where you're wrong,' Anthony replied. 'I've got better things to do with my time than salivate over some straight pop pin-up aimed at twelve-year-old girls.'

'I'm starting to worry about you,' Katy said. 'A bit of salivating might do you some good. It's months since I've heard any noises coming from your room, apart from the synthesiser that is. You'll be like me soon. A dried-up old spinster at twenty-one.'

Anthony pulled a face. 'If you must know, I've been too busy studying for my finals to go trolling around every club in town. I leave that to our friend James. From what I hear, he's getting enough for both of us.'

'Well good for him,' Katy smiled. 'At least someone's having sex around here. Maybe if you ask him nicely he'll introduce you to someone.'

'I don't need any help from James,' Anthony said crossly. 'Just because I don't bring a different man home every night of the week, it doesn't mean I'm not getting any.'

'What? You mean you're seeing someone?'

Anthony blushed. 'I never said that.'

'But you didn't deny it either. C'mon, Anthony! Don't hold out on me. Who is it? What's his name? What's he like? Have I seen him?'

Anthony laughed. 'What are you? My mother? You'll find out soon enough. I was thinking of maybe inviting him over for dinner. Actually, I was kind of hoping you'd cook. He's vegetarian and I'm no good with lentils.'

Katy grinned. 'Great. When?'

'This weekend?'

'I'm working Friday night. How about Saturday?'

'Saturday's perfect.'

'And does he have a name, or shall I just refer to him as "the vegetarian"?'

'Wilf,' Anthony said proudly. 'His name's Wilf.'

Wilf arrived at six that Saturday evening, and a pretty poor excuse for a dinner guest he turned out to be. Painfully thin, with a greased rockabilly quiff poking out from beneath a black leather cap, he wore a donkey jacket and had the fashionably wasted look that came from living in a squat in Camden on a diet of tea, toast and roll-ups. His skin was pale and there were dark shadows under his eyes, and probably in his soul as well for all she knew. He looked like he was suffering from an iron deficiency, which may have explained his troubled frown and apparent lack of humour. Katy hated him instantly.

The atmosphere didn't improve much over dinner. Wilf was the drummer in a band, and liked to boast that the sound he produced was so loud, he was forced to wear ear plugs on stage. Katy wondered if maybe he'd forgotten to take them out. For while he never seemed to tire of the sound of his own voice, he wasn't so good when it came to listening. She could easily picture him performing an extended drum solo, and drowning out the other band members around him.

'Wilf says the New Romantic scene is pretty much over,' Anthony managed to chip in at one point. 'He says the public is tired of poseurs pretending to be pop stars. It's time to get back to some real music.'

'The New Romantics are just a confederacy of punk failures hitching a ride on the next passing bandwagon,' Wilf said scornfully. 'At least punk had a political agenda. All this lot have is personal ambition and a pathetic obsession with clothes. Dressing to impress is such a bourgeois concept. Dressing to distress, now that's more like it.'

'Is that right?' Katy said. 'And what sort of music do you play, Wilf?'

'It's hard to categorise,' Wilf replied through a mouthful of vegetable lasagne. 'There's a lot of energy, a lot of guitars, a lot of feedback.'

Katy smiled. 'Sounds pretty aggressive.'

Wilf shot her a withering look. 'It's a sonic assault on crypto-fascist ideologies. Obviously it doesn't appeal to everybody.'

'And have you released a record yet?' Katy enquired innocently.

'Wilf doesn't believe in signing with record companies,' Anthony interrupted.

'And I've never had a job either,' Wilf boasted. He smiled smugly and recited: 'Employment is the surest sign of poverty.'

'So what exactly do you live on?' Katy asked.

'Dole money,' Wilf said, as if this was the most obvious thing in the world and she was an idiot for even asking.

'I see,' said Katy. 'So you don't have a problem with other people working and paying taxes to support you?'

'And there's the money from the gigs,' Anthony added quickly. 'Wages of Sin are amazing live.'

Katy's eyes widened as she turned to Wilf. 'Wages of Sin? Is that what your band's called?'

'Yeah,' Wilf muttered. 'It's a political statement, about capitalism and that.'

Katy smiled. 'I can see how it would be.'

'The fans go mad at their gigs,' Anthony gushed. 'People throw themselves at the stage and everything. We should go the next time they're on.'

'We should.' Katy nodded.

'We won't be doing any gigs for a while,' Wilf said mournfully. 'We lost our lead guitarist last week.'

'Never mind,' Katy said. 'I'm sure you'll find another one.'

'And when you do, we'll be there to support you,' Anthony said. 'Now, anyone for some more wine?'

The evening ended with Anthony and Wilf crawling off to bed drunk while Katy was left to do the washing-up. Not that she really minded. In fact, she preferred to linger in the kitchen for a bit, rather than lie awake trying to ignore the noises from Anthony's room. She took her time over the washing-up and left the lasagne dish to soak before making her way upstairs to the bathroom. She had just finished removing her makeup and was perched on the toilet when the door burst open and a naked Wilf walked in, his cock semi-erect and glistening wet.

'Oops! Sorry!' he said, making precious little attempt to avert his eyes or cover the evidence of his arousal.

Katy turned her head away. 'Get out!' she hissed, horrified at the sight of Wilf in all his naked semi-tumescence.

Wilf didn't budge. He simply stood staring at her for a moment, his eyes shiny with lust. Finally he sloped off, leaving Katy with the distinct impression that he'd enjoyed the interruption rather more than he should have.

The following morning over the breakfast table, Wilf was all sly smiles and sidelong glances. Katy avoided meeting his eyes, wolfed down her toast as quickly as she could and returned to her room. There she waited until she heard the front door slam before coming downstairs to find Anthony mooning about the kitchen.

'So what do you think?' Anthony said.

Katy blinked. 'About what?'

'About Wilf, stupid. Pretty sexy, huh?'

'He seems very nice,' Katy lied.

'Nice?' Anthony laughed. 'He's better than nice. He's gorgeous. And he's great in bed, I can tell you.'

Katy laughed nervously. 'That's good to hear.'

'Are you okay?' Anthony said. 'Only you hardly said a word at breakfast. I think Wilf thought that maybe you didn't like him.'

Katy swallowed hard. 'Are you sure Wilf's gay?' she said. 'Only I bumped into him last night in the bathroom and I thought he looked at me a bit funny.'

Anthony looked at her blankly. 'What do you mean, "a bit funny"?'

Katy hesitated. 'Well, not in the way a gay man usually looks at a woman. Sort of leering, I suppose, in a sexual way.'

Anthony laughed. 'Poor Katy. We really will have to find you a boyfriend one of these days. Fantasising about gay men isn't healthy.'

And so began the summer of Wilf. With his finals finally over, and the freedom to join his boyfriend on the dole and have his rent paid until fame beckoned or he found himself a suitable job, Anthony had little else to do but devote time to his relationship, and over the following few months Wilf's influence on him grew considerably. Everything was 'Wilf this' or 'Wilf that'. Slowly but surely, Anthony's relationship with Katy went from being one of close personal friendship to one of slightly distant musical partnership. Although they continued to share a house and the odd conversation over breakfast, Wilf's presence put a strain on things, to the extent that Katy found more and more excuses to hide out in her room whenever he was around. And since Wilf's band still hadn't found a new guitarist, he had plenty of time to spare.

From Katy's slightly embittered perspective, it seemed that much of this time was spent telling Anthony what to wear and how to style his hair, but gradually Wilf's influence spread until it was encroaching on her territory too. Spurred on by his boyfriend's suggestion, Anthony suddenly decided that it was time he and Katy found themselves a manager and tried to secure a record deal.

'But I thought Wilf didn't approve of managers and record deals,' Katy said.

'Not for his band, no,' Anthony replied. 'But that's different. Wages of Sin are a live band. We're more studio-based, or we would be if we could afford a studio.'

'And what about choosing a name for this band of ours, or has Wilf already thought of that too?'

'Actually, we did have a conversation about that. Wilf thought Bleeding Foetus would be good.'

Katy put her foot down. 'No way am I going to be part of a band called Bleeding Foetus. It sounds disgusting.'

'Okay, we'll leave the name for now. But let's try and find a manager. Maybe he can help us think of a good name.'

The search for a manager began with Malcolm McLaren, who turned them down flat.

'Wilf says Malcolm only wants people he can control,' Anthony said sniffily. 'We're better off without him. At least this way we're masters of our own destiny.'

As destiny would have it, they finally found a manager in the shape of Les – the same Les whom Anthony had encountered two years previously at Billy's. He hadn't changed much. Same haircut, same lecherous grin. Only now he was sporting a pencil moustache in the style of Midge Ure and managing a psychobilly band who'd just enjoyed their first chart success with a single called 'I Hate Your Face'. It seemed that Les wasn't lying when he said he could make people's dreams come true. And if his hands were prone to wander from time to time, Anthony figured it was a small price to pay.

'I love this girl's style,' Les said when Katy and Anthony came to his Soho office to sign the necessary paperwork. 'How does she put it all together?'

'The girl can speak for herself,' Katy said.

'And sing too,' Les replied. 'Honestly, she's such a diva.'

But Anthony wasn't paying attention. His eyes were drawn to a blond, skinny figure engrossed in a telephone conversation at the far end of the room. The hair was long and braided, and the face was turned away, but there was something familiar about the flamboyant hand gestures and the tilt of the head. 'Is that James?' Anthony said.

'Yes, of course, I'd forgotten you two know each other,' Les purred. 'James is my new PA. You know how he was thrown out of college for failing to attend lectures? As if lectures were all that mattered! Well, I couldn't see the poor boy starve. No experience, of course, but he tells me he's a very fast learner.' He shouted across the room. 'James! Look who's come to see us!'

James looked up and waved. Anthony was shocked to see that he was looking even more effeminate than usual. He'd obviously been plucking his eyebrows, and was wearing rather a lot of makeup – panstick, eyeshadow, lipstick, the works. Together with his braided hair, this gave him the appearance of a china doll. Anthony wasn't altogether disappointed when he failed to come over but redirected his attention to whoever was on the phone.

'So what happens now?' Anthony asked.

Les smiled. 'What happens now is that we put a demo tape together and send it round to the record companies. You've got some promising material there. I particularly like that song about the shadows exploding. It sounds a bit like Ultravox, which is no bad thing, obviously.'

'Obviously,' said Anthony.

'And then I think a little showcase somewhere should get the interest going,' Les continued.

'Showcase?' Katy said. 'You mean, sing in front of people?'

Les laughed. 'That is the general idea, my dear. If there

weren't any people for you to perform to, I rather think we'd be wasting our time, don't you?'

The demo tape was recorded at a small studio in Covent Garden and plans were made for a showcase at the Scala cinema in King's Cross. Everything appeared to be running smoothly. Then, a few days before the showcase, tragedy struck. Les rang to say that the demo tape hadn't gone down too well, and that under the circumstances it was best to shelve the showcase until a later date. Anthony was gutted, Katy was relieved, and Wilf suddenly lost all interest and stopped returning Anthony's calls. A week later he was spotted at the Marquee snogging a girl.

'But I thought he loved me,' Anthony sobbed when he heard the news.

Katy resisted the urge to say 'I told you so' and simply held him in her arms. 'I know you did,' she said soothingly. 'What a bastard, eh? He had us all fooled.'

It took Anthony approximately three weeks to get over Wilf. By the end of August he had a new love in his life. 'Tainted Love' by Soft Cell was the song of the summer, and for Anthony it marked the beginning of an obsession rivalled only by his devotion to David Bowie. Anthony had spotted Marc Almond at the Blitz and was already curious about this slightly androgynous northern soul boy with a background in performance art. He'd danced to 'Memorabilia' and wondered if the singer of the song was really as decadent as he sounded. Was it true that he once stripped naked on stage and smeared his body with cat food? Did he really live above a sex shop, and sleep in a room with padded walls?

But all this speculation was nothing compared to the thrill Anthony felt the first time Soft Cell appeared on *Top of the Pops*. There was none of that 'cheeks in' robotic posturing with Soft Cell. And there was none of that 'I'm a dandy highwayman' pantomime nonsense either. Soft Cell were everything the New Romantics weren't supposed to be – hyperemotional and wonderfully uncool. And they were everything Adam had forgotten how to be – overtly sexual and shockingly subversive.

The moment Marc Almond made his debut on *Top of the Pops*, a nation's jaws dropped in horror. Dressed all in black, with his trademark thick black eyeliner and metal bracelets up to his elbows, he had the look of someone who knew his way around the fleshpots of Soho. His hair was dyed an unnatural shade of black and had clearly been teased within an inch of its life (Anthony could almost hear it pleading, 'Don't touch me please, I cannot stand the way you tease'). Arms waving, head tossing, skinny hips wiggling beneath the folds of his baggy black trousers, his performance was the last word in camp overstatement. And when the camera zoomed in on his tortured face, eyes half-closed to reveal lashings of mascara, Anthony felt as if he were twelve again and seeing Bowie for the first time.

He played the twelve-inch version of 'Tainted Love' constantly for a week, and could barely contain his excitement when the single went to Number 1. And when the album came out, he played it to death, revelling in its celebrations of the seedier side of life. His favourite track was 'Sex Dwarf', partly because it reminded him of the poem he'd written years earlier.

'It's called "Never Trust A Dwarf (With Sex On His

Mind)",' he said, digging out one of his college notebooks and searching in vain for the aforementioned poem. 'It was inspired by my Auntie Alma. Remember that day we came back from King's Road with our fetish gear and she started going on about prostitution and dwarves?' He paused dramatically. 'God, I wonder if Marc Almond ever met Auntie Alma!'

Katy laughed. 'I doubt it. Isn't he from Leeds or something?'

Anthony frowned. 'All I know is, when I still lived in Bridgend there was a carpet shop called The Pink Flamingo. You can't tell me that's just a coincidence!'

And so it continued. Every twelve-inch single, every TV appearance, everything Marc Almond said or did was soaked up by Anthony on a daily basis. By now it was clear to him that the majority of the so-called New Romantics were simply a bunch of old-fashioned straight ponces with a leggy model on each arm and their sights on the high life. He'd seen them on *Top of the Pops*, the Durans and the Spandaus, dressed in straight-edge suits and advertising their heterosexuality at every opportunity. Soft Cell were a different story altogether. The only women Anthony ever saw them with were either prostitutes or tarty-looking backing singers with names like Cindy Ecstasy. And they sang songs about sex. Not the kind of sex practised by beautiful people on yachts and foreign beaches, the other kind. Sex in bedsits, in porno cinemas, in the back seats of cars. Sex involving 'dumb chauffeurs' and 'lurid disco dollies'. The kind of sex that left a nasty taste in your mouth and a hole in your wallet. The kind of sex that sold.

'I've had an idea,' Anthony announced one Thursday

evening, marching into the living room with his hair a deathly shade of blue-black. Katy was busy watching *Top of the Pops* and trying to decide whether she still fancied Adam now that he'd ditched the dandy highwayman look and reinvented himself as Prince Charming.

'Mind you don't overexert yourself,' she said without taking her eyes off the screen.

'I think it's time we sexed up our image,' Anthony continued. 'Leather, chains, the whole works. Really rub people's faces in it.'

'By "people", I take it you mean our imaginary audience?'

'Not for much longer,' Anthony said. 'Trust me, get the look right and in a few months we'll have a proper fan base. I'll have a word with Les, see if he can get his hands on some bondage gear. Just promise me you'll follow Adam's advice.'

'What?' Katy said, finally looking up at him.

Anthony lifted his chin and held his arms crossed above his head in imitation of Prince Charming. 'Don't chew leather,' he said, and ran laughing from the room.

CHAPTER FIFTEEN

'Day one in *The Clink* and already there are signs of trouble. Our ten celebrities have been under lock and key for less than twenty-four hours, and the tension is mounting. One celebrity has already threatened to leave!'

At this, the woman with the microphone paused for dramatic effect, tossing back her long blonde hair extensions.

'But don't worry, we've still got them all banged up and bang to rights! Later tonight we'll be giving you the chance to vote for your least favourite celebrity, who'll be given the task of winning food rations for the group. More on that later. But first, here's today's action from *The Clink*.'

Kelly Gibbon stepped away from the camera and let out an enormous sigh. She hated this job. Whoever said reality TV was a fast track to fame and fortune was wrong. The job of a TV presenter wasn't nearly as easy as some people thought. Reading the autocue without her glasses was hard enough. But this wasn't about reading. This was about acting. How else was she supposed to summon enthusiasm for some stupid show about a bunch of celebrities with nothing better to do than humiliate themselves on TV in the pursuit of popularity? Nobody thought she actually cared about these people, did they? The truth was, she'd rather be thrown into a snake pit than spend five minutes in the company of these losers.

No, Kelly was meant for far greater things than this. All her life she'd nursed the dream of becoming a famous actress. It was written in the stars right from the start. She'd sparkled in the school nativity play as Mary, and shone in the village hall production of *Cinderella*. Everyone said she was meant for the stage. Then when no acting school would take her, she was forced to find an alternative route. What was it the rejection letters had said? 'No natural ability as an actor.' 'Too self-conscious to ever really convince.' Showed how much they knew. People watching tonight's show at home probably thought she was some ditzy blonde who actually cared what happened to some of these celebrities. As if that were the scale of her ambition!

Her only hope was that someone, somewhere, would see this show and recognise her for the great undiscovered talent she was. All she needed was that one big break, the chance to prove herself once and for all. Maybe then her stepfather would stop complaining about all the money he'd wasted on her education. It wasn't even as if he couldn't afford it. At the last count he was worth well over £100 million. What were a few school fees when you owned half of Shropshire? At least she hadn't followed in the footsteps of so many of her school chums and snorted her way through the best part of her inheritance. Then again, maybe if she had, there'd be more people out there willing to give her a break. The public loved that kind of thing. Poor little rich girl, snorting coke to numb the hurt inside. It appealed to their sense of justice, somehow compensating for the fact they would never have her kind of wealth, no matter how much overtime they did.

Friends wondered why she even bothered working at all.

'What's the point?' Petra asked her one day over lunch at The Ivy. 'You're already filthy rich. If I had half your money I'd never work another day in my life.'

But girls like Petra would never understand. For them, work was that irritating thing they did in between facials and appointments at the hairdressers. For Kelly, it was a different story altogether. She needed to work, not for the money, but for the sense of worth it gave her. She wasn't simply her stepfather's daughter, heiress to a small fortune and survivor of childhood sexual abuse. She was Kelly Gibbon, TV presenter. It wasn't quite Kelly Gibbon, Oscar-winning actress. But at least it was a step in the right direction.

She looked around for the assistant producer and, spotting him chatting with one of the makeup girls, marched up and tapped him on the shoulder.

'Andrew,' she said. 'About this script. Could I have a word?'

Katrina stared in disbelief at her computer screen. She'd been avoiding checking her emails for days, worried that some well-intentioned letter of condolences would open the floodgates and she'd be like a drowning woman, swimming against a tide of her own tears. That was the last thing she needed right now. She'd already lost it a few times in front of Rose. She'd kept her mouth shut, of course. And she was confident that Rose didn't suspect anything. But she had to hold it together for a few more days. She couldn't afford to fuck up now. Too much depended on it.

Rose had retired to bed early tonight, so Katrina had crept

into her study, figuring that now was as good a time as any to face whatever horrors lay ahead. What she hadn't expected was this. An email from a man she hadn't spoken to in over twenty years. An email from someone more dead to her now than the man whose funeral she was helping to arrange. An email that brought back memories she'd struggled for years to forget.

'Hello, Katrina,' it began. 'Or should I call you Katy? I'm not sure how to start really. Twenty years is a long time! I only hope the years have been kind to you, and that you can find it in your heart to extend a little kindness my way. Forgiveness is a lot to ask, I know. But we all make mistakes – especially me! In fact, I may be about to make another mistake. I'm taking part in this TV show called *The Clink*. You've probably read about it in the paper. Everyone's telling me it'll be good for my career, but we both know what managers are like . . .'

Katrina stopped reading and looked at the gold discs hanging on the wall. She took a deep breath, and then she hit the delete button.

Tony gritted his teeth and told himself that there were cameras watching. In fact, reality TV being the tightly controlled, highly artificial environment it was, it wouldn't have surprised him to learn that there were more cameras dotted around this converted television studio in London's docklands than would normally be found in a working maximum-security prison. There were cameras in the grey-painted cells and in the stark white bathroom. There were cameras in the TV room with its plastic chairs and wall-mounted TV, and in the games room with its ancient board games and ping-pong table. There were cameras outside in the prison yard where inmates would face a variety of physical challenges, and inside 'the Cooler' where they were threatened with solitary confinement if they broke the terms of their contract or the rules of the game. And here in the canteen, where they were summoned three times a day, a multitude of cameras allowed the show's producers to zoom in on every facial expression, every tic, every sign of tension as Tony and his fellow inmates sat down to a breakfast of porridge, imaginatively thought up by the producers and served by a scowling Scotsman who looked as if he was on day release from Broadmoor.

Seated around a long trestle table, dressed in matching orange prison uniforms which carried distinct overtones of Guantanamo Bay, it was all a far cry from the usual celebrity soirée of champagne, canapés and designer dresses. Tony's only hope was that the prison food would help him shed a few pounds, provided of course that he stayed the distance and wasn't voted out on the first day. Right now there was the distinct possibility that he wouldn't be eating porridge for very long. This wasn't the first time in his life that Tony had been required to perform for the cameras. But as he was quickly discovering, there was a world of difference between miming to a three-minute pop song and having your every move monitored 24/7.

He knew, of course, that this was all part of the challenge, part of the price he was required to pay for appearing in a primetime, heavily promoted show like *The Clink*. He knew also that a show like this was little more than a popularity contest, and that the way to win friends and influence the voting public was to be as inoffensive and innocuous as possible. Past winners of reality TV shows were usually the blandest of people, those without strong opinions, barely capable of thinking for themselves in some cases.

And God knows he'd tried to keep his mouth shut. He pretended not to notice when weather girl Tamsin, oblivious to the irony of the situation, gave the assembled inmates a little lecture on animal conservation and how difficult it was to get people to care for creatures that weren't cute and cuddly, before suddenly clapping her hands in the air and passing an instant death sentence on a passing house fly. He paid no attention when Tyrone, a rapper from south London, compared the inside of the prison to conditions inside the youth detention centre he'd attended when he was twelve and had been rapping about ever since. He smiled politely when Kim, eager to flex her lesbian credentials, started banging on about patriarchy, phallocentrism and other words designed to shame men into shutting up and listening to her drone on.

But now his patience was starting to wear a bit thin.

Hercules, desperate for some attention and unable to hold his own in the conversation, had begun removing the top half of his uniform and was inviting Tamsin to inspect his tattoos.

'This one remembers me of Rio,' he said, pointing to a figure of Christ tattooed across his left pectoral muscle. 'And this one' – pointing to an elaborate hearts and daggers design on his right bicep – 'this one was made in Los Angeles.' Evidently pleased at the gasps of admiration he was generating, Hercules stood up from the table and peeled his uniform right down to his waist, revealing an even greater number of tattoos on his back. Floating above his buttocks were two cherubs with a banner bearing the legend '100% Satisfaction Guaranteed'. Scrawled across his shoulders in huge black letters was the word 'Rebel'.

'This one's beautiful,' Tamsin cooed, reaching out and touching one of the cherubs. What she really wanted to know, but didn't dare ask, was whether Hercules was as confident of his ability to satisfy a woman as his tattoo proclaimed. And if so, why had he chosen to advertise the fact on his lower back, rather than on his front where more women would be inclined to see it as they knelt down to administer a blow job?

Finally Tony's patience ran out. 'I'm sorry,' he said, sounding more irritated than apologetic, 'but I'd like to ask Hercules a question. No offence, but what exactly are you rebelling against?'

Hercules looked confused. 'Sorry?'

'All these tattoos of yours,' Tony went on. 'Are they actually supposed to mean something? Because I really don't see what's so rebellious about having the word "rebel" tattooed across your back.'

Hercules frowned. 'What you mean?'

'Yes, Tony,' Tamsin said accusingly. 'What do you mean?'

'Well, tattoos are hardly a sign of rebellion, are they? Not any more. If you ask me, the truly rebellious thing for you to do now would be to have them all removed.'

'You don't like?' Hercules looked mortally wounded.

'It's not that I don't like them,' Tony replied. 'I just think they're a bit passé, that's all.'

'Well I think they look lovely,' Tamsin cooed.

'Tony does have a point, though,' Kim chipped in. Tony noticed she had a bit of porridge caught in her lip ring.

'Tattoos are very last century,' she went on. 'We had quite a heated discussion about this on my radio show not so long ago. In some parts of the world, tattoos still signify something transgressive and socially unacceptable. In Japan, for example, they insist that you cover them up before entering a steam room or public baths. But here in the West all that has changed. Tattoos may have signified rebellion fifty years ago. Now they're just decoration, devoid of any real meaning.'

'I don't care if they mean anything or not,' Tamsin pouted. 'Everything doesn't have to mean something.'

'Well put,' Tony said snidely. 'Though I hope you aren't quite so laissez-faire when it comes to reading the weather. I'd hate to discover that those little symbols you stick on the map of Britain have ceased to mean anything. Am I right in assuming that a little cloud still means it's going to be cloudy and a little sun still means it's going to be sunny?'

Bored with the way the conversation was developing, and possibly dreaming of the time he'd next feel the sun on his skin, Hercules had now pulled his uniform back on and was seated at the table, poking at his porridge with a spoon and a look of disgust.

'Come on, Hercules,' Tony said. 'I'm sure you've had worse things in your mouth.'

Hercules looked at him blankly.

'So is it true that you're a porn star?' Tamsin said. 'That must be a very demanding profession.'

'Rubbish,' Kim said tartly. 'Porn is just a metaphor for the menace of male power. Porn is the theory and rape is the practice. It degrades women.'

'Not the sort of porn he's involved in,' Tony smirked.

'What do you mean?' Tamsin's eyes widened. She turned

to Hercules. 'Are the women in your films treated nicely, then?'

Tony sniggered. 'There aren't any women in his films. That's the whole point. You're not just barking up the wrong tree, you silly bint. You're in a completely different part of the forest.'

Hercules frowned. 'What is this forest? There is no forest. Only studio.'

'It's a metaphor,' Tony said patiently. 'You know, like your tattoos?'

Hercules shook his head. 'No, no forest. A farm? Yes, one time. And two times in prison. But a forest? No.'

Judging by the look on her face, it was clear that Tamsin was every bit as confused as Hercules. Tony decided to put her out of her misery.

'He makes gay porn films,' he said, far louder than was strictly necessary. 'He makes the kind of films where he's paid to shove his cock up other men's arses. Women don't enter into it.'

By now, the entire table had turned to watch as Hercules blushed and Tamsin blanched. At the far end of the table, Finella the daughter of the famous politician and Gary the disgraced game show host stopped swapping hard luck stories and sat with mouths agape. Seated directly opposite them, Shelley the former soap star and Lisa the least famous member of a forgotten girl band were similarly stunned into silence.

'But that's disgusting,' Tyrone the rapper said, pushing his porridge away and staring hard at Hercules. 'I thought you was the man, having all that pussy and that. But what you're doing is gross, man.'

These words were music to the ears of Gary the game show host, who'd recently been accused of sleeping with underage girls and, despite having his case thrown out of court when a key witness refused to testify, had been torn to pieces by the tabloids and still felt the weight of public disapproval wherever he went. Having narrowly escaped a prison sentence, he'd come on to *The Clink* in the hope that, by seeing him ritually humiliated, the viewers would take pity on him and welcome him back on to their screens in a new game show, the details of which his agent was currently discussing with one of the free digital channels.

'I'm afraid I have to agree with Tyrone,' Gary said, grateful to be part of the baying mob for a change. 'It does all sound rather unpleasant.'

'Are you telling me that such films actually exist?' Finella piped up. 'How extraordinary.'

Shelley and Lisa exchanged knowing looks but said nothing. As the youngest females in the room, they'd grown up with Madonna and weren't the least bit shocked at the thought of two men having sex together. In fact, they found the idea positively exciting.

Finally, Ritchie Taylor spoke. 'Well I don't think there's anything remotely disgusting about what Hercules does for a living. What I find disgusting are some of the attitudes around this table. Sex is a natural part of life, and if Hercules is comfortable having sex on camera I don't see how it's anybody's business but his own. Whether it's gay sex or straight sex is totally irrelevant.'

Shelley and Lisa gazed at Ritchie in adoration. Here was one gay man they'd be happy to see having sex, on camera or not.

Sensing that the mood was shifting in favour of Hercules and his controversial career choices, Tony made a last-ditch attempt to save face and side with the winning team.

'Too right,' he said heartily. 'I couldn't agree more.'

Ritchie stared across the table at him with a look bordering on contempt. 'If that's how you feel, why have you spent the past ten minutes pandering to the sort of prejudices gay people like yourself know only too well?'

Tony blushed. 'What? But I . . .'

Ritchie smiled sadly. 'I'm disappointed in you, Tony. Take my advice and keep your internalised homophobia to yourself. It's not very attractive.'

And with that, Ritchie rose from the table and walked off, leaving his porridge half eaten and Tony with egg on his face.

CHAPTER SIXTEEN

Nineteen eighty-two dawned bright and full of optimism. The Human League were enjoying their third week at the top of the charts with 'Don't You Want Me?', and Anthony was confident that it wouldn't be too long before he and Katy would have the world at their feet, that success would be as easy for them as it had been for Phil and the girls. Only they weren't actually called Anthony and Katy any more. On the advice of Les, Anthony had shortened his name to Tony, while Katy's had been lengthened to Katrina.

'It sounds better,' Les insisted when she protested. 'More sophisticated. Sophistication is what's in now. Think Bryan Ferry in a white tuxedo. Think Bowie in a black fedora. Glamour, that's the name of the game.'

Glamour was very nearly the name of the band too, until Tony pointed out that, these days, most people took 'glamour' to mean 'topless modelling'.

'And I don't think Katy's ready to bare her boobs just yet.'

'Katrina,' Les corrected him. 'Katy is the girl she used to be, before stardom beckoned. Katy is no more. Now she's Katrina.'

Finally, after much heated debate and a few unwelcome suggestions from James, Les hit on the name A Boy and His Diva.

'Perfect,' James announced, clapping his hands.

'Indeed it is,' Les agreed. '"Boy" because you're still only a boy, Tony, despite that stubble on your chin. And "boy" always sounds much sexier than "man", especially to the all-important teenage girl market. And "diva" because I've always thought of our Katrina as a bit of a diva, right from the moment I first clapped eyes on her.'

Privately, Katy/Katrina wondered if A Boy and His Diva made it sound like she was Tony's possession, but by now Les was quite clearly on a roll and she didn't dare interrupt.

'Are you sure about this, Les?' Tony asked. 'You don't think it sounds like some sort of cabaret act?'

'So what if it does?' Les replied. 'Cabaret is an essential part of today's pop landscape. Think Cabaret Voltaire. Think *Non-Stop Erotic Cabaret*.'

The first reference passed Tony by completely, but the reference to Soft Cell was enough to convince him. And when Katrina complained that the name didn't sound edgy enough, Les was quick to put her right on a few things.

'Forget edgy, my dear. Forget spitting and vomiting and all that anarchy rubbish. Never mind the Sex Pistols, here's the way things will be in the future. Think aspiration. Think style. Think New Pop. Trust me, a year from now it'll be like punk never happened.'

Loath as she was to admit it, even Katrina could see that Les had a point. It didn't matter how many times people repeated the tired old mantra 'Punk's Not Dead'. She only had to look around to see that the punk era as she knew it was officially over. Sid Vicious was dead and buried, and although his ghost still walked the streets in every town centre across the country, there wasn't the same excitement that had greeted him when he was alive. Johnny Rotten was Rotten no more, and apart from a few petrified mohicans who still loitered around the King's Road, posing for tourists, punk's legacy was disappearing fast. Post-punk had already been and gone, and the more successful of the New Romantics were busy cleaning up their acts. Duran Duran had swapped their panstick and velvet knickerbockers for pastel suits, and Spandau Ballet were no longer wearing kilts and ponchos but dressed like Edwardian gentlemen in pin-stripe trousers and dangly watch chains. Rotten was wrong when he sang about there being 'no future'. There was a future, just not one he'd ever have wanted to be part of. And nobody, least of all the futurists Katrina counted as friends, had smelled that one coming.

Les might have had his finger on the pulse of popular culture, but by the time June came around and Adam Ant completed his transition from wild frontiersman to 'Goody Two Shoes', his plans for world domination hadn't met with much success. Nor had Tony's strategy of dressing in black leather and hanging around the Blitz, waiting to be discovered. The Blitz kids were last year's news, and while the club might have provided a convenient launching pad for both Steve Strange and Spandau Ballet, the days when anyone walking through the door was guaranteed a recording contract were long gone. The Blitz kids may have acted like stars, but nobody was casting around the club for the Next Big Thing.

Still confident that the more traditional route could yet yield results, Les booked a series of small club gigs and hired a studio to record a second demo tape. But even John Peel refused to give the new demo air time, and a much-publicised gig in the upstairs room at Heaven failed to attract more than thirty people, one of whom was the *NME*'s Paul Morley, who took great delight in trashing the band in words of three syllables or more.

'I don't get it,' a disillusioned Tony complained to his manager one night over a pint at the Chelsea Potter pub on King's Road. 'I even saw Bow Wow Wow on *Top of the Pops* last week! Bloody Bow Wow Wow! What have they got that we haven't? Apart from Malcolm McLaren as manager?'

If Les was wounded by the mention of the man in whose shadow he operated, he didn't let it show. In fact, he oozed cool. Lately he had taken to dressing the way he imagined a country squire might, should he happen to live in a flat off the Fulham Road – riding breeches, pocket watch, tweeds and an enormous overcoat fashioned from soft brown leather. He looked both slightly ridiculous and extremely well connected at the same time. For a young man from Tony's humble background, the effect was strangely disconcerting.

'Patience, my boy,' Les assured him. 'Your time will come. So long as you have faith in yourself, and you keep working hard at it, the rest of the world will catch up eventually.'

'But will it, though?' Tony said. 'How can you be so sure?'

Les took out his pocket watch and studied it carefully. 'See this watch, Tony? See how the second hand keeps ticking away? If there's one thing I've learned in this life, it's that everything comes to those who wait. Look at Adam. He didn't become the biggest pop star in Britain overnight. It took years. But what matters is that he got there in the end. And you will too. Trust me. I'm never wrong about these things. Never.'

Tony smiled weakly. Now probably wasn't the time to

mention all those acts Les most certainly had been wrong about – the psychobilly band who failed to follow up their one chart entry with anything even remotely resembling a hit; the Japanese girl duo who screamed blue murder over a backing track of electronic bleeps; the Latin quartet who beat out their rhythms on a bass guitar and a set of bongos.

'So how's the lovely Katrina?' Les went on. 'Will she be joining us this evening, or has she had a better offer?'

'She's not feeling too well,' Tony replied. 'Women's troubles.'

'Nothing serious, I hope,' said Les. 'We wouldn't want an unplanned pregnancy getting in the way of our plans for world domination.'

'No, nothing like that,' Tony said quickly. If the truth be told, he'd begun to question Katy's commitment to her new role as the diva Katrina. But now wasn't the time to be voicing such concerns, not when Les was the only one who appeared to have any faith left in the idea of them ever becoming famous.

'You know Katrina,' he added. 'She spends so much time with gay men, the chances of her ever getting pregnant are about a million to one. It's just period pains, that's all.'

'Glad to hear it,' Les said. 'A Boy without his Diva would be like Sonny without Cher. No offence meant, but without her I can't see you going very far.'

Tony felt as if he'd been slapped in the face, but was determined not to let it show.

'We're hardly the talk of the town now, are we?' he laughed nervously.

'No, you're not,' Les said. 'But stick with me and you soon will be.'

Sadly, 'soon' was a vague concept. And for Tony at least, it was never soon enough. His frustration peaked that October, when Boy George made his debut appearance on *Top of the Pops*. While the rest of the country was staring in disbelief at the TV, debating whether the vision in ribbons and braids was a boy or a girl, Tony was threatening to burst a blood vessel.

'Can you believe this?' he said, turning to Katrina. 'That bloody drag queen from the Blitz is on *Top of the Pops*! And he looks fat.'

'His voice is lovely, though,' Katrina said.

'It's not nearly as good as yours,' Tony replied.

'Yeah, right.'

'I'm serious. You have a fantastic voice. Les certainly thinks so.'

'Les,' Katrina repeated, and rolled her eyes.

'What about him?'

'Well, do you trust him? I mean, really trust him?'

'Yes, I do,' Tony said. 'Don't you?'

Katrina shrugged. 'I dunno. I suppose so. I mean, I know he believes in us, otherwise he wouldn't still be hanging around. And when he says he thinks we can make it big, I want to believe him. I really do. I just wish I shared his confidence.'

'Now isn't the time to start losing faith,' Tony said. 'We're on the edge of something big. I can feel it.' He couldn't really, of course, but there was no point in telling Katrina that.

'You know what we need?' he went on. 'Hair extensions.'

Katrina laughed. 'Hair extensions? So I can look like even more of a drag queen?'

'You don't look like a drag queen,' Tony said, then broke

into a grin. 'Well, maybe a bit, in the wrong light. But at least you're not fat.'

Katrina sighed. 'It's a wonder there's anything left of me at all. I haven't slept properly in weeks. I can't remember the last time I ate a proper meal. I feel like I'm constantly on the go, running from one job to the next. And I never seem to have any money to show for it.'

'You will,' Tony assured her. 'A year from now you'll be rolling in money. We both will. We just have to keep working at it, stay focused. The right opportunity will present itself eventually, and when it does we need to be ready to grab it with both hands.'

'What we really need are some new songs,' Katrina said.

Tony looked crestfallen. 'What do you mean? What's wrong with the ones we've got?'

'If you ask me, nothing,' Katrina said. 'But it's not me you have to convince, is it? We've made two demo tapes, and neither one has convinced anyone to sign us. So either we're kidding ourselves and we're just not cut out for this, or it's the material that's wrong. Either way, I think it's time for a bit of a rethink, don't you?'

Tony forced a smile. 'And you don't think hair extensions are the answer to all our problems?'

Katrina laughed. 'No, I don't think they are.'

'Then I suppose I'd better write some new songs, hadn't I?'

She nodded. 'And Tony?'

'Yes?'

'Don't take this the wrong way, but try not to get too bogged down in sounding clever. Try to let your feelings show a bit more.'

'What do you mean?'

'Write about the things you really care about.'

'Like what?'

Katrina hesitated. 'Oh, I dunno. Like Wilf, for instance.'

Tony frowned. 'Wilf? But we broke up over a year ago. I haven't thought about him in months.'

She smiled. 'I don't believe that for a moment. Besides, that's not the point. All I'm saying is that maybe you should write about how you felt when things ended between you two. It'll be good for you to put it into words, kind of like therapy but without the whopping great bill at the end. And people relate to that sort of thing. It's what pop music is all about. You know, boy meets girl, boy meets boy . . .'

Tony grinned. 'Boy loses boy to girl and turns bitter heartbreak into million-selling single?'

Katrina nodded. 'Exactly.'

Tony leapt to his feet. 'Right, well, I'd better go and write it then.'

She looked surprised. 'Don't you want to watch *Top of the Pops*?'

'I've seen enough,' he replied, heading out of the door. 'Besides, we should be *on Top of the Pops*, not watching it.'

The following morning he was one step closer to achieving his goal. At seven o'clock he came knocking on her door, desperate to share the fruits of his labour. She answered the door in her dressing gown, unprepared for the wild-eyed vision awaiting her.

'You look like shit,' she said. 'Did you forget to go to bed or what?'

'Never mind that,' he said, grabbing her hand and leading her up the stairs to his room. No sooner were they inside the door than he'd taken his place behind the keyboard.

'Okay,' he said. 'Listen to this.'

She listened, and within a matter of moments she began to share his enthusiasm. 'That's fantastic!' she said when he'd finally finished. 'I love that thumping, slightly sinister sound at the beginning. And that "bleep bleep" bit before the chorus is great. What's it called?'

'It's called "Love Is A Pain (In The Heart)". The second bit is in brackets.'

She smiled to herself. 'I had a feeling it might be.'

Anthony struggled hard to contain his excitement. 'And I know I shouldn't tempt fate, but I really think this could be the one. I think this could be it.'

She reached for the lyric sheet. 'Well let's give it a go, then, shall we?'

CHAPTER SEVENTEEN

'Day two in *The Clink*, and things are really hotting up. Following yesterday's catfight between Ritchie and Tony, a lot of viewers were expecting to see Tony voted out. But last night's surprise eviction saw Finella fall at the first hurdle, which means the boys are both still in there. Will it be hairdryers at dawn?'

Kelly paused to allow her little joke to sink in. That last line wasn't in the script. It had just popped into her head a moment ago, and being the spirited, spontaneous creature she was, she'd made a split-second decision to run with it.

Of course it was possible that her spontaneity wasn't entirely of her own making but had something do with the fat line of coke she'd snorted shortly before stepping in front of the camera. This stuff was a lot stronger than the crap her girlfriends routinely shoved up their surgically enhanced noses. It just went to show that money couldn't buy you everything. In this life, it was all about making the right connections, and clearly she'd made the right connection when she went back to that dealer's flat in Covent Garden last night. It was a pity he couldn't get it up, but when his coke was this good, she was more than willing to forgive him.

Behind the camera, Andrew the assistant producer was

waving his arms frantically. Kelly ignored him. She'd been around long enough to know that live TV was where a girl could really make her mark. It was simply a matter of taking control, of daring to step outside her comfort zone and being true to herself. Wasn't that what she'd learned at all those drama classes? Nobody wanted to see an actor simply regurgitating their lines. It was all about following your gut instinct. Improvisation, that was the key. Feel what you say and say what you feel. Provided you were honest, you couldn't go far wrong.

'What a day it's been,' Kelly said, ignoring the autocue and the script agreed by everyone less than an hour ago. 'I know one thing, girls. I wouldn't mind being in close confinement with that Hercules for an hour or two. No wonder Tony got so uptight yesterday. If you ask me, he's got the hots for Hercules and is simply bitter because that prime piece of Brazilian beefcake isn't gay.'

By now, Andrew's attempts to distract her were reaching epic proportions, his arms waving like wind turbines. Kelly could hardly fail to notice him. Still she remained focused. This was her moment, her chance to shine, and no working-class oik with a media studies degree was going to ruin it.

'And as for that Tamsin! Who on earth does she think she is? As if a stud like Hercules would go for her! I've checked Tamsin's forecast, and let's just say it's not looking too good. She'd be better off aiming her sights a little lower. I hear Gary is available, now that he's been cleared of fiddling with little girls. Apparently his wife took a dimmer view of the situation than the judge who presided over his court case, which just goes to show why we need more women judges.

Or there's Tyrone, of course. He has a girlfriend, but we all know what rappers are like. Can't keep it in their trousers, can they, girls?'

Suddenly Kelly's mind went blank. All she could think of was Gary the game show host and the terrible things he was alleged to have done to those little girls. Her face froze, her lips went dry, and when she tried to speak her tongue stuck to the roof of her mouth like Velcro. She looked at Andrew, who was purple with rage, still waving his arms. She looked at the camera and tried to smile. She felt a burning sensation at the back of her throat and attempted to swallow. Seconds later, the viewers at home were treated to the unmistakable sound of a lump of snot passing from her sinuses to her oesophagus.

Finally she spoke. 'Now it's over to *The Clink* for all the day's action.'

Tony woke to the sound of snoring from the bunk below. Daylight was breaking through the tiny barred window above his head, casting a grim shadow on the wall opposite. Suspended from the ceiling in the far corner of the room, the unblinking eye of a TV camera stared down blankly. The contestants had been assured that the cameras were switched off during the night, though Tony wasn't convinced. He'd seen enough reality TV shows to know that producers weren't always true to their word when it came to matters of privacy.

There were no clocks in the room, and his watch had been confiscated along with his wallet and other valuables. Still he was certain that he couldn't have slept for more than three or four hours at most. His eyes burned and, after thirty-six hours on prison rations, his stomach felt as if his throat had been cut. In short, it wasn't a good start to the day.

It was bad enough that he'd been forced to share a cell with Ritchie Taylor. The producers of *The Clink* had kept some of the interactive elements of the show a closely guarded secret. Only last night was it revealed that the viewers at home had even greater voting powers than previously thought. Not only did they vote to decide which celebrity to evict, they also determined the sleeping arrangements of those still remaining. After the way he'd behaved yesterday with Hercules, Tony knew he was lucky to have survived the first eviction. But the viewers obviously wanted to see him punished in some way and thought it would be funny to force him and Ritchie to spend some quality time together.

Ritchie obviously thought so too, and was actually far friendlier than Tony had been led to expect. When the announcement was made, he'd grinned and yelled, 'Nice one,' as if sharing a cell with Tony was some kind of honour and not the booby prize it clearly was. Later, as they lay in their respective beds, he'd even attempted to strike up a conversation, asking Tony what he thought of the state of British pop and complimenting him on his choice of pyjamas (pure silk, hand-stitched by one of the finest tailors on Savile Row). But Tony wasn't ready to bond with him just yet. He still hadn't forgotten the way Ritchie had reprimanded him yesterday. He hadn't forgotten, and he certainly hadn't forgiven. And it didn't matter how many porn movies he'd seen where prison buddies shared a bunk and helped one another to relieve their frustrations. Under no circumstances would he allow himself to find Ritchie Taylor sexy.

The bed below creaked and he heard the sound of Ritchie shifting in his sleep. He peered over the edge of the mattress and stared at the younger man asleep in the bottom bunk. Ritchie's eyes were closed, and the bedclothes had been kicked off to reveal a tight, muscled torso in a white ribbed vest. His skin was pale, almost luminous, as if his own personal spotlight were shining on him even as he slept. There were smudges of mascara in the corners of his eyes, and his thick blue-black hair was pointing in several different directions at once, like an ad for some revolutionary new sculpting gel. His arms were raised and folded on the pillow above his head, inviting closer inspection of his armpits with their cute little tufts of black hair. The scene put Tony in mind of the first time he saw Adam Ant perform on *Top of the Pops*, bare-chested with arms aloft and that strange blend of male beauty and feminine grace. It was no wonder so many people wanted to fuck Ritchie Taylor so badly. The boy was sex on legs, as beautiful now as Adam had been all those years ago.

'Morning,' Ritchie said and opened one sleepy eye.

Tony blushed and turned his head away. 'Morning,' he said with an extravagant yawn, as if he'd just this minute woken up and hadn't been leering like some dirty old man. His cock told a different story, straining so hard against the silk fabric of his pyjamas, he feared the stitching might split.

'Sleep well?' Ritchie asked.

'Not bad,' Tony replied. 'I miss my own bed, though. You?'

'Oh, I can sleep anywhere,' Ritchie said, and if Tony wasn't mistaken, there was a suggestive tone to his voice, as if the mere mention of Tony's bed was enough to send his pulse racing.

'Can I ask you something, Tony?'

'Sure,' Tony said, his penis straining even harder now.

'Why were you so mean to Hercules yesterday?'

Tony felt his erection begin to wilt. 'Oh, that.'

'I didn't mean to have such a go at you,' Ritchie said. 'Only I was bullied a lot when I was at school, and whenever I see someone picking on someone else like that, it just makes my blood boil.'

'I wasn't really picking on him,' Tony said. 'Not really.'

'Yes you were,' Ritchie said, gently but firmly. 'It's weird, because usually people only pick on people they feel threatened by in some way, and for the life of me I can't think of any reason why someone like you would feel threatened by someone like Hercules.'

'Then either your theory is wrong, or you completely misread the situation and I wasn't really picking on him.'

Ritchie didn't sound too convinced. 'Right,' he said. 'I guess we'll just have to agree to differ then. No hard feelings, though, eh?'

By now, Tony's erection had dwindled to nothing. 'No,' he said. 'No hard feelings.'

The evidence of his arousal now gone, Tony felt it was finally safe to climb out of bed and check his hair in the tiny mirror above the washbasin. And immediately he wished he hadn't. His heart sank as he studied the thinning, straw-like arrangement covering the top of his head. A few days ago he'd actually convinced himself that his new hairstyle had taken years off him, that somehow it had enabled him to recapture something of his youth. Who was he kidding? He might have looked okay in the salon. But next to Ritchie he looked ridiculous, like some tired old queen who did his hair with an egg whisk.

'God, I look awful!' Tony said, dismayed. 'And I forgot to pack my hairdryer.'

'You can borrow mine,' Ritchie offered, and swung his beefy legs out from under the blankets. The bulge in his boxer shorts suggested that maybe this was where he stored his personal grooming products. But no. The hairdryer was tucked away in his suitcase under the bed. A monstrous metallic thing with several speeds and a variety of attachments, it looked like something you'd find in the basement at Clone Zone, designed for men with chewed nipples to maximise their pleasure at the weekend.

'This should do it,' Ritchie said with a smile. 'And there's some extreme style texturing gum in my toilet bag, or some rock-hard hairspray if you prefer. Help yourself.'

'Thanks,' Tony gulped. 'That's really kind of you.'

Ritchie laughed. 'Are you kidding me? Tony Griffiths using my hairdryer? The pleasure's all mine. It's an honour, really.'

'Thanks,' Tony said again, and for the first time in a long time he actually felt like a star.

An hour later, the inmates were gathered in the canteen, putting on their bravest faces as they filled their rumbling stomachs with another helping of porridge, colder and even lumpier than yesterday's. Tamsin, Shelley and Lisa were comforting Gary over the loss of his friend Finella, whom he'd only known for thirty-six hours but to whom he'd formed a deep and lasting attachment, the way fellow celebrities were wont to do in such trying circumstances. Tyrone was describing his favourite lesbian porn movie to Kim, who seemed both appalled and strangely fascinated at the same time. Ritchie and Hercules were comparing armpits and discussing gym routines. Tony was deep in thought, wishing there were more mirrors so he could check his hair and wondering why Ritchie was directing all his attention towards Hercules and none towards him. Finally, he could take it no more.

'Listen, Hercules,' he said, interrupting a conversation about free weights and their advantages over multigym equipment. 'Sorry if I was a bit hard on you yesterday. I didn't mean anything by it. This place takes a bit of getting used to, and I was just feeling homesick. I didn't mean to hurt your feelings.'

Hercules looked across at Tony and smiled warily. Nobody said anything for a moment.

Then Ritchie spoke. 'Well I for one think that's really decent of you, Tony.'

'You would,' Gary muttered under his breath.

'What do you mean?' whispered Tamsin.

'Well these queers all stick together, don't they?' Gary replied. 'Look at the way the press rallied around George Michael. If that had been a girl he'd flashed his cock at, he'd be locked up by now.'

'Just like us,' Tamsin whispered gleefully, totally missing the point of Gary's little rant. 'Actually, I wouldn't mind being locked up with George Michael. "Careless Whisper" is one of my favourite songs of all time.'

'I prefer "Different Corner",' said Lisa. 'We did a cover of that on our first album. Well it was our only album, actually. But it's a great song, that.'

'So can we start over?' Tony said to Hercules. 'Friends?'

Hercules paused, then held out a big paw and took Tony's hand. 'Friends,' he said, and smiled.

At that precise moment, a tannoy buzzed into life and the disembodied voice of a male authority figure boomed around the canteen.

'Good morning, inmates. This is the prison warder with an important announcement. Today one inmate will be given a special task to perform. If they complete the task they'll be rewarded with a luxury hamper containing enough food for the group and sufficient alcohol for a party. If they fail, they must face a penalty. The public have been voting all night. The votes have been counted and verified, and I can now reveal that the inmate chosen to perform the task is . . . Tony!'

There was a smattering of applause from the other inmates, most of whom were simply expressing their relief at not being chosen for the task, whatever it was.

'Tony, you have been chosen to perform today's task,' the announcement continued. 'Please make your way to the warder's office, where you will be given further instructions.'

Tony smiled weakly and rose from the table. 'Well I guess this is it,' he said. 'Wish me luck.'

'Yeah, good luck, Tony,' said Gary, sounding about as sincere as the average game show host.

'Good luck,' said Shelley and Lisa in unison.

'You won't need luck,' said Ritchie. 'You can do it. I know you can.'

'And if you can't, don't worry,' said Tamsin.

That's easy for you to say, thought Tony.

Hercules grinned and gave a thumbs-up.

Tyrone nodded.

Kim forced a smile.

There was another smattering of applause from the younger members of the group, rising to a chant of 'Go, Tony, go, Tony, go, Tony!'

As he left the canteen and made his way to the prison warder's office, Tony was suddenly struck by the absurdity of his situation. Being famous never used to be like this.

CHAPTER EIGHTEEN

'God, I love being famous,' Tony said through a mouthful of peppered steak. 'Isn't it just the most amazing feeling in the world?'

Katrina smiled and poked at her crab salad. 'Yeah, fantastic.'

She wasn't as hungry for fame as Tony, not by a long way. But even she was forced to agree that this was the kind of lifestyle she could quite easily get used to. Just this morning she'd been stopped in the street by a group of schoolgirls eager for her autograph. Afterwards she'd gone shopping for clothes, and spent more in one afternoon than she would normally spend in a year. And now here she was enjoying a slap-up meal on record company expenses while Tony held forth about the fabulous future they had together. And it wasn't just any record company either. This was Icon Records, a subsidiary of EMI, and one of the hippest, most powerful labels in the land. She had every right to feel a little pleased with herself, and she did.

Who'd have thought that one day she would appear on *Top of the Pops*? Certainly not her father, who greeted the news with a certain amount of scepticism, as if she were still fifteen and this was simply her latest scam for skipping school. But sure enough, the following night there she was, sandwiched between Spandau Ballet and Kajagoogoo on the nation's favourite music show. Of course any pride she may have felt was compromised by the fact that she fluffed the intro to the song. If she'd had her way, they'd have stopped filming and done it all over again. But the producer insisted that there wasn't time for another take, and the performance was broadcast complete with her standing idly by as the backing track started and her disembodied voice echoed around the studio. They did try to obscure the mistake with a cutaway of the audience, but if you looked closely you could still tell.

Not that it seemed to have mattered. Three weeks had passed since that fateful *Top of the Pops* appearance, and despite some of the unkinder comments in certain sections of the press, there was no denying the fact that, as of now, A Boy And His Diva were indeed famous. Not as famous as David Bowie, who'd recently made a triumphant return to the charts with 'Let's Dance' – blond, bland and immediately branded a turncoat by everyone who preferred Aladdin Sane to A Lad In A Suit. Not as famous as Boy George, who much to everyone's surprise had outlived the initial media hysteria to become a regular face in the tabloids and on peak-time television. But a damn sight more famous than Pete Burns, or Tasty Tim, or any of the other so-called gender-benders eager to hitch a ride on the latest bandwagon.

'The gender-benders are last year's news,' Tony announced in their first interview with *Smash Hits*. In the same in-depth interview he confirmed that he wasn't any good at marbles, he'd never owned a stuffed Alaskan timber wolf, he didn't know anyone called Tarquin and his favourite sandwich filling was tuna and mayonnaise. But it was his comments about Boy George that made headlines. 'People like Boy George have reduced pop stardom to the same level as soap celebrity,' he was quoted as saying. 'We're here to put the glamour back into pop music, and to inject a little danger. We're not interested in appearing cuddly. We're here for the kids, not the grannies. I'd prefer sex to a nice cup of tea any day of the week, and I don't care who knows it.'

No sooner had the magazine hit the newsstands than Tony's comments were leapt on by the tabloids and he and Katrina were thrown into the queasy mix of outmoded New Romanticism, outsized shoulder pads and outright bitchery that constituted the pop landscape of 1983.

'Tony Griffiths should check his makeup before he goes out in the morning,' Boy George spat back through the pages of the *Mirror*. 'I've seen better blusher on a Cabbage Patch Doll.'

'I'd rather look like a Cabbage Patch Doll than My Little Pony,' Tony told the same *Mirror* reporter the following day. 'At least I haven't got an arse like the back end of a pantomime horse.'

Spats like this didn't strike Katrina as particularly edifying, but then as Tony tried to explain to her, it was one way to keep their names in the papers. And sure enough, with each bitchy exchange, their popularity seemed to grow. A week after their appearance on *Top of the Pops*, 'Love Is A Pain (In The Heart)' had risen from Number 32 to Number 9. A week later it was at Number 4, then at Number 2, where it stalled while Spandau Ballet enjoyed their third week at the top with 'True'.

When Tony wasn't busy bitching about Boy George, he and Katrina followed Les's instructions to the letter and were seen at all the right places. Having signed his young charges to Icon Records for a tidy sum, Les was determined that they should put themselves about a bit. Living the dream was one thing, but what really mattered was that they were *seen* to live the dream. As Tony had already discovered, the tabloids had a new role to play in promoting the country's pop stars, and plenty of pages to fill. For him and Katrina, that meant late nights, bright lights and an endless whirl of photo-opportunities. Monday was the Limelight club, where George Michael was often seen parading young pretties in an attempt to squash the rumours about his homosexuality. Tuesday was Camden Palace, where the stars gathered under the watchful eye of Steve Strange (still enjoying a modicum of chart success, much to Tony's annoyance). Wednesday was Heaven, where Marc Almond was often spotted swinging a bottle of Dom Perignon (Katrina had to hold Tony back from rushing over and singing a chorus of 'Tainted Love'). Thursday was back to Camden Palace, where the regulars included everyone from Kim Wilde to David Van Day of Dollar.

Today was Friday, and they were enjoying an early dinner at Le Caprice before Les came to whisk them off to an industry party at the Embassy club. Katrina was dressed in her summer goth look, an image largely inspired by Siouxsie's sojourn in the Far East around the time of 'Arabian Knights' – all charm bracelets and psychedelia, with silk scarves floating at her wrists and rags tied in her hair. Tony was wearing an ice-blue Antony Price suit and sporting a snood – a sort of half-scarf, half-hood affair which would soon prove enormously popular, despite its obvious short-comings as a fashion accessory.

'You look like that girl from Haysi Fantayzee,' Tony said as he polished off his steak.

'Thanks,' Katrina replied. 'And that snood really suits you.'

'Yeah?' Tony said.

'Yeah. It looks like a foreskin wrapped around your face. I always said you were a knob head. Haysi Fantayzee? Fuck off!'

Tony laughed. 'More champagne?'

She held out her glass. 'I don't mind if I do.'

'A toast,' said Tony. 'To fame. And to friendship. And to being Number Two in the charts!'

'To fucking up on *Top of the Pops*,' Katrina added.

Tony smiled. 'And to carrying it off beautifully.'

'Thanks,' she said. 'At least I'll know what to expect next time. If there is a next time.'

'What do you mean, "if"? Didn't you hear what Les said? We're here for the long haul. Another year or two and you'll know that studio like the back of your hand. We'll be on so often, we'll practically be living there.'

She laughed. 'God, I hope not.'

'I know what you mean,' he said. 'A bit grim, eh? It was funny, though, seeing the guys from the record company sucking up to the producer like that. I thought that publicist was going to crawl right up his arse at one point.'

'He was just doing his job.'

'If you can call it a job. I'd sooner stick pins in my eyes than spend my entire life sucking up to people.'

Katrina raised an eyebrow. 'That much is obvious.'

Tony studied her for a moment. 'Do I detect a little crush developing here?'

She blushed. 'I don't know what you mean.'

'I think you do. The way you leapt to his defence just then. It's obvious. You've got a crush on our publicist.'

Katrina blushed even brighter. 'Steve? Don't be so ridiculous.'

'He's cute, though, isn't he? His eyes are bluer than my suit, and he's got a nice little arse on him. That Essex accent is pretty sexy too. Come on, don't tell me you don't think he's cute.'

Finally she caved in. 'Cute? He's fucking gorgeous!'

'So what do you reckon?' Tony asked. 'Gay or straight?'

'Straight,' said Katrina.

'I'm not so sure,' Tony said.

'I am,' Katrina said firmly. 'Very sure.'

Much like the band's success, Katrina's affair with Steve didn't just happen overnight. Despite what Tony would later claim, it wasn't going on the night he and Katrina had dinner at Le Caprice. Nor was it going on the following month, when they flew to Sri Lanka to film the video for their second single, 'Touch'. When Katrina sat astride an elephant and sang about 'a lover's touch, burning my skin', she wasn't speaking from recent experience.

Like many great love affairs, the story of Steve and Katrina took a while to develop. At first they tiptoed around one another, nervously flirting but never really getting anywhere. Then after a few weeks the flirting became a kind of in-joke, the way it often does with people who decide to become friends rather than risk everything on a relationship. By this point, Katrina couldn't really tell if Steve fancied her or not.

It was years since she'd been on the receiving end of so much male attention, and she was having trouble reading the signs. But as it was Steve's job to accompany them on the publicity trail, the opportunities presented themselves time and time again, until finally one night the inevitable happened.

They were in Newcastle, where Tony and Katrina had performed a short set for Channel Four's new youth music programme *The Tube*. Tony had sloped off to bed early complaining of a headache, and Steve and Katrina were perched at the hotel bar sharing a joke and their second bottle of wine. Katrina was still feeling a bit giddy from her TV appearance, and had drunk rather more than she was used to.

'So what do you reckon to this pop star lark?' Steve said, his tone suggesting that he found it all a bit of a laugh. 'Is it everything you always dreamed it would be?'

'Mostly,' she replied, suddenly catching herself staring into his eyes and redirecting her attention to the glass of wine in front of her. 'Don't get me wrong. The record company have been brilliant. And I know how lucky we are to be doing this for a living. A lot of people struggle for years and never get anywhere. So I am grateful, really I am. But it's hard work. The hours are long, and the travelling really wears me out.'

Steve leaned forward on his bar stool. 'At least you've got Tony for company, though, eh? It's a lot tougher if you're all on your own.'

Katrina bit her lip. 'I suppose so,' she said. 'The thing is – and please don't tell Tony I told you this – but if I'm really honest, it can still feel a bit lonely sometimes.'

'Really?' Steve smiled. 'I thought you two were as close as it gets. Without the sex, that is.'

Katrina blushed. 'We are,' she said. 'We are close. Tony's my best friend. I'd do anything for him. But that's not the point. It's tough being away from home all the time, staying in hotels, sleeping in different beds. It can be lonely. You must find that too.'

Steve nodded gravely. 'It's a terrible thing, loneliness. But I think I may have a solution.'

'Oh yes?' she said. 'What's that?'

'We should stop sleeping in different beds. That way, neither of us would be lonely.'

Katrina blushed a brighter shade of crimson and tried to disappear behind her hair.

'Hey, don't go all shy on me,' Steve said, reaching for her shoulder. 'It was just a joke.'

She looked up at him. 'Was it?' she said.

'No,' he replied, and the next thing she knew, his tongue was lodged halfway down her throat.

'Promise me something, Steve,' she said, coming up for air.

'Of course I will, whatever you want.'

'Promise me you won't hurt me.'

He grinned. 'Hey, I don't know what you've heard, but it's not that big!'

'I mean it, Steve.'

He looked her straight in the eyes. 'I know you do,' he said. 'And you needn't worry. I won't hurt you, I swear.'

Minutes later they were upstairs in his hotel room, tearing each other's clothes off. It was a while since she'd felt a man's naked body next to her own – well, two years actually – and there were a few moments where she froze, not knowing what to do or where to look. But with Steve stroking her breasts and whispering assurances, it wasn't long before it all slipped into place. And when it did, she found it was quite big enough for her needs. When she came, it was like having sex for the first time, only without the soreness in her groin or the chewing gum stuck in her hair.

She'd been walking around with a big smile on her face ever since. Six weeks into their relationship, she was happier than she'd ever been. Steve was everything she could have asked for in a boyfriend – strong but sensitive, cute but kind, and not so full of himself that she constantly worried about what he was getting up to when her back was turned. His blue eyes and pert little bum meant that he was never short of admirers, but he never gave her any reason to doubt him. He showered her with gifts and told her over and over again that she was beautiful. Privately, she thought that he was the beautiful one, but of course she never told him that.

Nor did she confide very much in Tony. He'd been in a funny mood lately. At first she put it down to the pressures of their schedule, a simple case of too much work and not enough hours in the day. But more recently she'd started to wonder if it might have something to do with Steve.

'Is everything okay, Tony?' she asked him one night in Manchester. Today's round of radio interviews and press promos had gone well, not that she'd have guessed it from the look on Tony's face.

'Of course,' he replied. 'Why shouldn't it be?' He was on his third martini of the evening and his breath reeked of gin.

'No reason,' she said. 'You just seem a little quiet, that's all.'

They were in the hotel bar (of course). Steve was off somewhere making phone calls, arranging radio slots for the following morning. Later tonight they'd be performing their new single at a trendy new club called the Hacienda. But for now it was just the two of them, her and Tony. They seemed so different to the way they had been that night at Le Caprice, when the conversation had flowed as easily as the champagne. Could it really only have been ten weeks ago? How the time flew when you were a busy pop star with a hit single under your belt and a boyfriend to boot.

'I think I'll join you in a martini,' she said, taking a seat next to him. 'I could do with a stiff drink. It's thirsty work talking about yourself all day.'

Tony didn't say anything. He simply sat staring in the opposite direction. Nervously she looked around for a waiter and ordered herself a drink.

'Make it quick,' she told him. 'I'm gasping.'

As the waiter hurried away, Tony turned to her with a drunken expression and started singing. 'You were working as a waitress in a cocktail bar, when I met you.'

She blushed and giggled. 'Not me, Tony. That was the girl in the Human League song.'

'My mistake,' he said. 'Wrong girl.' And there was a nasty edge to his voice that cut her laughter dead.

Suddenly Steve appeared.

'All right, Tony?' he said, and patted him on the shoulder. Then he turned to Katrina with a quizzical look. 'All right, babes?'

'Great,' she replied and forced a smile. Then the waiter arrived with her drink and Steve ordered a beer and soon any tension was soothed away in a blur of alcohol and male bonding gestures.

Later that night, as they left the Hacienda, Steve asked her again if things were okay with Tony.

'Of course,' she lied. 'Why wouldn't they be?'

CHAPTER NINETEEN

'Day three in *The Clink*, and what an action-packed twenty-four hours it's been! First, Tony was forced to confront his fear of heights as he faced yesterday's task. More on that in a moment. And as if that wasn't excitement enough for one day, last night saw not one, but two evictions, as both Gary and Kim had their sentences reduced and were shown the door.'

The identikit blonde flashed her teeth and caught the eye of the assistant producer, who winked at her reassuringly. Heather Marsh had been drafted in at the last minute to replace Kelly Gibbon (described in this morning's tabloids as 'the troubled television presenter'), and already she'd won the respect of the production team by learning to read the autocue and flirting outrageously with every man present who wasn't gay (the gays, of course, were treated as girl-friends).

Heather was a sweet-natured good-time girl, with none of the artistic pretensions of her predecessor. No sooner was her appointment announced than she was offered a spread in *FHM* magazine. At this rate she'd be a bona fide celebrity in a matter of weeks, and could publish her autobiography in time for the all-important Christmas market. In fact, her agent was already in talks with several major publishers. Not

185

that Heather's story was particularly interesting. But as her agent told her, if your face was on the telly you were guaranteed to shift at least one autobiography by the time you were thirty. Two if you adopted an AIDS baby or developed an eating disorder.

'Later we'll be catching up with Gary and Kim as they adapt to life on the outside,' Heather continued, thinking of all the fake tan she could buy with the proceeds from her book sales. 'But first it's time for today's action from *The Clink*.'

Watching from her sofa at home, Katrina felt her stomach lurch as she caught her first glimpse of Tony in over twenty years. She hadn't planned to tune in to tonight's show. She hadn't planned to watch any of this dreadful rubbish. But Rose was soaking in the bath, leaving her alone for the first time all day. And despite telling herself that she would just catch up on the news, Katrina's curiosity had got the better of her and she'd quickly changed channels. She regretted her decision already. That presenter was nauseating enough, but when Tony appeared, she felt that she might actually be sick. Seeing him at all was unsettling. Seeing him degrading himself like this brought up feelings she didn't know she had. She felt angry with him and embarrassed for him and protective of him, all at the same time.

Dressed in a bright orange boiler suit which clashed horribly with his black and blond dye-job, he was attempting to scale a forty-foot stone wall, cheered on by a bunch of vaguely familiar faces and that cute singer from Fag Endz. Katrina was alarmed to see that he wasn't wearing a safety helmet, though knowing Tony, he was probably worried that it would spoil his hair. Suddenly the cheers turned to cries of alarm as Tony lost his grip on the wall and fell twenty feet, saved only by the guide rope tied to his waist. Sadly, even this couldn't prevent him from bashing his head against the wall several times before being lowered to the ground, where he was attended to by a couple of medics and carried off on a stretcher.

The next scene seemed to confirm the presenter's assurances that there was 'no real damage done', as a sheepishly grinning Tony was led towards something resembling an electric chair and strapped in by two out-of-work actors dressed as prison guards. Only then was it announced that his punishment for failing today's task was to have his head shaved, at which point his smile vanished completely. With the prison guards still standing by, a sinister figure with a bald head and a butcher's apron emerged from behind the chair, brandishing what looked to Katrina like the kind of mechanical device usually reserved for shearing sheep. Moments later, Tony was as bald as his assailant and the nauseating blonde presenter was back on the screen, reminding everyone at home of what they'd just seen and trying desperately to extract some humour from the situation.

Katrina didn't much feel like laughing. Tony's public humiliation on national television had given her no pleasure whatsoever – a fact that surprised her almost as much as it would have surprised him.

A few miles away, in Mayfair, the woman previously described as 'troubled television presenter Kelly Gibbon' hurled a zebra-print cushion at the high-definition plasma

TV screen and reached for the remote. Kelly was indeed troubled. Not troubled in the way Katrina was now feeling troubled. Not troubled in the tabloid sense of 'suffering from nervous exhaustion'. But troubled in the sense that she had been unceremoniously dumped from *The Clink* and had her name dragged through the mud thanks to an anonymous tip-off alleging that she had a problem with cocaine. The nerve of it! As if television companies weren't crawling with people who spent half their lives huddled over the toilet seat in the staff washroom! She'd tried calling the production office to find out who was responsible for leaking the story to the press, but of course they all stuck together and not a single person would take her call. In the end, she'd had to content herself with shouting at the receptionist, whose sing-song tones suggested that her words had made very little impact.

To make matters worse, her own solicitor had advised her against suing for breach of contract and her agent, normally so quick to offer his thoughts, was suddenly unavailable. Eight times she'd called him today, and each time she was told he was in a meeting and would call her back. She'd have fired him if it weren't for the fact that good agents were so hard to come by. And she ought to know – she'd been turned down by over a dozen.

All things considered, Kelly wasn't in a very happy place right now. And when Kelly wasn't happy, memories of the abuse she'd suffered as a child had a nasty habit of coming back to haunt her. She'd been battling with them all day, drowning out the voices with a bottle of cherry brandy she'd found hidden at the back of the kitchen cupboard. She hadn't dared go to the off-licence, not when there might be photographers waiting outside, and for a while the cherry brandy seemed to do the trick. But now the bottle was empty, her head was still full, and it was time to face her demons or brave the world beyond her front door, neither of which sounded particularly appealing.

She walked over to the window and peered through a crack in the curtains. The street below was quiet and still, with no parked cars except for those she recognised as belonging to her neighbours. It was a good job she lived in Mayfair, where traffic wardens were known for their vigilance and local residents were up in arms at the first sign of an illegally parked vehicle.

The lack of parking had never been a problem for Kelly. She made it a rule never to drive in London. Taxis were well within her budget, and there were plenty of shops within easy walking distance. Still, she daren't risk walking to Oddbins. For all she knew, there could be a photographer lurking on the corner of Curzon Street. But maybe if she called a taxi?

Suddenly she had an idea. If she had to venture outside, she might as well reward herself properly for the effort. Somewhere in her purse was a piece of paper with the number of the dealer she'd met a few nights ago. She ran into the bedroom, retrieved her purse from under the dressing table and dug out the piece of paper. She flipped open her mobile and made the call. Then she ordered a taxi to take her to Covent Garden.

'How's the ankle?' Ritchie asked. 'Has the swelling gone down yet?'

'Never mind the ankle,' Tony snapped. 'Look at my bloody hair!'

He was standing at the washbasin, staring at his reflection in the mirror. Ritchie was sitting on the edge of the bed. Neither of them had any idea what time it was. All they knew was they'd gone to bed on an empty stomach, and now the sun was up and they were so hungry they couldn't wait for their daily helping of porridge.

Ritchie smiled reassuringly. 'It doesn't look so bad.'

'Doesn't look so bad? Are you having a laugh? I've got no fucking hair left. Thanks to those bastards, there isn't a single person watching who hasn't seen my bald spot!' Tony scrutinised his reflection in the mirror and sighed dramatically. 'God, I look fat!'

Ritchie grinned. 'You do not look fat. If anything, you look thinner now than the day you arrived. Maybe going to bed hungry last night wasn't such a bad thing.'

'I bet the others aren't thinking that.'

'Bugger the others. You did your best. That's all anyone can ask of you. I can't see any of them scaling a prison wall, no matter how much food is on the other side.'

Tony shrugged. 'Thanks.'

'You're welcome. Besides, it's not as if the whole world thought you were a natural blond. And if you're worried about going bald, the bastards have probably done you a favour. They do say the best way to deal with hair loss is to take control of the situation and chop it all off.'

'Do they indeed?' Tony said. 'Well that's easy for you to say, you with your thick black hair and your boyish hips. Just wait till you're my age. Then you'll understand.'

Ritchie smiled coyly. 'If I look half as good as you when

190

I'm your age, I'll be more than happy. Things could be a lot worse, y'know. Look at Boy George. At least you haven't started painting your neck black.'

Tony pretended to look shocked. 'Poor George. Though I think you'll find he was shading in his jawline as long ago as 1983. There was even a *Boy George Fashion and Makeup Book*, showing you how to achieve the same effect. I used to know him in the old days, y'know. Before he was famous.'

Ritchie grinned. 'Don't you mean, he used to know you?'

'Well, he was famous before me – just. We used to bitch about each other constantly. We'd review each other's records on *Round Table*, then slag each other off in *Smash Hits*. Then the following week George would have a go at Marc Almond, and Marc would have a go at George, and Jimmy Somerville would have a go at the both of them. There wasn't much solidarity between gay pop stars then. It was handbags at dawn. Of course that all changed when AIDS came along. Suddenly we were lining up to do benefits together.'

Ritchie's smile faded. 'The big wake-up call.'

Tony nodded. 'Something like that. How does that Joni Mitchell song go? "You don't know what you've got till it's gone"? We didn't have a clue how lucky we were. The early eighties was an amazing time. And so queer. We had New Romantics, gender-benders, Frankie Goes to Hollywood. By the late eighties it was all faceless dance acts, stadium rockers and Kylie and Jason. From 1986 onwards, pop started straightening up its act. It wasn't cool to be queer any more. AIDS saw to that.'

Ritchie shifted position on the bed. 'Did you know a lot of people who died?'

'We all did,' Tony replied, staring into the mirror and seeing the bald heads of dead friends reflected back at him. 'You couldn't avoid it. By the time we knew what was happening, it was already too late for some of us. Between 1985 and 1987, I went to thirty funerals. That's more than most people go to in a lifetime.'

Ritchie frowned and shook his head. 'I can't begin to imagine what that must have been like. I don't think I could cope.'

'Yes you could,' Tony said, turning to face him. 'You cope because you have to. What's the alternative? You're just going to curl up and die? What a waste that would be. And what an insult to those who died. You owe it to them to go on, and make the best life you can for yourself.'

'I suppose . . .' Ritchie began.

But Tony wasn't listening. 'I read this article once,' he continued in a distant voice. 'It was explaining how gay men in the eighties experienced death on a scale not witnessed since the Second World War. And what made it worse was that the rest of the country was just carrying on as normal. Here we were, surrounded by all this death and disease, and everyone else was busy waving wads of cash and swilling champagne like it was going out of fashion. Not that I have anything against people swilling champagne. I've swilled my fair share of the stuff. But there was a time when I hated the sight of people enjoying themselves. I wanted everyone to feel what I was feeling. I wanted everyone to share that sense of loss. I even wrote a song about it.'

'I remember,' Ritchie said. '"Generations of Loss". Great song.'

Tony gave a wry smile. 'A pity more people didn't think so. It bombed.'

'But you survived,' Ritchie said. 'That's the important thing. You didn't just curl up and die. You kept going. That took enormous courage. People respect that.'

Tony shrugged. 'And now here I am pissing away what little credibility I have left on a dumb reality TV show.'

'So what made you decide to do it?'

'I dunno. Vanity, I suppose. Though given the state of my hair, my faith in the restorative power of TV was obviously a little misplaced. But let's face it. My career could use a little push at the moment. And it'll make a nice change to see my name in the papers without the word "cocaine" attached to it.'

Ritchie grinned. 'I remember that story. Written by some tabloid hack who's never been near a line of coke in his life, of course.'

'Of course.' Tony smiled back. 'So what about you? What possessed you to sell your soul to reality TV?'

'Honestly? I heard you were taking part and I wanted to get to know you.'

Tony blushed. 'No, seriously. The rest of us are either here for the money, or to drum up some publicity. I can't imagine you need much help in either department.'

'I am being serious,' Ritchie said. 'The main reason I agreed to do this show was because you were involved. The other day, when you were having a go at Hercules, the reason I got so annoyed was because I was disappointed in you. I used to idolise you growing up. I'm serious. You're the reason I wanted to become a pop star in the first place.'

Tony shifted uncomfortably. 'But you probably weren't even born the last time I was on *Top of the Pops*.'

'Yes I was,' Ritchie replied indignantly. 'It was in 1986 and I was four.'

Tony laughed. 'Four? Four! Weren't you a bit young to be watching *Top of the Pops* unattended?'

'I was an early developer,' Ritchie said proudly. 'It must have made a pretty big impression on me, 'cos I can still remember what you were wearing. You had these black and yellow cycling shorts, Doc Marten shoes with steel toecaps and a yellow top with Russian lettering across the chest. But it's the cycling shorts I remember the most. I begged my mum to buy me a pair, but she refused.'

Tony gave a dramatic sigh. 'Mothers can be so cruel. I hope you reported her to Childline.'

'Very funny. Anyway, it wasn't until later that I really got into your music. From about twelve onwards I'd say. When all my friends were listening to Oasis, I was addicted to A Boy and His Diva.'

'Smart boy,' Tony said. 'I never cared much for Oasis.'

Ritchie pulled a face. 'They were awful. Music for Neanderthals.'

'And one of them looks as if he has a chromosome missing,' Tony added. 'At least Blur were pretty.'

'And they wrote better songs. I mean, if you're going to rip off The Kinks, you might as well do it properly.'

'The Kinks?' Tony said. 'Now I am impressed. What are you? Some sort of walking pop encyclopedia?'

Ritchie grinned. 'I just happen to have good taste in music, that's all.'

'So who else did you used to listen to when you weren't fantasising about owning a pair of cycling shorts?'

'Oh, the usual suspects. Bowie. Velvet Underground. Roxy Music. But I always had a soft spot for eighties synth-pop. Soft Cell. The Human League. And you, of course. I have every record you ever released, including the twelve-inch singles. I used to go to the record and tape exchange in Kensington Market. I even have the limited edition picture disc of "Lovers and Losers", the one with the gatefold sleeve.'

Tony looked surprised. 'God, I don't think even I have that.'

'Like I said, I'm a huge fan. There's just one thing I never understood. What happened to you and Katrina? Why did you guys split up? It was all going so well for you, and then suddenly it was all over. What happened?'

Tony eyed the camera warily.

'It's all right,' Ritchie said. 'It's off.'

Tony sighed. 'It's a long story.'

'C'mon, Tony,' Ritchie said, 'What have we got to lose?'

'Okay,' Tony said, 'but you might not think so highly of me after this.'

CHAPTER TWENTY

The reviews of 'Touch' weren't good. 'Lingers in the brain like syphilis' was one critic's considered opinion. 'An irritating cacophony of clichés' was another. But it wasn't all bad news. *Record Mirror* quite liked it, and the lyrics to the song were about to be reprinted in *Smash Hits*. To hear the way Tony talked, praise didn't come much higher than that.

'Who cares what some inky old rag like *NME* thinks?' he said dismissively when Katrina alerted him to the paper's less than glowing review. 'The last band they got off on were Joy Division, and they can't even see the irony in that. We're a pop band, not a bunch of northern doom merchants in raincoats. Of course they hate our single. I'd be disappointed if they didn't.'

As if to prove their pop credentials, they were in a television studio in Holland (or was it Belgium?), waiting to film their third promotional spot of the day. A few hours earlier they'd performed against a blue screen and a picture of Rodin's *Kiss* for some French television producer's arty interpretation of the song's lyrics. Immediately afterwards they'd flown to Belgium (or was it Holland?) for an encounter with an overexcited TV host and a studio full of mannequins. Six months ago, they'd have found this sort of thing exhilarating. But by now the novelty was starting to wear off.

'God, I'm knackered,' Katrina yawned.

'What's the matter?' Tony asked. 'Not getting enough sleep?'

Katrina's relationship with Steve had been the butt of more jokes than she cared to remember. But in the interests of diplomacy, she decided to let this one pass.

'How many more of these things have we got left?' she asked.

'Just one,' Tony replied. 'The bad news is, it's in Germany. But at least we're flying first class.'

Katrina sighed. 'All this flying is playing havoc with my skin. If it wasn't for the makeup, I dread to think what people would be saying about me. I must have aged about ten years.'

'Me too,' he laughed. 'But look on the bright side. At least now we'll be able to afford facelifts at forty.'

'I'm not sure I can wait that long. Another six months of this and I'll be pushing fifty.'

Tony grinned. 'You don't look that bad. I'd say forty-five tops.'

She grinned back. 'Thanks. You really know how to boost a girl's ego.'

He raised an eyebrow. 'I'd have thought your ego was receiving quite enough boosting these days. How is the lovely Steve? Don't tell me he's neglecting his duties.'

'Steve is fine, thank you,' she replied tightly.

'Glad to hear it,' Tony said. 'We can't have our diva going short in the bedroom department. That wouldn't do at all.'

Katrina gave him a warning look. 'Maybe it's time you had a sex life of your own,' she said. 'Then perhaps you'd take a little less interest in mine.'

'I do have a sex life of my own,' Tony shot back. 'I just choose not to parade it in public, that's all.'

'You mean you're afraid of being labelled a poof,' Katrina said. 'What was all that nonsense you told that journalist yesterday? Bisexual? You're no more bisexual than I am.'

'I was being enigmatic,' Tony said. 'Anyway, how do you know I'm not bisexual? For all you know, I could have several women on the go as we speak.'

'Go on then. Name the last woman you slept with!'

'A gentleman never discloses that kind of information,' Tony replied airily.

Katrina laughed. 'No, and a gay man never sleeps with women. Because that's what you are, Tony. You're gay. You always have been, and you always will be. So play silly buggers with the papers if you want to, but don't expect me to buy that bisexual crap. I know you too well.'

'Have you quite finished?' Tony snapped.

She faltered. 'Yes.'

'Good,' he said. 'Because I think they're ready for us.'

The video for 'Touch' received its first airing on *Top of the Pops*, and was immediately dismissed as a pale imitation of Duran Duran. It wasn't that it was bad, exactly. There were certainly worse videos shown that night, including another absolute stinker from the Thompson Twins. And there was never any doubt that a lot of money had been spent spiriting Tony and Katrina away from the seedy London setting of their first single and into altogether more salubrious surroundings. The wardrobe budget alone ran into thousands of pounds. Tony wore a white Vivienne Westwood suit and a bottle of fake tan, his spiky hair bleached blond on top and dyed black at the sides. Katrina continued the theme in a floaty white outfit complete with an ivory silk headscarf and white plastic bangles up to her elbows. Her hair was black, with a few blonde braids woven in for good measure. The elephants played their parts beautifully, and the beaches were even whiter than those featured in a recent edition of *Wish You Were Here*, where Judith Chalmers sailed the South Pacific in search of the ultimate beach holiday. Compared to Wham's Club 18–30 video for 'Club Tropicana', the video for 'Touch' was the absolute height of sophistication.

But still there was something missing. Partly it was the song. A follow-up single hastily produced in less time than it took for 'Love Is A Pain (In The Heart)' to find its way into the remainder bins, 'Touch' was all pomp and no circumstance. Lyrically, it found Tony reworking themes from their earlier hit. Musically, it lacked the all-important hook. And then there was the video. Lavish it may have been, but original it most certainly wasn't. Duran Duran had already marked out this territory as their own, and even Bowie's video for 'China Girl' ended with the freshly tanned, not so Thin White Duke cavorting naked on a beach with the girl of the title. Compared to that, Tony and Katrina's exploits in Sri Lanka seemed rather tame. The screening on *Top of the Pops* failed to ignite the public's imagination, and nobody was surprised when the single stalled at Number 12. Nobody, that is, except Tony.

'That song should have made the Top Five at least,' he complained when the chart position was announced the following Sunday. 'It's a thousand times better than Paul fucking Young!'

'You don't need to tell me that,' Les assured him. 'Whenever I hear that record I want to take that hat of his and shove it right up his arse. But the worst thing you could do now is get hung up about it. You need to move forward. Concentrate on the next single. Concentrate on the album. Don't let some temporary setback knock you off course. You've got three weeks until you start recording the album. I'll see to it that you aren't distracted. No promotional engagements, no interruptions. But use the time wisely. Show the world what you're capable of. Claim your place in musical history. Now go home and don't come back until you've written a Number One single.'

Furiously energised by this sudden assault on his rapidly expanding ego, Tony threw himself into a frenzy of creativity, staying up all night as he delved deep into the darkest recesses of his soul and came up with song after song about loveless sex, rotting flesh, alienation and despair, none of which would have sounded out of place on the second Soft Cell album. He then changed tack completely and churned out half a dozen tracks that put the cloying cuteness of Culture Club's recent output to shame. One song, provisionally titled 'Boy Talk', even had the same harmonica-based intro as 'Karma Chameleon'!

Clearly, drastic measures were called for. So for the next few days Tony developed his own version of the 'cut-up' method of songwriting made famous by David Bowie, tearing pages of other people's lyrics from copies of *Smash Hits*, cutting them up and arranging them in no particular order until exciting word combinations or fresh new ideas presented themselves. He would later deny ever having done this, of course, fearing that any mention of Bowie would lead to accusations of plagiarism or, worse, a terminal lack of hipness. Bowie's name didn't carry quite the same cachet in 1983 that it did in 1973, as a confirmed Bowie-phile like Tony knew only too well. But slowly new songs began to emerge, songs that had all the hallmarks of classic pop yet somehow seemed to sum up the mood of the times. If he was going to get technical about it, then Tony would have taken a leaf out of many a pop theorist's book and said that the secret lay in the way traditional hooks and trim verse/chorus song structures were combined with new technologies to create a sound that was both ultramodern and curiously old-fashioned, hinting at the Euro-aesthete's exhaustion from life yet poppy enough to withstand comparison with Abba. But for now he was just happy to have got over his writer's block.

Finally, at the end of the three weeks, he returned to Les's office with the evidence of a dozen sleepless nights etched into his face and half a dozen new songs on a rough demo tape. The first track he played his manager was a song called 'Lovers and Losers'.

'That's it!' Les said, leaping up from behind his desk. 'That's your next single! That's the one!'

'But don't you want to hear the rest first?' Tony said, taken aback.

'Don't need to,' Les said. 'That's the track that'll take you to Number One. All it needs is the right producer, someone who can maximise the drama and make it big in every respect. How do you feel about Trevor Horn?'

Of course Katrina was hurt. To make matters worse, it wasn't Tony who phoned with the news, but James.

'I suppose you've heard it as well, have you?' she asked.

'Well, naturally I've heard it,' James replied. 'I am Les's second in command after all. He doesn't keep a thing from me.'

'Unlike Tony' was the implication, but Katrina refused to rise to it. 'Well thanks for letting me know, James,' she said sweetly and hung up.

She wasn't so cagey with Steve. As she told him, it was she who'd always been Tony's sounding board, the one person he trusted enough to comment on his new material when it was still in the embryonic stages. And since she was the one who'd be singing the damn song anyway, it was only fair that she should hear it first.

'You should say something to him,' Steve advised her. 'Tell him how you feel.'

But Katrina had never been very good at telling people how she really felt. At times she wondered if she was in danger of turning into her mother, meekly accepting everything life threw at her and barely raising any objections while the men in her life stormed ahead making all the decisions.

'There's no point arguing about it now,' she said, desperately trying to shrug the whole thing off and failing miserably. 'What's done is done.'

'That's as may be,' Steve replied. 'But if you don't stand up for yourself now, you'll be storing up a whole host of problems for later. Trust me, I've seen it happen before. People go into this business as friends, and if they're not careful they wind up as enemies.'

But Katrina wasn't convinced, and the weeks passed by without so much as a word of complaint from her or a word of apology from Tony. Instead they talked about the things that really mattered – the inexplicable rise of Paul Young, Boy George's appearance on *Wogan*, the new-look, sexually ambiguous Depeche Mode and their anti-capitalist anthem 'Everything Counts'. And of course they talked about all the things they'd buy when 'Lovers and Losers' was a massive hit. Because there was never any doubt in either of their minds that it would be.

Given the circumstances, Katrina had wanted to hate the song, but in all honesty she couldn't. It was the best thing Tony had written by far, as up tempo and infectious as Heaven 17's recent hit 'Temptation', yet with all the doom-laden, industrial Gothic splendour of Depeche Mode. And it gave her the opportunity to really let rip with the vocals. When the chorus came and she urged listeners to 'love before you lose', she felt as if she was singing from the heart for the very first time.

Tony had ideas about everything, including what they should wear in the video.

'I've seen this amazing black leather suit in Vivienne Westwood,' he said. 'Big shoulder pads. Tight waist. Really masculine.'

'Sounds perfect,' she replied. 'But what will you wear?'

'Actually that's not such a bad idea,' he said excitedly. 'We could change sex in some way, really show the world what gender-bending is about. I'll have a word with Les, see what he thinks.'

By now, she was used to Tony plotting with Les without so much as a thought for her feelings. But when the day came to finally record the track, it soon became apparent that she wasn't the only one who felt crowded out of the picture. With Trevor Horn at the helm, Tony began to feel like a guest on his own record. Sound effects were added, then taken away, then added again – all without his say-so. Old instruments were hauled into the studio, and their sounds sampled for future arrangements. Vocal tracks were repeated ad nauseam, and mixed in a hundred different ways. At one point a seventy-piece orchestra was assembled and a choir flown in from Hamburg. And at various intervals, the producer would decide that nothing he'd done so far was working, and announce that he was scrapping everything and starting again.

Throughout all of this, Tony wore a frown like a cable-knit sweater and Katrina took what little satisfaction she could, knowing that he was getting a taste of his own medicine. But all was forgiven when the work was finally done, and the producer played them the finished track. They were stunned. Katrina's voice had never sounded better, and the production had to be heard to be believed. Crashing synths gave way to lush string arrangements and the rumble of thunder. When Tony's backing vocals warned of 'love's bitter tears, bigger than the sea', there was the unmistakable sound of waves breaking on a distant shore. In short, the song had everything except the kitchen sink, and neither Tony nor Katrina was under any illusions that even that might have been added had the producer deemed it necessary.

The single was a hit even before it was released. Advance copies were biked over to Radio One and played on heavy rotation. A video was filmed with directors Godley and Creme, with Tony and Katrina entering a porn cinema and being so seduced by the images on the screen, they appeared to actually swap genders with each other. Although no genitals were actually shown, the mere suggestion was enough to provoke a moral outcry from the usual quarters. Mary Whitehouse declared it an affront to decent licence-payers everywhere and very likely to encourage promiscuity in the young. The video was immediately banned by the BBC and was shown instead on *The Tube* on Channel Four, where it was introduced by an overexcited Paula Yates. Ultimately the ban did very little to dissuade people from supporting the record, and by the time the single was finally made available to the record-buying public, advance orders were so high it went straight in at Number 1.

Suddenly the copycat fans started to appear – boys with hair like Tony's, girls who copied Katrina's increasingly elaborate eye makeup. And with the single outselling the Number 2 record by two to one, they made a triumphant return to *Top of the Pops*. There were no nervous hiccups this time, no technical hitches. Expensively dressed and elegantly coiffured, they looked like a couple of old pros. Indeed, one journalist later commented that Katrina's makeup made her look just like an old pro. But what did it matter? By the time this remark appeared in print the single was enjoying its third week at Number 1 and their place in pop history was guaranteed. They were officially the biggest band in Britain. Nothing could stop them now. Nothing.

CHAPTER TWENTY-ONE

The morning of the funeral, Rose woke at five o'clock with her face pressed against a damp pillowcase. She was confused at first, thinking that maybe she'd reached for a glass of water in the night and spilled it without realising. Hauling herself out of bed and looking in the mirror, she saw that her eyes were also wet and suddenly it dawned on her that she'd been crying in her sleep. It must have been a terrible dream, whatever it was, but no worse than the reality she was waking up to. Today was the day she cremated her son. It didn't get much more terrible than that.

She washed her face, dressed herself, tidied her hair and wandered into the kitchen to find Katrina sitting at the table with a packet of ten Silk Cut, smoking furiously. Her eyes were puffy too, Rose noticed. Anyone would think it was her son they were cremating. Such thoughts weren't very charitable, she knew. But if she wasn't allowed to feel a little selfish on the day of her son's funeral, when was she?

'Did I wake you?' Katrina asked from inside a cloud of cigarette smoke.

'No,' Rose replied. 'Have you been awake long?'

'I couldn't sleep,' Katrina said, fanning the smoke away with her hand. Then, smiling wryly, 'I'm always like this before a performance.'

Rose didn't know quite what to make of this last comment, so she chose to ignore it. 'Cup of tea?'

'Please,' Katrina answered. 'The kettle's not long boiled.'

'I didn't know you smoked,' Rose said as she switched the kettle back on and waited for the steam to rise.

Katrina looked sheepish. 'I don't. I gave them up years ago. Filthy habit.' She stood up, walked over to the sink and ran the cold tap over the glowing cigarette stub.

Rose looked away in disgust. 'Mark started smoking when he was fourteen,' she said. 'He thought I didn't know, but I did. If you ask me, he only did it to impress the other kids. He was always so easily led, even then. He'd come home from school, have his tea, and then be off for hours with some of the older kids from down the street. Playing football, they said. Then he'd come in stinking of cigarette smoke. No grass stains, and never any mud. Just that awful smell. I'd have to wash his clothes just to get it out, and I only had a twin-tub in those days. It used to drive me mad.'

'Why didn't you say anything?' Katrina asked.

'What would be the point? He obviously didn't want me to know, and it was his lungs he was polluting.'

'That helps explain a lot,' Katrina muttered under her breath.

Rose took two mugs from the cupboard above the sink. 'What was that, dear?'

'I said I was just wondering, have you thought about what you're going to say today, at the funeral?'

Rose busied herself with the tea bags. 'I've thought about nothing else,' she said briskly. 'It's not every day you're asked to speak at your own son's funeral.'

'No,' Katrina said. 'Of course not.'

'So we'll just leave it at that for the moment, shall we? No point dwelling on it now.'

Katrina's hand reached for the cigarette packet. 'No,' she said. 'No point dwelling on it.'

It was possible for a deeply bereaved person to make it through an entire funeral without shedding a single tear. Katrina had seen it before, more times than she cared to remember. There had many funerals before Mark's. In the dark days before protease inhibitors and combination therapy, funerals were a regular occurrence. She'd seen men weep uncontrollably, and she'd seen men numb with grief, unable to shed a single tear. So she could hardly blame Rose now, if she seemed a little disconnected from her surroundings.

The first part of the service had gone off without a hitch. The minister had led the congregation in a hymn (a concession to Rose, though she didn't know it), and there had been readings from several of Mark's closest friends. Someone read a poem by W. H. Auden, written many years ago, for a man laid to rest during a different kind of war. Someone else read the lyrics to a song about house plants, composed by Mark one night at the piano. Then there was a musical interlude as 'Being Boring' by the Pet Shop Boys flooded the crematorium chapel. No prayers, though. Mark had specified that there be no prayers. Hymns he could just about tolerate. They reminded him of his childhood.

Now it was Katrina's turn. Nervously, she rose from her seat and made her way to the front of the chapel.

'Some of you may know me,' she began, and a ripple of laughter spread around the room. 'A long time ago, I sang on a hit record called "Lovers and Losers". We're gathered here today because we've lost someone we all loved very much. Mark didn't think of himself as anyone special. He didn't have any great achievements to boast of. He didn't make vast amounts of money or leave the kind of legacy that would ensure his name was remembered by those who'd never even met him. But he wasn't a loser either. Mark came into my life at a time when I'd pretty much lost faith in humanity. He taught me to love again, and for that I'll always be grateful. And it's out of love that I'd like to sing this song for him.'

And then she sang. The words were familiar to most of the people in the room. They'd heard the song a hundred times before, either when they were still at school, or starting their first job, or moving into their first flat with only a rubber plant and a radio for company. Some had danced to it only last weekend, at Duckie's perhaps, or Popstarz, or any of the places where gay men of a certain age congregated to wallow in a shared sense of nostalgia. Hearing it sung now, without the big production, without the multitracking or the sound effects, the words seemed to take on a whole new meaning. What was once a cheesy pop song celebrating love suddenly sounded like an anthem to a lost generation. Soon there wasn't a dry eye in the house.

'Don't lose heart before you love,' Katrina sang. 'Learn to love before you lose.'

At the second verse, she felt a catch in her throat, and her eyes filled with tears. But still she struggled on. She owed it to Mark to make it through this performance, and all the tears in the world wouldn't stop her. She stared out into the crowd and saw a dozen faces mouthing the words back at her. Together they made it to the final chorus.

'Don't lose heart before you love,' she sang for what she knew would be the last time. 'Learn to love before you lose.'

She held the final note for as long as she could, as if the mere act of holding on to it somehow defied the meaning of the word. As the sound faded, she took a moment to compose herself before continuing.

'Now I'd like to welcome a very special woman, Mark's mother Rose.'

There was a deathly silence. Heads turned. A few people coughed. Katrina scanned the front row but Rose was nowhere to be seen. Her seat was empty. And then she spotted her. She wasn't walking towards the podium. Instead she was walking briskly in the opposite direction, straight to the back of the crematorium and out of the door.

It was no surprise to Tony that he was evicted from *The Clink*. He'd never been the public's favourite inmate, and once it was revealed that the producers had lied about the cameras being turned off at night and his conversation with Ritchie had been broadcast to the nation, it was only a matter of time before he was given his marching orders. The only real surprise was that the eviction was announced not during the evening, as previous evictions had been, but the following morning over breakfast. Maybe the producers were hoping that another night in the cells would bring further revelations, or maybe they were just messing with his head. Either way, he was given an hour to pack his things and say his goodbyes, and then a uniformed guard handed back his valuables in a plastic bag and showed him to the door marked 'exit'.

Cameras flashed as he passed through the prison gates, the morning sun glinting off the top of his head. Despite Ritchie's best efforts, there was only so much you could do with half a millimetre of hair, and all the texturing gum in the world couldn't disguise the fact that Tony wasn't quite the man he used to be. Still, he felt an odd sort of pride as he posed for the photographers, shorn of his crowning glory yet strangely elated. So what if the world could see his bald patch? His secrets were all out now. There was nothing left to hide, and little left to lose. He felt like a man reborn. This, surely, was how a real prisoner must feel, the day his sentence was finally served and he was released back into the community. And Tony had been a prisoner in a way. Not a prisoner of *The Clink*, of course, but a prisoner of his own fame, and the guilt and shame he'd carried with him for so many years. And now it was all over. His sins had all been confessed on national television. The public had spoken, and he'd taken his punishment. The slate had been wiped clean. It was no wonder he felt so liberated. How did the song go again? 'I'm coming home, I've done my time.' He knew the feeling well.

Someone called his name, and he turned and posed for the last of the photographers. Then the crowd finally parted and he saw Dan waiting for him just beyond the prison gates. He wasn't bearing flowers or a yellow ribbon, but he was wearing an enormous grin.

'Sorry I was so crap,' Tony said, milking the self-deprecating angle for all it was worth.

Dan laughed. 'Are you kidding me? You were fabulous! I've got offers from several tabloids for your story. They want to know what you really think about the other inmates. And they're particularly interested in what went on between you and Ritchie Taylor.'

Tony smiled. 'Of course they are.'

'So what did go on? You two seemed pretty chummy in there'.

'You tell me, Dan,' Tony said. 'The way I understand it, there wasn't a fart under the bedclothes that wasn't broadcast.'

Dan grinned. 'What, so nothing happened? You didn't have a quick grope in the shower?'

'He's a nice kid,' Tony said. 'But that's as far as it goes.'

Dan looked doubtful. 'Right.'

'Seriously, Dan. There's nothing else to report. He's half my age, for fuck's sake!'

Dan frowned. 'Well, I'm sure we can spin it out a bit. Tell them you're planning to hook up at some point in the future, maybe release a single together or something.'

'Sure,' Tony scoffed. 'Like someone's going to give me a recording contract.'

Dan shook his head. 'O ye of little faith, Tony my son. What if I was to tell you that I've been in touch with the record company, and they're planning to rerelease "Lovers and Losers" in a matter of weeks? There's even talk of a new single, and maybe an album to follow if all goes according to plan.'

Tony could hardly believe his ears. 'But that's amazing,' he said. 'Fucking hell, Dan! That's the best news I've had in years!' He frowned. 'There's just one problem.'

'Katrina?'

Tony nodded. 'She didn't reply to my email. Obviously I haven't checked for a few days, but I don't hold out much hope.'

Dan's face broke into a cocky grin. 'Forget the email,' he said. 'I think this calls for a more personal approach.'

Tony looked confused.

'Oh for fuck's sake, Tony! I've found her! I know where she lives!'

As the mourners filed out from the crematorium, Katrina found Rose seated on a bench next to the car park.

'Well that was just great,' she said, her voice rising as the emotions of the past few days welled up inside her. 'Just fucking great. I thought we had an understanding, Rose. I thought we had a deal. What the hell is wrong with you? What kind of woman walks out of her own son's funeral?'

'I . . . I . . .' Rose sniffed. 'I just couldn't cope.'

Katrina was unmoved. 'You never can, can you? You couldn't cope with having a gay son when he was alive, and you can't cope with paying your proper respects to him now he's dead. When will you learn to cope, Rose? Because I hate to break this to you, but life is all about coping. Few of us sail through life having it easy all the time. Most of us have shit to deal with at some point or other. We might not like it, but we deal with it. We do our best. It's what makes us human.'

'I don't need a lecture from you on what life is about,' Rose snapped. 'I'm not a child.'

'No, you're not,' Katrina said. 'A child could be excused for what you did today. But you, you're a grown woman. What's your excuse? God knows I've tried to make allowances for you, Rose. I know things haven't been easy for you, and I've tried not to judge you too harshly. I've bitten my tongue so many times these past few days, it's a

213

wonder I didn't bite it off. But I'm not going to bite it now. This was it, Rose. This was your chance to pay your final respects to Mark, and show the world how much you cared. And you fucked it up, Rose. You fucked it up really badly.'

Rose couldn't have looked more shocked if she'd been slapped across the face. Her eyes stared wildly and her chest heaved as she gulped for air. For a moment, Katrina feared she was about to have a heart attack. But then her eyes narrowed and her face flushed red with rage.

'You think you're so clever, don't you?' she spat. 'You with your fancy flat and your gay friends and your gold discs on the wall. You think you know it all. But you don't know the first thing about me or my life. You don't know how it feels to have your husband walk out on you and your dreams shattered. You don't know what it means to be left on your own to raise a child, and to have people stare at you and wonder who that child's father is and what you did to drive him away. You don't know what it's like to watch that child grow more like his father every day, until suddenly he turns fifteen and becomes a stranger. You don't know what it's like to have people whisper behind your back when they discover that your son is queer, or wonder what you did to make him turn out like that. You don't know anything!'

Rose's eyes glittered, and as the anger subsided, the grief she'd refused to show finally came pouring out of her. Tears rolled down her cheeks and landed in her lap. She reached into her handbag for a handkerchief and buried her face in it, weeping uncontrollably.

Katrina studied her for a moment, her face a mixture of emotions. 'Right,' she said finally. 'There's something I need to discuss with you, Rose. Something very important. But now isn't the time. People will be arriving at the flat in the next half-hour. The caterers will have everything ready, but I need to be there to greet people when they arrive, and I want you to be there with me. I'd like us to do this bit together, for Mark. What do you say?'

Rose wiped her eyes. 'All his friends will be thinking badly of me.'

'They'll think even worse of you if you're not there. The day isn't over yet. There's still time to put things right. Will you at least try?'

Rose thought for a moment. 'Okay,' she said finally. 'I'll try.'

CHAPTER TWENTY-TWO

'Ten, nine, eight, seven, six, five, four, three, two, one . . . Happy New Year!'

Tony popped the cork and showered the room with champagne. And none of your cheap stuff, either. This was Cristal, the best champagne money could buy. By Tony's estimation, that meant he'd just sprayed his guests with around £100 worth of bubbly. But it was worth every penny. He had a lot to celebrate. All things considered, 1983 had been a great year. Twelve months ago, he and Katrina were just another synth-pop duo struggling to make themselves heard. Now they'd notched up two Number 1 singles, including the sappy ballad 'Angels At My Table', which had just been knocked off the top spot by Paul McCartney and the even sappier 'Pipes of Peace'. Still, if you were going to be knocked off the top spot by anybody, it might as well be a former Beatle and one half of the most famous song-writing duo that ever lived.

There were few songs approaching the classic simplicity of Lennon and McCartney on the first album from A Boy and His Diva, which had been rushed out for the all-important Christmas market and had already gone gold. Calling the album *Lovers and Losers* had obviously helped, although in all honesty there wasn't a song on it that matched the quality of the title track. Even the better numbers were buried in a mess of production, Trevor Horn having left the project to concentrate on a band from Liverpool called Frankie Goes to Hollywood. But the reviews had been surprisingly kind, and sales of the album meant that Tony could rest on his laurels for a while. And to top it all, he was now the proud owner of a stunning new house in Fulham, the setting for tonight's New Year celebrations, and the kind of property he'd never imagined owning even in his wildest dreams – five bedrooms, three floors and a white stucco front that conveyed wealth and class in equal measure.

And it wasn't as if this was just any old New Year. Finally it had arrived – 1984, the mythical year of George Orwell and David Bowie, of *Nineteen Eighty four* and *Diamond Dogs*. Contrary to both men's predictions, the world hadn't been enslaved by a fascist dictatorship or descended into sexual anarchy. True, Mrs Thatcher was still in power and Annie Lennox was giving Boy George a run for his money in the gender-bender stakes. A recent newspaper item even claimed that Lennox was cross-examined by an American customs official, who took one look at her prison-issue haircut and immediately mistook her for a man. But compared to Orwell's vision of a totalitarian super-state, or Bowie's vision of a post-nuclear hell populated by marauding gangs of proto-punks whose own mothers weren't sure if they were boys or girls, the reality of life in Britain was remarkably upbeat. Yes, there were people who protested about the closure of the coal mines or complained about rising unemployment. But from where Tony was standing, the future had never looked brighter.

'Great party!' Les said, sidling over with a glass of champagne in one hand and a pretty blond boy in the other.

'Thanks,' Tony replied, sizing up the blond boy as he spoke.

'And you can keep your eyes off the merchandise,' Les said. 'This is all paid and accounted for, and nobody is sampling the goods except me. Unless of course you fancy a threesome?'

'No, you're all right', Tony smiled politely. 'I have other guests to attend to. Who knows? Maybe later I'll find some pretty blond boy of my own.'

'Good luck,' Les said. 'Judging by the look of this crowd, you'll need it. Where did you find these people? Sleeping rough on the streets of Soho?'

Tony laughed. 'They're mostly just friends.'

'Hangers-on, you mean. Don't get me wrong. Who you mix with is your own business. But with your money I'd have thought you could afford a better class of friend than some of these people. There's a man in the kitchen who looks as if he just came out of prison. Now I'm as big a fan of jailbait as anybody, but you have to draw the line somewhere. Speaking of which, I suppose you've heard about Terry.'

Terry was an old friend of Les's, a notorious leather queen with a private income, who spent much of his time cruising the Coleherne in Earls Court.

'No,' Tony said. 'What about him?'

'He's only gone and got himself AIDS. I told him he should steer clear of Earls Court. Far too many Americans. It was bound to happen sooner or later.'

Tony looked for some sign of emotion in Les's face, but found nothing to go on. 'Christ, I'm really sorry to hear that,' he said eventually. 'Give him my regards when you see him.'

'Oh, I won't be seeing him,' Les said. 'Good lord, no! I can't stand hospitals. Depressing places. I suppose I'll have to attend the funeral. God knows what I'll wear, though. A black suit looks so uninspired.'

'You could always wear black leather,' Tony offered. 'It would be a fitting tribute.'

'So long as nobody mistakes me for a leather queen.' Les shuddered. 'I've already had to shave off my moustache. I don't want people getting the wrong idea.'

'No,' Tony said. 'Of course not.'

'Actually, you should probably think about toning your image down a bit,' Les continued. 'Just until this whole AIDS thing is out of the way. I fear a backlash may be in the air, and we don't want the record company getting nervous.'

'I'm not sure Katrina will go for that,' Tony joked. 'You know how she loves everyone thinking she's a lesbian.'

'Where is the lovely Katrina?' Les asked. 'Busy practising her heterosexuality with Steve?'

Tony nodded. 'They just got back from Morocco. They'll be along later.'

'Good.' Les smiled lasciviously. 'It's always such a pleasure to see Steve, and I imagine he'll be looking especially devastating with a tan. Now, can I interest anyone in a line?'

The party continued until the middle of March. It was then that Tony was forced to put his social life on hold as rehearsals began for the upcoming British tour. He and Katrina had played a few small live dates before, but never anything on this scale – eight weeks, twenty-four cities, starting at the Edinburgh Odeon Theatre and ending with three nights at Earls Court. A rehearsal space was booked, and plans developed for a multimedia extravaganza involving a dozen dancers and an ever-changing backdrop of slide projections. It wasn't quite as theatrical as Bowie's Diamond Dogs tour of 1974 (still the benchmark so far as Tony was concerned, despite the fact that he'd only ever seen a few clips on the telly). But it was certainly a cut above the recent panto put on by Culture Club. As Tony told *Record Mirror*: 'A live show should offer something more than just a chance to see your favourite band getting fat on your dinner money.'

The Lovers and Losers tour got off to a shaky start. Katrina was suffering from a sore throat, and on the first night the slide projector broke down. Not that anyone seemed to mind. The Scottish crowd screamed from the moment the band first appeared, and didn't stop screaming until long after the final encore. For the tour, Les had roped in a couple of session singers to provide backing vocals and a second keyboard player to help flesh out the sound. Katrina was happy to give the singers a share of the spotlight, while the keyboard player was obliged to hover in the shadows, a good four feet behind Tony and his bank of synths.

By the third week, the travelling was beginning to take its toll and Tony's drug intake had increased considerably.

'I don't know why you keep doing that stuff,' Katrina said to him one night when they came off stage at Sheffield City Hall. 'You know cocaine damages your vocal cords.'

'Nonsense,' Tony replied. 'Listen to the records Bowie produced in the mid seventies. *Young Americans*, *Station to Station*, even *David Live* for that matter. Coked off his head, and he never sounded better. Now compare that to *Tonight*. I rest my case.'

Katrina knew Tony well enough to recognise that now probably wasn't the best time to be having this conversation. She knew, also, that he had a self-destructive streak and would probably get a lot worse before he got better. She said as much to Steve that night in Sheffield.

'I'll have a quiet word with him,' Steve assured her. 'I'm sure it's not as bad as you think. Tony's not stupid. He'll soon sort himself out.'

What Katrina didn't know, at least not then, was that Tony wasn't the only one who needed sorting out. Steve had also developed a fondness for cocaine. It began at Tony's New Year's Eve party when Steve, drunk on champagne and flattered by all the attention he was receiving, wandered into the bathroom to find his host hunched over the toilet seat with a rolled note in his hand.

'Oops, sorry, mate!' Steve had said, and backed away.

But Tony wasn't the least bit embarrassed. 'Come in,' he'd said, and proceeded to lay out two massive lines of coke. Steve's protests that he didn't do drugs had fallen on deaf ears.

'How can you not do drugs, Steve? You work in the bloody music industry. Shut the door, and don't be such a party pooper. It's New Year's Eve, for fuck's sake!'

And so it continued, week by week, line by line, gram by gram, until the end of April and the middle of the Lovers and Losers tour. By now, Steve's drug intake was averaging two grams a week, aided and abetted by Tony. Coke loves company, as Tony knew only too well. Holed up on his own with a gram and a few hours to kill, he was beginning to experience feelings of self-doubt, the nagging suspicion that he wasn't nearly as talented or half as popular as he liked to think he was. With Steve there to share his addiction and shore up his ego, he felt better about himself and his growing dependency on the ever-growing white lines that promised so much but delivered so little. He was supposed to be writing songs for the next album, but all he had so far were a few notes on scraps of hotel stationery. Those, and the wraps of coke that arrived each afternoon and were gone by the following morning.

One night at the Britannia Hotel in Manchester, Katrina came knocking on Tony's door. She and Steve were staying in the adjacent suite, but the days when they left the adjoining door unlocked and wandered freely into one another's rooms were long gone.

'Have you seen Steve?' she said. 'He was supposed to collect me ten minutes ago. It's our one night off this week, and I'm sick to death of room service. We're supposed to be going somewhere nice for dinner.'

Tony flicked nonchalantly through a copy of *The Face* with Frankie Goes to Hollywood on the cover, his expression one of vague disinterest. 'Have you tried the bar?'

Katrina frowned. 'He said he'd meet me in our room. Oh well. I guess I'll try downstairs.'

No sooner had she left than the bathroom door was prised open and Steve emerged, grinning sheepishly. 'Thanks for that, mate.'

Tony looked up at him. 'No problemo.'

'I owe you one,' said Steve.

Tony grinned. 'Careful. I might hold you to that.'

One morning in September, Tony woke up to some surprising news. It was Les, trying hard to sound cool and professional and failing miserably.

'Are you sitting down? 'Cos you're not going to believe this.'

'I'm in bed, Les,' Tony replied. 'It's where I tend to be at eight o'clock on a Saturday morning. What could be so important that you're willing to interrupt my beauty sleep?'

'Pack your bags,' Les said. 'We're going to New York.'

Tony yawned. 'Whatever for? The Americans hate us. Nobody plays our records, and the press are vile. What was it *Rolling Stone* said about us? "Their biggest hit is a song called 'Lovers and Losers'. They got that half right." Forget it, Les. I'm not going where I'm not wanted.'

'But that's just it,' Les said. 'You *are* wanted. You're wanted so much the record company are even talking about an American tour. Some DJ started playing an extended mix of "Lovers and Losers" in the clubs in New York, and it's really taken off. They're predicting a Top Thirty entry in next week's *Billboard* chart.'

Tony sat up. 'Fucking hell, Les! Are you sure?'

'And that's not all. They're throwing a huge party for you next week at the Danceteria.'

Tony tried to conceal the excitement in his voice. 'Well, better later than never, I suppose.'

'Oh, we won't be late,' Les gushed. 'We're flying on Concorde.'

The party at the Danceteria was hosted by New York socialite Diane Brill, a big-busted blonde in a rubber dress who glided effortlessly between the human sculptures and caged go-go boys, shaking hands and making introductions. By midnight, the downtown glitterati were out in force and attention-seeking outfits. Lady Bunny was there, and Joey Arias.

'Who's he again?' Katrina asked.

'Performance artist,' Tony replied. 'Sang with Klaus Nomi. They did *Saturday Night Live* with Bowie a few years ago.'

Shortly after one a.m., debutante Cornelia Guest arrived, together with a familiar ghostly figure in a platinum wig. It didn't matter to Tony that the wigged figure stood around for an hour looking bored, or that when they were introduced he radiated all the warmth of a wet weekend in south Wales. Andy Warhol had attended his party, which could only mean one thing – A Boy and His Diva had finally arrived in America.

As predicted, 'Lovers and Losers' entered the *Billboard* chart at Number 27, and within a matter of weeks Tony and Katrina were back in New York, checked in at the Columbia Hotel in preparation for a series of live dates. Their whistlestop tour of America was scheduled to take them from New York to Philadelphia, Detroit to Chicago, Atlanta to Los Angeles. And it would have done, had it not been for what happened that first night at the Columbia.

Katrina had woken from a jet-lagged snooze and was looking for Steve, something she seemed to do rather a lot of these days. She checked the bathroom, phoned the front desk, and when it was confirmed that he hadn't been seen leaving the hotel, she went and knocked on Tony's door. There was no answer, but she could see a light under the door so she turned the handle and entered the room.

Steve was asleep in Tony's bed. His chest was bare and his clothes lay in a heap on the floor. As she approached, Tony's face appeared from under the covers. He gaped at her, speechless with shame.

A look of mild incomprehension settled on her face, turning to one of disbelief, then hurt, followed by anger. In the far corner of the room, the TV burbled away. With bitter irony, she noted that the Eurythmics' 'Sexcrime (Nineteen Eighty-four)' was playing on MTV.

She struggled for something to say, but couldn't find the words to express the enormity of what she felt. Tony was supposed to be her friend, so what was he doing in bed with her boyfriend? Steve had sworn he'd never hurt her, so why did it feel as if her heart had been ripped out? How could he do that to her? How could either of them do that to her?

Choked with pain, she lurched towards the door, then stopped and turned to take one last look. Her parting words were, 'Goodbye, Tony.'

CHAPTER TWENTY-THREE

'Hello, Tony,' Katrina said. 'I was wondering when you'd show up.'

Tony stood in the doorway, a fixed grin spread across his face. His head was shorn, and the years of cocaine addiction had clearly taken their toll. He had the skin tone of someone whose liver was working overtime. But at least he'd swapped that hideous orange prison uniform for something more flattering – a bottle-green suit, probably from Paul Smith or some other designer favoured by middle-aged readers of *GQ*.

'Katrina,' he said, a little too familiarly for her liking. 'You're looking well.' He glanced past her at a group of gay men with plates of canapés and glasses of wine, hovering in the hallway. 'Having a party?'

She answered flatly. 'It's a funeral party, Tony.'

His face dropped. 'Oh, right. Shit. Sorry, I didn't realise. This obviously isn't a good time. I'll leave you to your guests. I'll come back another time, when you're less busy.'

'There'll never be a good time, Tony. So why don't you just say what you came to say?'

He forced a smile. 'Well, aren't you going to invite me in? We can't really talk in the doorway.'

She thought for a moment. 'We can talk in the study,' she said finally, and ushered him inside. 'It's this way.'

'More guests, Katrina?' one of the gay men said, eyeing up Tony as they passed in the hallway. A portly man with a shaved head and a grey goatee, he'd been around long enough to know that funerals were a bit like doctors' waiting rooms – unlikely places to pick up, but not without the odd frisson of excitement.

'Just a bit of business,' Katrina replied briskly. 'Won't take long.'

As they walked, Tony studied her from the corner of his eye. She'd put on a bit of weight, but other than that she wasn't looking too bad for her age. The blonde hair suited her, and the eyes were still as seductive, despite the crows' feet. Nothing a bit of Botox and a few fillers couldn't fix. Assuming she was amenable to a little retouching, he couldn't see any reason why she shouldn't be allowed back on TV.

'It's here,' she said suddenly, opening the door to a large study with views overlooking Russell Square. Stepping into the room was a bit like stepping back in time, and it wasn't just the memories of the square before the trees were chopped down. Tony's eyes were immediately drawn to the eighties black ash furniture and the gold discs on the wall.

'Nice room,' he said, lying through his teeth. 'I see you kept your gold discs.'

'My name's on them,' she replied sharply. 'Why shouldn't I have kept them?'

'No, I'm glad you did,' he said quickly. 'I mean, it's good to see them. And you too, of course. It's good to see you.'

'What do you want, Tony? You didn't come here to admire my taste in home furnishings. You came because you want something. What is it?'

'Right.' Tony hesitated. 'Well, you know I've just been on this TV programme, *The Clink*?'

'I think I may have read something somewhere.'

'Didn't you get my email?'

Katrina glanced at the computer. 'I might have done. To be honest with you, I've had other things on my mind besides your stab at reality TV stardom.'

Tony blushed. 'Yes, of course. Well, the thing is, I actually did pretty well in there. I mean, I was more popular than I thought. So much so, in fact, that the record company want to rerelease "Lovers and Losers".'

'You don't need my permission for that. It's your song. You own the rights.'

'Yes, but that's not all. If it does well, and a lot of people seem to think it might, then there may be an opportunity to record some new material.'

Katrina stared at him.

'Obviously we'd need to work out the terms,' he went on. 'I mean, I could have my new manager go over it with you. Unless of course there's someone you'd rather discuss it with first. A manager or an agent or something.'

Katrina continued staring.

'Anyway,' Tony said, 'this is probably all a bit premature. But I thought I'd raise it with you now. That way, you have more time to think about it. Not a huge amount of time, obviously. You know how record companies are. But, well, you know what I mean.'

Finally Katrina spoke. 'Let me get this straight,' she said stiffly. 'You walk in here after twenty years and you expect me to just drop everything and pick up where we left off? That's what you came here to say?'

Tony frowned. 'Well, I wouldn't put it like that exactly, but I suppose that's the gist of it, yes.'

Katrina's eyes blazed. 'Well, you've certainly got a nerve. I'll give you that. If my memory serves me correctly, where we left off was with you fucking my boyfriend.'

Tony stared at the floor. 'Oh, that. I was hoping you'd have got over that by now. It was more than twenty years ago.'

'I don't care if it was fifty years ago. And of course I've got over Steve. I'm not some lovesick teenager. What I haven't got over is the fact that you betrayed me. You of all people. You broke my heart, Tony. I lost my boyfriend and my best friend, both at the same time. Do you have any idea how much that hurt?'

'Of course I do,' he said, clearly wishing he could get this part of the conversation over and done with. 'And you've every right to be angry. But I lost something too, y'know. I lost you. And I'm sorry for what happened, I truly am. But what could I do? By the time I'd come to my senses, you were gone.'

'Of course I was gone,' she snapped, turning away from him and walking over to the window. 'What did you expect me to do? Stick around and risk further humiliation? I was hurt enough, Tony. Trust me.'

'Where did you go?'

'Everywhere. Nowhere special. I just kept moving about, hoping I could leave it all behind me. But of course I could-n't. The places changed, but the pain was always there. It felt as if my insides had been torn out, and here I was running around like something from *The Evil Dead*, with my guts hanging out and half my vital organs missing.'

He chuckled at this and she glared back at him. 'It

wasn't funny, Tony. None of it was funny. Just because it happened a long time ago, it doesn't give you permission to laugh.'

He wiped the smile from his face. 'No, of course not,' he said. 'So where did you end up?'

'I spent the best part of a year in Swansea with my mother, listening to her prattle on about what bastards men were and what a mistake she'd made marrying my father. Then when that all got too much, I came back to London and started piecing my life together again.'

'I wish you hadn't gone,' Tony said. 'Maybe if you'd hung around, you and Steve could have worked things out. I know he wanted to. He tried calling you a million times. We both did.'

'I'll bet you did,' Katrina sneered. 'Because of the tour. Not because you cared about my feelings.'

'Of course I cared.'

'So why stop?'

'What?'

'You could have tracked me down any time. What stopped you?'

Tony looked away. 'I had a few problems of my own by then. And I had no way of knowing if you'd still want to hear from me.'

'Nothing to gain, more like. The band was finished, so you had no use for me.'

'How can you say that? It was never only about the band. Our friendship meant a great deal to me.'

'Tony, I caught you in bed with my boyfriend! If our friendship meant anything to you at all, that situation would never have arisen in the first place.'

'It wasn't as simple as that,' Tony insisted. 'There were other factors involved.'

Katrina shot him a withering look. 'You mean coke.'

'Among other things, yes.'

Her eyes widened. 'Christ, what else were you on? Heroin?'

'No, not heroin. Never heroin. I meant there were other factors involved. I was having trouble adjusting to the whole pop star thing. Fame takes a lot of getting used to, and you weren't really there for me any more. It was always "Steve this" and "Steve that". I suppose part of me was jealous that you'd found someone else to share it all with. It was meant to be our big adventure, but you left me to go through it all on my own.'

'So you decided to get back at me by fucking my boyfriend! After everything we'd been through together! All the years we were friends, all the dreams we shared and the plans we made. I loved you like a brother, and you threw it all away for the sake of a few lines and a quick fuck!'

'I didn't mean to,' Tony protested. 'It wasn't planned. But like you say, there was coke involved. Coke can do terrible things to a man's libido.'

'Screw your libido!' Katrina snapped. 'So there was coke involved. Big fucking deal. That still didn't give you the right to seduce my boyfriend.'

Tony looked surprised. 'But I didn't seduce him,' he said.

'What? Oh fuck off, Tony. How else do you explain the fact that you ended up in bed together?'

'I didn't seduce him,' Tony said again. 'That's not what happened, Katrina. That's not how it was at all. Yes, we were doing coke. And yes, I did a shitty thing. I know that. But he came on to me. Not the other way around.'

Katrina stared at him in disbelief. 'Steve came on to you? Bollocks! He wasn't gay. Why would he do that?'

Tony shrugged. 'I'm buggered if I know. Why would a straight boy sleep with me at all? I wasn't like Boy George, all ribbons and bows and girly dresses. No man ever bought me drinks thinking I was a woman. They all knew exactly what they were getting.'

'So now you're telling me that Steve was really gay?'

'Not necessarily. But maybe there was a part of him he was repressing, and the coke brought it out.'

Katrina narrowed her eyes. 'And where did he get the coke from, Tony?'

'What?'

'He got it from you, didn't he? You had your eye on him from the start. The coke was just a means to an end. And don't try and blame your behaviour on me, saying that I wasn't there for you any more. Did it ever cross your mind that the reason I got together with Steve in the first place was because you weren't there for me?'

'Of course I was there for you,' Tony replied. 'We were a double act, the same as we'd always been.'

'No we weren't,' Katrina said crossly. 'There were three of us in that double act – you, me and Les. And I might as well have been a session singer for all the attention you paid me. It was always you and Les deciding everything.'

Tony fell silent for a moment. 'He died, y'know. Les. About a year after you left. AIDS. His was one of the first funerals I went to.'

Katrina felt her anger subside. 'No, I didn't know,' she said in a quieter voice. 'I'm sorry to hear that.'

'I tried to reach you,' Tony said. 'Of course I wasn't sure if you'd want to attend the funeral or not.'

'Probably not.' She sighed, feeling a tinge of guilt and the need to explain herself further. 'Me and Les, we weren't close the way you two were.'

Tony smiled. 'No, I suppose not.' His mind drifted off for a moment, thinking of all the funerals he'd attended since, all the people he'd lost. He looked at her in her dark dress. 'So who's the party for today?'

'A friend,' she replied. 'A very dear friend.' She thought of Mark and the special bond she had with him. And then she looked back at Tony, remembering the time when he too had been special. 'There's one thing I never understood about you,' she said.

Tony raised an eyebrow. 'Just the one? What was it?'

'I never understood how you could write such sensitive lyrics, and still be such an insensitive bastard. There you were, singing songs about sex and relationships and how love was the only thing that mattered. And all the while you were too busy chasing your own fame to let anyone get really close to you. The way you behaved, anyone would think you didn't know what those lyrics meant.'

Tony smiled. 'It was the eighties, Katrina. We all sang lyrics we didn't mean.'

'I didn't,' she replied flatly. 'I meant every word.'

There was a long pause.

'I think you should go now,' she said finally.

Tony looked her in the eye. 'I'm really sorry about what happened with Steve. If I could go back and change things, you know I would.'

She held his gaze. 'Would you?'

'Of course I would. Hurting you was the biggest mistake I ever made. I was selfish and thoughtless, and I hate myself for it. I only hope that one day you'll be able to forgive me.'

'That's a lot to ask, Tony.'

'I know it is. But it's no good dwelling on the past, Katrina. You have to live for the present.'

'I know that,' she said.

'So you'll try to forgive me?'

'I'll think about it.'

'And the band?'

'The band?' Katrina smiled. 'The band is in the past, Tony. Let's leave it there.'

As soon as he stepped outside Katrina's building, Tony phoned his manager.

'Bad news, I'm afraid, Dan. She's not interested.'

'That's not the only bad news', Dan said. 'I've just had a call from the *News of the World*. I'm not sure how to say this, Tony, so I guess I'll just come straight out with it. They have photos of you snorting coke off someone's cock.'

Watching from the window above, Katrina had no idea of the trouble Tony had landed himself in. Her mind was elsewhere – a different time, a different place. Seeing him again had brought it all back – the band, the betrayal and the bitterness that had set in soon after, eroding her faith in human nature. It was that she hated him for most – the loss of faith, the fear of ever trusting anyone again. For years afterwards she'd kept her gold discs hidden away in the back of a cupboard, reminders of a time she'd sooner forget. It was only recently that she'd brought them out again, proud of her achievements and finally able to enjoy the awards for what they were, irrespective of the memories attached to them.

Now, as she watched Tony climb into a taxi and speed away up Southampton Row, it suddenly struck her that seeing him today was a bit like dusting off those gold discs. For years the thought of ever seeing him again had filled her with dread. And when that email had arrived, she could barely bring herself to consider the possibility that he might turn up on her doorstep. It had taken her a long time to recover from what he'd done to her, and her greatest fear was that all that pain and anger would rise up again and she'd be right back where she started. But now that she had seen him, and she hadn't been sucked through a wormhole and thrown back to 1984, she was surprised at how much better she felt. She wasn't ready to forgive him – not yet, maybe not ever – but for the first time in years she felt free from the burden of hating him. And for that she was profoundly grateful.

Tony's apology was largely self-serving. She wasn't under any illusions about that. Knowing him as she did, she doubted it could have been any other way. But there was also an element of sincerity to it, an acknowledgement of the fact that what he'd done was wrong. It wasn't the best apology in the world, but it was enough for her. Enough for now. The past had been laid to rest. It was time to face the future. She picked up the phone and dialled.

'Hi, it's me. Yes, I think I'm ready for you now. Okay, see you shortly.'

She left the study and rejoined the party, searching for Rose. Finally she found her, alone in the kitchen, clearing plates.

'You don't need to do that, Rose. The caterers will see to it.'

'I'm just trying to make myself useful,' Rose said.

'But there's really no need,' Katrina said, taking her firmly by the hand. 'You'll only be putting someone else out of a job. Besides, your job is to help me play hostess. Come on, I'll introduce you to some people.'

She led Rose into the living room, where a small group of men and women were congregated around a man with red hair and a mellifluous voice, busy recalling a conversation he'd had with the man they'd all loved and lost.

'Well, you know how green-fingered he was. He could make anything grow just by looking at it. And of course I'm the complete opposite. I dread to think how many plants I've killed off over the years. So I asked him where I was going wrong. Was it the compost? Too much water? Or was it simply that I was impossible to live with? And do you know what he said? He turned to me and he said, "Who am I to cast nasturtiums?"'

The man laughed at the memory, and the others nodded politely.

'God, I'm going to miss him,' the man said, his eyes glistening. 'His choice of puns was terrible, but he had a heart of gold.'

'John?' Katrina said. 'Can I introduce you to someone? This is Mark's mother, Rose.'

John turned to face her, and for a moment Rose feared he might tell her to leave, that she had no place here. But instead he smiled and held out his hand.

'Pleased to meet you, Rose. And I'm very sorry for your loss. Your son was a wonderful man.'

'Thank you,' she said, and without warning the tears welled up again and began pouring down her face. She wept for all the years she'd wasted, and for the times she never had. She wept for all the hurt she'd caused him, and all the hurt she'd caused herself. She wept for the way she'd lived, and for the way he'd died. She wept uncontrollably, not caring who saw her or what they thought.

Suddenly she felt a steadying arm around her shoulder as Katrina guided her to the sofa and offered her a tissue to wipe her eyes.

'I'm sorry,' Rose sniffed.

'Don't be.' Katrina smiled. 'It's better out than in. Can I get you something to drink? A glass of water? A stiff brandy?'

Rose shook her head. 'No. I'm fine, really.'

'Sure?'

Rose nodded.

'Just take a moment,' Katrina said. 'Then when you're ready I'd like you to come with me to the spare bedroom.'

Rose wiped her eyes. 'What for?'

'Because there's someone I'd like you to meet.'

The spare bedroom was situated next to Katrina's own bedroom, at the opposite end of the hall to where Rose slept. When they arrived, Katrina knocked and opened the door to reveal a bedroom that didn't look very spare at all, but was crammed full of children's toys. Sitting among them were a blond man and a little girl in a blue dress. Rose recognised the man immediately. And the little girl looked familiar too. It was the same girl she'd seen in that photograph at Mark's flat, only now she was a few years older.

'You remember Peter, Rose. You met at the hospital.'

Rose looked at the man who had once been on intimate

terms with her son. 'Yes,' she said, offering her hand. 'Nice to see you again. And who's this?'

'This is someone very special,' said Katrina. 'Someone you should have met a long time ago. This is Grace. My daughter. Your granddaughter.'

CHAPTER TWENTY-FOUR

'I remember the first time I felt childless,' Katrina said. The party was over, the guests and caterers had all left, and in another part of the flat Peter was busy putting Grace to bed. Soon he would join them in the living room, and the conversation would continue late into the night. But for now it was just her and Rose, a bottle of brandy, and the story of how she and Mark came to be parents.

'I was on a plane,' Katrina continued, 'coming back from New York. I was in business class, and there was a woman sitting across the aisle from me with two small children. Gorgeous, they were. And really well behaved. I must have been staring at them without realising it, because just as we were about to land the woman turned to me and said, "I know what you're thinking. There's nothing worse than bloody kids in business class." I told her I wasn't thinking that at all, I was just thinking how sweet and quiet they were. "No you weren't," the woman replied. "You were thinking they shouldn't be here. I know. I was childless myself once." She was smiling as she said it, so I wasn't sure if she was joking or what. But the words really stuck in my head.

'That was in 1992. And it's funny, because I'd never really thought about having kids before. But after that I couldn't

239

stop thinking about it. Of course I didn't think it was going to happen. I'd already turned thirty by then, and my life wasn't exactly geared towards motherhood. I'd been working on a solo album. The record company wanted to call it *Diva*, to remind people of my former glories. Then of course Annie Lennox released her *Diva* album and things went a bit belly-up. There was only room for one diva in the charts, and it wasn't me. The album sold a few thousand copies, but not enough to secure my future as a solo artist. So that was it – the end of my recording career. If it hadn't been for my investments, I'd have been sunk.

'As for my personal life, that was even worse. I'd had one proper relationship, and that had ended in tears. I didn't want to repeat the same mistake twice. Most people seem to end up with the wrong person, and I was determined that wouldn't happen to me. I wouldn't settle for second best. And of course the fame thing didn't help. Everyone talks about how fame changes you, but nobody talks about how it changes the people around you, especially if you're a woman. Men don't know how to deal with it. Either they feel threatened, or they see you as a meal ticket. I knew how to spot the gold-diggers. It was the others I wasn't prepared for.

'So there I was – the wrong side of thirty, single and seriously wondering if I was destined to spend the rest of my life alone. And that's when I met Mark. He wrote to me after hearing my solo album, saying it was the best thing I'd ever recorded. Of course I knew that wasn't exactly true. But I enjoyed the flattery, and I knew he was gay from his letter, so I wrote back and pretty soon we became pen pals. Then one day he wrote and asked if we could meet for a coffee or something and I arranged to meet him at this little place in

Soho. We sat and talked for hours. Some people say you should never strike up personal relationships with fans, but Mark was different. He wasn't some starstruck kid. He was younger than me, but he was wise beyond his years. He saw me for me, not the person I was on *Top of the Pops*. So we became friends.

'I think part of the reason we got along so well was that Mark was as unlucky in love as I was. Shortly after we met he started dating a guy called Tim. It took him eighteen months to discover that Tim was a cheating, lying bastard, and after that he was convinced he'd never meet another man again. We used to say how all men were the same, gay or straight, and how the only people we could rely on were each other. He'd tell me that I was his ideal woman, and I'd tell him that he was my ideal man, and we'd joke about how we should settle down together and start a family. That's how it began – as a sort of joke. But deep down he knew how much I wanted a child, and one day he just popped the question.'

Rose, who'd been silent until this point, suddenly perked up. 'You mean he asked you to marry him?'

Katrina looked puzzled. 'No. He asked if he could be my sperm donor.'

Rose blushed. 'Oh, I see.'

'I didn't need to think about it for very long,' Katrina continued. 'I mean, I wanted a child, and I wanted the child to know who its father was. And Mark was the obvious choice. We'd been friends for about five years by then. He was someone I loved and trusted, and he was great with kids.'

'But what about his health?' Rose asked. 'Weren't you taking a terrible risk?'

'He hadn't been exposed to the virus then,' Katrina said. 'He was tested twice, and both tests came back negative, so there was no risk to me or the baby.'

Rose frowned. 'I see. So when . . .?'

'When did I get pregnant? Pretty quickly, actually.'

'No, I meant when did Mark find out that he'd been . . . exposed to the virus?'

Katrina's eyes fell. 'Oh. It was shortly after Grace was born. It was a shock, obviously. I mean, he was always so careful. You hear of people contracting HIV these days and you think, haven't they heard of safer sex? But it's not always as simple as that. Accidents happen. Condoms break. Mark was proof of that. He took it pretty badly at first. But meeting Peter helped him a lot. They were together for three years. The first time Mark got sick, we were all worried. But then when the new drugs came along it looked as if everything would be all right. We didn't know that the virus could mutate, or that the drugs could stop working. They don't really tell you about that.'

Rose's face darkened. 'Why didn't anyone tell me? I had a right to know when my son was ill. I had a right to know I had a granddaughter.'

'I wanted to,' Katrina said. 'God knows I wanted to. But Mark was adamant. And at the end of the day, it was his decision. I had to respect that. I only hope he'd understand why I'm telling you now. I'd like to think he would.'

Rose thought for a moment. 'But where have you been hiding her? I've been staying here for a few days and I haven't seen hide nor hair of her until today.'

Katrina smiled. 'She's been staying at Peter's for the past week. He's like a second father to her anyway, and with Mark in hospital and me coming and going at all hours, I thought it best she stay there. Then when you arrived I really felt that I needed some time alone with you, for us to get to know each other. So I asked Peter if she could stay a bit longer. She came to the funeral. Peter brought her. She wanted to come, and we both felt it was important that she be given the chance to say goodbye to her father.'

Suddenly Rose broke down. 'I've missed out on so much,' she sobbed. 'I could have been there for him. I could have watched my granddaughter grow up.'

Katrina squeezed the older woman's hand. 'You still can,' she said with a smile. 'She's only ten. She's still got a lot of growing up to do.'

The headlines were lurid even by tabloid standards. '*Clink Star In Cocaine Shame*' read one. 'Coke-Hungry Tony Blows His Chances' read another. Tony could barely bring himself to look beyond the headlines, but of course his curiosity got the better of him. Judging by the tone of the writing, you'd have sworn that the journalist responsible had never been within a ten-mile radius of a line of cocaine, or a penis for that matter. And that was just the Sunday papers. By Tuesday the story showed no signs of dying, with some leader writers calling for the police to intervene and make an example of 'pampered celebrities who flout our drugs laws'.

It was Kelly who was behind it, of course. It didn't take Tony long to work out that the former presenter of *The Clink* was the one responsible for leaking the photos to the press. Kelly's own drug problems were well known, and it didn't take a genius to work out that she was the only one with an axe to grind and access to the relevant people, Alex among them. Apparently, the dealer had taken the photos himself, with one of those hidden spy cameras, concealed inside the entertainment system in his living room. Evidently he got quite a kick out of this sort of thing. Not that he had conspired with Kelly in any way. Clearly it wasn't in his interests to provide the constabulary with evidence of his activities. But according to the press reports, when the police raided his flat, in addition to the kilo of cocaine and the fat wad of cash he kept locked in his safe, they also found a collection of polaroids of various men chowing down on the 'evil drug pusher's' undeniably photogenic cock. Among those photographed with their mouths full were two well-known TV personalities and the former lead singer with a boy band.

In the wake of what was soon described as 'a tabloid storm of disapproval', the record company got cold feet and plans to rerelease 'Lovers and Losers' were shelved.

'I'm really sorry about this, Tony,' Dan said when he called with the news. 'But you know what the industry is like these days. Anything verging on criminal behaviour and they drop you like a hot brick. Unless you're a rapper, of course. Then it's par for the course.'

'Thanks for the tip,' Tony said. 'I'm not sure how good a rapper I'll be, but it's certainly worth considering.' When his manager didn't respond, he laughed. 'I'm joking, Dan. Somehow I don't think rap is my forte.'

'Oh, right.' Dan laughed. 'Well, if you want my advice, I'd put the whole music thing to one side for a while. Ride it out for a few months, then see if we can't capitalise on your notoriety and get you to host a late-night show on digital.'

Tony smiled to himself. 'That's great, Dan. But I think I'll just lie low for a while, maybe finish off some songs I've been working on.'

Dan didn't sound convinced. 'Whatever works for you, Tony. But don't rule out the TV thing just yet. A pop career isn't for life, y'know. These days if you want to keep working you have to add new strings to your bow. A bit of ballroom dancing. A bit of presenting. Anything to keep your face in the public eye.'

'I'll bear that in mind,' Tony said, and hung up.

The following three weeks were a living hell of doorstepping tabloid hacks, bottomless pits of self-pity and endless hours of daytime television. Then one day Tony was in the bathroom experimenting with a new hair colour when he heard the distant ringtone of his mobile. He removed his rubber gloves, grabbed a towel and ran down the stairs and three times round the living room before finally finding the phone buried under a pile of newspapers. There was a voice message.

'Tony, it's Ritchie. Ritchie Taylor. Listen, I know this is a bit out of the blue, but I wanted to ask you a big favour. We're just about to start work on our new album, and I'm running short on ideas. I was wondering if you'd consider writing some tracks with me, and maybe even doing a duet. Who knows? We could end up like Marc Almond and Gene Pitney, or the Pet Shop Boys and Dusty Springfield! You'll have to play Dusty's part, obviously. Hope I can talk you into it. Call me.'

The last thing Katrina expected to see when she turned on the television one wet Wednesday afternoon was Tony having a cosy chat with Richard and Judy. It was six months since he'd turned up on her doorstep, and a lot had happened. After a shaky start, Grace was adapting to life without her dad but with her new grandma. Rose came to London as often as she could, and once a month Katrina and Grace would drive down to visit her in Swindon.

And judging by the stories in the press, Tony had been coming to terms with a few changes too. If she was honest, Katrina was disappointed that 'Lovers and Losers' hadn't been rereleased. Each time she turned on the radio, she could hear the eighties influence on some of the younger bands who dominated the charts. It would have been nice to hear one of the originals on heavy rotation too. But however disappointing it might have been for her, it must have been far worse for Tony. The tabloids had been particularly vicious to him over that episode with the drug dealer. And knowing him as she did, she'd feared that the loss of the record deal would be enough to tip him over the edge.

But six months later here he was sharing a sofa with Ritchie Taylor from Fag Endz and happily discussing his cocaine addiction with the reigning king and queen of daytime television. His hair had grown back, but it was his skin tone that surprised Katrina the most. Clearly he'd made some major changes these past six months. Gone were the hollow eyes and pallid complexion. Blond and tanned, he looked fitter and healthier than she'd have thought possible.

'Yes, I have been in rehab,' Tony confirmed in answer to Judy's somewhat hesitant line of questioning. 'And I would seriously suggest that anyone with a cocaine problem seeks help as soon as possible. Coke is a pernicious drug. I'm not saying that everyone who touches it will end up where I did.

Some people can control it. But if you're an addictive personality like me, the chances are it'll end up controlling you. And when it does, you'll lose everything – your friends, your fortune, even your septum if you're not careful!'

At this point, he held up his nose to allow closer inspection of his reconstructive surgery. And that wasn't the only surprise he had in store. As the interview drew to a close, Richard interrupted to say that Ritchie and Tony would end the show with a live performance of their new single, 'Prisoner of Love'. But before the camera panned away, Tony asked if he could make a quick announcement.

'This is for you, Katrina,' he said, staring straight into the camera. 'Sorry for being such a loser.'

'Thank you, Tony,' she murmured to herself. And though she knew in her heart they could never be friends, the smile on her face showed there was still some love there.